HUNTER'S MOON

THE KATE SHUGAK MYSTERIES

OTHER BOOKS
BY DANA STABENOW

A KATE SHUGAK MYSTERY

HUNTER'S MOON

DANA STABENOW

G. P. PUTNAM'S SONS   NEW YORK

G. P. Putnam's Sons
Publishers Since 1838
a member of
Penguin Putnam Inc.
375 Hudson Street
New York, NY 10014

Library of Congress Cataloging-in-Publication Data

Stabenow, Dana.
     Hunter's moon / Dana Stabenow.
          p.   cm. — (A Kate Shugak mystery)
     ISBN 0-399-14468-4
     I. Title. II. Series: Stabenow, Dana. Kate Shugak mystery.
     PS3569.T1249H86   1999
     813'.54 — dc21   98-33465 CIP

Printed in the United States of America

10   9   8   7   6   5   4   3   2   1

This book is printed on acid-free paper. ∞

"Bright Shining" by Mary TallMountain reprinted from
The Light on the Tent Wall, by permission of the
American Indian Studies Center, UCLA,
© Regents of the University of California.

Book design by Ellen Cipriano

My thanks to Chris Pepe,
who helped this butterfly
fight its way out of the cocoon,

and to Dad, Gary Porter,
Mark Rousch, Ralph Young, Hank Carlson
and all the other Alaskan hunters
who bring home the meat to fill my freezer
and the stories to hang books on,

and to Chris Copeland,
without whose help
nobody would have shot anybody in this book,

and to Dad again, for buying the gold camp
and letting me use it as the setting,

and to Jeannie,
for running my butt ragged over every inch of it.
Kate doesn't know how easy she had it.

For Sarah and Joyce,
who taught me everything I know
about loyalty and generosity,

and for Lulu,
who is gone but not forgotten

HUNTER'S MOON

There's just something so
irresistible about a woman with a gun.

"What's the Bush word for Renaissance woman?"

A handful of cranberries, glowing red in the afternoon sun, showered into the plastic bucket. Kate looked over at Jack. "What?"

He was leaning against the water pump housing, arms crossed over his chest, a speculative look on his face. "You're what, thirty-three?"

"Thirty-four next month," Kate said. "What's that got to do with the Renaissance?"

He grinned. "Nothing. It just seems like you ought to be older. You know too much for thirty-three."

"Uh-huh." Kate licked her reddened fingers. The juice was tart to the tongue. She made a mental note to buy more sugar on the way through Anchorage.

"Being a Renaissance woman means you're good at more than one thing. If you lived in England in the fifteen hundreds, you'd be good at poetry, fencing and navigation. Move it up four centuries and west one hundred eighty degrees and what do we get?"

"Kabbibity-bobbity-boo?" Kate suggested.

He laughed, but shook his head. "You deckhand for Old Sam in the summer, you guide climbers up the Big Bump in the spring, you can skin a Cat, mine for gold, butcher a moose, fix an engine." He gestured at the bucket dangling from her right hand. "Make jam. And now here you are, fixing to guide a big-game hunt. You can do anything. You're a Renaissance woman, Kate."

"That's not ability," Kate said, disconcerted. "It's not even talent. It's just . . . geography."

"What?"

"It's where I live. I'm not special, or different. Not from anybody who lives like me. When you live in the Bush, you do what you have to to get by." She shrugged. "I live two hundred miles from the nearest town of any size. If the engine off a 747 falls through my roof, there aren't any carpenters within calling distance, even if I had a phone. I do it myself or it doesn't get done. Same goes for—what did you say?—butchering a moose, fixing an engine. If I want to eat, I get my moose. If I want to drive, I service my truck. No big deal." She turned back to the berries.

"And that's probably what is most amazing," he said, more to himself than to her. "You actually believe that."

She cast a baffled glimpse his way. "What else would I believe?"

He held up both hands, palms out. "Nothing. Just talking to myself. How long have we got, anyway?"

"George said he'd be back tomorrow morning with the next party."

"Who this time?"

"A bunch of Germans, he said."

"Oh goody," Jack said without enthusiasm, "urban cowboys, Euro-style. Do they speak English?"

"I don't know, but Demetri's coming back. He'll be one of the guides."

"Oh." Demetri Totemoff had spent twenty years in the military, most of it in Germany. Few people knew he spoke fluent German because he spoke as little of his native Aleut tongue as was humanly possible already.

The sun warmed her skin, the flannel of her shirt, the denim of her jeans. She wriggled out of her shirt and knotted the waist of her T-shirt so that several inches of concave belly were exposed above the snap of her jeans. She was not entirely unaware of her audience.

Jack said hopefully, "Why don't we lay a blanket next to the creek, catch some rays while they last?"

Kate looped her braid off her neck with a rubber band fished from one pocket. "You go ahead. I want to fill up this bucket."

Jack trailed off to the lodge, pouting. She smiled to herself and waded back into the berry patch.

Breathing martyrdom from every pore, Jack put away the breakfast dishes and swept out the lodge before fetching a blanket and a book and spreading out at the edge of the creek bank. Mutt flopped down next to him with a voluptuous sigh. "Don't get any ideas," Jack told her. Mutt, half husky, half timber wolf, stretched out her full 140 pounds so that every possible square inch was exposed to the sun, closed her yellow eyes and lapsed into a satisfied coma. She'd been doing her share to reduce the spruce hen population near the lodge, and her belly was tight beneath the thick gray pelt.

Kate waded deeper into the brush, fat globes of radiant red berries clustering together everywhere she looked, the rays of the sun causing them to glow with luminous beckoning light. The weather, incredibly, was still holding, although there was a wisp of something on the southeastern horizon that Kate was keeping an eye on. For now, there was the merest breath of a breeze brushing at her cheek. The berries fell into the pail by the handful. An errant wasp buzzed contentedly nearby, and in the polished branches of a tall, dead cottonwood two immature eagles sat silently, immobile, looking half asleep but no less fierce for that.

It was so still that she could hear the page in Jack's book rustle when he turned it, even over the sound of water flowing downstream, a flow diminished from spring torrent to summer gush to a comparative fall trickle. It was narrow and shallow enough to wade across, barely sufficient water for the last exhausted silver salmon to fight her way upstream to lay her eggs and her burden down forever.

Kate paused to flex her shoulders. She'd worked her way down to the edge of the camp, next to the last cabin, the one almost but not quite falling into the Nakochna.

The hunting lodge sat 125 miles northeast of Anchorage, 10 miles south of Denali National Preserve, 75 miles southwest of the mountain itself. It had been the rapidly deteriorating remains of a defunct gold mine when George Perry stumbled across it on a deadheader back from a freight trip/visit to a girlfriend in McGrath in June about twelve years back. His 180 started losing oil pressure, so he looked around for an airstrip and found this one jutting north from just before the confluence of the Nakochna and the Kichatna rivers. It was overgrown with alders, surfaced with round river rocks the size of dinner plates and sported a distinctly uphill grade, but there was enough clear space to put the Cessna down before the engine quit on him. He did, promptly, and if not quite without incident then without any permanent damage to the gear. Any landing you walked away from was a good landing.

When he'd repaired the oil line, he looked around for a reason for the airstrip and found one main building, a shop, a two-story garage and seven small cabins. None of the build-ings had foundations, being temporary edifices constructed on skids made of twelve-by-twelves. The yard was a jumble of dumped equipment and supplies, ranging from a disassem-bled, rusted-out steam engine to rotting two-by-fours to dis-carded screws and nails. The undergrowth, consisting of a dozen tangled varieties, from alder to white spruce, was all but marching into the various doors.

He took off again and surveyed the area from the air. The strip and the camp sat on a wedge-shaped piece of land that began where the Nakochna ran into the Kichatna and gradu-ally widened as it rose into the foothills of the Alaska Range, the first of which was the 3,020-foot Blueberry Ridge and es-calating in vaulting, geometric leaps to the higher peaks of Gurney, Lewis, Agustin and Dall beyond. The Nakochna bordered the wedge of land on the west, the Fourth of July and Gagnan creeks on the east. There was faint evidence of a rough road that paralleled the river all the way up the foothills, probably leading to one of the mine entrances and, from George's point of view, the perfect place for a spike camp. He saw a grizzly with two yearling cubs swiping salmon out of the river, startled a pair of eagles out of a dead cottonwood, surprised a black bear with three cubs into stampeding for the sheltering branches of the nearest spruce, stopped counting moose after he got to ten and caught sight of a black streak that might have been a wolf, although he was too high by then to be sure.

He leveled the plane out and set a course for home. The buildings were in good enough repair to be salvaged, and a couple of swipes with the blade of a bulldozer would clear the yard. Best of all, the runway was long enough to accommodate a Herc.

A Lockheed Hercules four-engine turboprop was the archetypal Bush freight plane, with a capacity to haul twenty tons a trip, providing it had four thousand feet of runway to land on. George estimated that the gold camp runway was about forty-five hundred, if he could take out that stand of alders that had sprung up at about the twenty-five-hundred-foot mark. With a runway that would accommodate a Herc, anything was possible.

He stopped in Anchorage long enough to put a trace on the owner of the property. The gold miner was all too glad to be rid of it, and George understood why when, after he sold it to George for sixty thousand dollars cash and got on the first plane south, the miner's creditors started boiling out of the woodwork.

Eighteen months and a hefty legal bill later the old mine and the twenty-five acres surrounding it belonged to George free and clear—after two fishing trips to the camp for the presiding judge. George considered it fuel well spent, even if the judge had required an additional flight into Anchorage for more beer. Before rod, before reel, before tackle, beer was the indispensable ingredient for a successful venture into combat fishing, making the days you didn't catch anything easier to bear and the days you did a celebration.

Of course, it was also a primary factor in fishermen falling into streams and drowning, but no one was ever tactless enough to say that out loud.

The nearest neighbor to the gold mine was a man named Crazy Emmett who lived in a cabin on a tiny lake five miles away. Crazy Emmett, an ex–history teacher from West High School in Anchorage, had retired at his earliest possible date of eligibility and fled the city for the peace and security of Bush life. Years of teaching indifferent students had inured him to loneliness, while his study of history had led him to a deep-seated belief in the hidden agenda of the United Nations in collusion with the Trilateral Commission to take over all the world's governments, thereby jeopardizing his Second Amendment right to keep and bear arms. He believed that secret operatives working on behalf of the U.N. had put directions in invisible ink on the backs of all government highway signs, readable only by U.N. troops wearing special government-issue goggles. Crazy Emmett saw everyone as the point man for the invasion and if you didn't want to be used for target practice you kept your distance. George kept his distance.

George's day job was the owner and operator of Chugach Air Taxi, flying freight, passengers and the U.S. mail in and out of Niniltna, the village twenty-five miles up the unmaintained road from Kate's homestead. It was no sinecure; he was in the air more often than not. But over the years, when he could snatch a day here or a weekend there, he would fly to the gold camp site with the girlfriend or wife du jour and put them to work replacing the windows, painting the walls and cleaning the yard. Not to mention clearing the airstrip, which, it was speculated, may have been indirectly responsible for the failure of his fourth marriage.

Once the alders were gone, he loaded a borrowed Herc with a backhoe and flew it into the gold camp. A small bulldozer required wings with a bigger payload, and after some dickering with the same people who owned the Herc, he traded four hours' use of a Sky Van for a week's fishing. This had proved so successful that he got an offer of a trade every subsequent year, and this year used the Herc to haul in, among other things, two snow machines and two four-wheelers.

With the backhoe, George convinced a small tributarial creek not to run straight down the airstrip, and with the dozer, he built a dam to bolster the creek's conviction and to level the brush around the buildings and to plow the strip in winter. The snow machines and the four-wheelers would take care of local transportation year-round. When someone pointed out that the snow machines were liable to scare off more game than they snuck up on, George replied laconically, "There's always a choice. We can ride our snow machines when and where we please, or we can have caribou to hunt." But Kate had noticed that the most common means of transportation from Taiga Lodge was on foot.

After eight years of work undertaken in fits and starts, he had a rough but serviceable hunting lodge, with one big main house for eating, six smaller cabins for sleeping, two bunks each, one shop, one garage, and two spike camps. One of the spike camps was four miles northwest of the lodge, reached by four-wheeler via the rudimentary road that ended in a secondary mine entrance. He had used the dozer to extend the road to the plateau-like surface of the ridge, from which there was a breathtaking view of the Alaska Range and the Skwentna-Yentna-Susitna river deltas. The second spike camp was on another ridge three miles east of camp, the only geographical hump of any size between the camp and an enormous and extensive swamp, an area rich in moose.

Alaska big-game guides made a ton of money and wanted to keep on making a ton of money, and big-game guides' licenses became available only when a current licensee died, and sometimes not even then. George had never volunteered an explanation and Kate had never asked, but she had long suspected his license had had something to do with ex-wife number four, Ramona Halford, the right-wing state senator whom no one admitted voting for but who was reelected every four years by an embarrassing majority of Park residents. Ramona knew where all the bodies were buried and how most of them got there, and if she were married, however briefly, to someone who wanted a big-game guide's license for a wedding present, she was one of the few people in the state who could get him one.

Having a big-game guide's license meant you could sign off on someone else's Class A Assistant guide's license, which George promptly did, for Kate Shugak, Demetri Totemoff, Jack Morgan and Old Sam Dementieff, his stable of assistants. This entitled them to a pale blue square of paper with the state of Alaska's seal on the watermark. It bore the license number, the effective and expiration dates, two years apart, and the game management units in which it was valid, and if such a thing had been allowed, these could have been auctioned off on the open market for a fortune.

From that time forward, George's gold camp was set for guiding big-game hunters to meat, trophies and, if they were lucky, fame of a kind, at least in Boone and Crockett. Officially called Taiga Lodge (*taiga* was Athabascan for bear shit), George had been doing business for four years now. He specialized in Europeans who had read a lot of Ernest Hemingway when they were young and impressionable and their parents should have known better. They had the armament to prove it, and, more to the point, a shitload of money.

George was happy to help them spend it, or he was for four weeks out of the year, the last two weeks of September (moose) and the first two weeks of October (bear). Guiding hunters from the lodge for four weeks out of the year meant he could write off the expenses for the other forty-eight, when it served its primary purpose as a romantic getaway *a deux*, and sometimes *trois*. The rest of the time he left the main house stocked and unlocked, as per Alaska law, in the event some yahoo on a snow machine got lost and needed shelter.

It was George's contention that owning and maintaining such a wonderfully romantic getaway was worth any amount of trouble, even guiding hunting parties with more money than brains, although there were hunts that did severely test that premise. There were hunts when the clients were pleasant and good sports and helped pack out the meat, but there were also hunts when the clients' most important piece of equipment was the tape measure and who shot at everything that moved regardless of size, sex and sometimes species— once he'd had to physically disarm a British hunter who had taken his rifle down to the creek to blast away at a king salmon. These hunters took their trophies and left the meat for carrion, or would have, given the chance.

This irritated George and infuriated Kate, especially when they had to make the long trek back to the site of the kill to recover what wasn't spoiled or hadn't been eaten by bears, wolves and coyotes. The trophy hunters, Kate was quick to point out, were always the same hunters who left their trash scattered the length and breadth of the campsite and who looked impatient when George made them clean up after themselves. Some refused. Some were invited by George to walk back to Anchorage. These were not likely to be repeat customers.

Back in Niniltna, Kate could always tell how irritated George was with his current hunting party by how much her checks were, which represented forty percent of his gross divided by the amount of assistants. Hunters George liked paid through the nose; the ones he didn't were lucky to escape with enough for cab fare from Merrill Field to Anchorage International Airport. "The charges are dependent on the customer's attitude," he told her once. "The more they piss me off, the higher the price."

It was a sentiment Kate understood and embraced wholeheartedly. She wouldn't guide for anyone but George.

And then there were hunts when they couldn't find anything to shoot, miserable stretches out in the woods when the only living things present were themselves and the mosquitoes and an occasional porcupine. It always seemed to rain on those hunts, too, not a torrent, which might end when the clouds ran out of water, but a steady drizzle that went on and on, dampening the underbrush and the spirit in equal proportion.

It wasn't going to happen this week, although that wisp seemed almost imperceptibly larger than it had the last time she'd looked at it. She shrugged. Wasn't here yet. Here, it was still sunny. Here, it was still hot. She picked berries steadily until the bucket was almost full.

She returned to the yard around which the shop, the garage and the main house were built. There was a twenty-foot log two feet in diameter lying on its side, the upside worn smooth from years of fannies sitting on it while their owners knocked back cases of beer and lied about rack widths. She got another bucket and went down to the well, the old-fashioned pump handle sprouting from the square, flat-topped wooden well housing. She worked it a few times, bringing up water, and shoved the bucket underneath the spout when water began to flow.

The bucket was almost full when two arms slid around her waist and started working at the buckle on her holster. "There's just something so irresistible about a woman with a gun," a voice growled in her ear.

She laughed, and let her head fall back against Jack's shoulder and his hands go where they would. He turned her around and took her there, sitting on the well housing, the sun dazzling his eyes and gilding her skin. It was urgent without being desperate, both of them so in tune that they came almost as one, and when it was over Kate sat with her legs wrapped around his waist, his hands cupping her ass, her ear against his thudding heart, satisfied, drained and incapable of movement, even of bolting when he said, "I love you, Kate."

She nuzzled her face against his chest, and felt it rise and fall in a sigh.

"I know. The three most terrifying words in the English language."

The tone of his voice was light-hearted and accepting, but before she could respond to the feeling beneath them he had reached behind her to work the handle of the water pump, causing a stream of ice cold water to cascade down her back. She yelped, and he ran for his life.

TWO

Oops.

Most of the German hunters, thankfully, spoke impeccable English, with only the faintest trace of an accent, some stilted diction and occasionally putting their verbs last to give them away. "Some kind of corporate retreat," George said when they had off-loaded the last of the group.

"What kind of corporation?" Jack said.

"What are they retreating from?" Kate said.

"I don't know, Kate, pressures of business, reporters from *Wall Street Week*, their auditors? And the company is the German equivalent of Radio Shack or something like that." George pulled out the manifest, squinting at the fine print. "*Deutches Radio Gessellschaft*, it says here."

"DRG?" Jack said. "They make computers?"

George shrugged and held out the manifest.

Jack read it. "Yeah, that's them all right, DRG. They

make computers—the operating systems for them, anyway. I think we've got a couple in the office."

"I don't care if they make ladies' lingerie," George said. "The check cleared the bank first time."

Jack handed the manifest back. "You're lucky."

"Why?"

Jack grinned. "Because DRG is under investigation by the FBI, the SEC and probably the CIA for tax fraud, bribery and industrial espionage. It's rumored that DRG's playboy president, whom I recognized from the front page of the *Enquirer* when he got off the plane, is under investigation for improprieties in his own personal finances. The IRS has frozen all their American assets pending resolution of the court cases. Dell is suing them for patent infringement, and Microsoft is suing them for loading an illegal—so they claim—Windows99 clone on all their PCs. And that's only in this country. Don't you ever read the papers?"

"If it isn't in *Aviation Week*, George doesn't see it," Kate said.

"And doesn't worry about it," George agreed. He wiped the dipstick, reinserted it and closed the hood of the Cub, giving it an affectionate pat. "Like I said, the check cleared the bank first time."

"So, who's the boss?"

George waved a vague hand in the direction of the lodge. "Dieter. The big blond guy."

The three of them turned to survey the group. "They're all big blond guys, George," Jack said. "Except for the woman."

George smiled, a long, slow, anticipatory smile, and managed, barely, to refrain from licking his chops. "I noticed." He stretched, working out the kinks caused by a day's worth of flying. "Guess I better go help her with her luggage."

There were ten in the group, the one woman and nine men, and there was a lot of luggage. It had been steadily accumulating from flight to incoming flight over the day—gun cases, rod cases, fly cases, creels, valises, suitcases, a case of schnapps, ten cases of beer, another ten of Evian, and boxes and bags of groceries. It was now in a haphazard pile in the center of the yard. Demetri and Old Sam had begun carrying the supplies into the lodge while their guests used the two outhouses and explored. A shout came from the creek, followed by sounds of hurried feet. "Dieter, there are fish in the water!"

"There better be fish in the water," Dieter said, shooting George a challenging glance, as if to say that if there weren't, George would be held personally responsible for the migratory habits of the Alaska silver salmon.

They all had last names, of course, but Kate considered that she was doing well to have mastered their first names, and if they considered that to be disrespectful of their august positions—what the hell, they had only to suffer her impudence for a mere ten days. Jack was right, they were all big and blond, including their token woman, who, if she'd been wearing a brass brassiere, would have looked just like the Ice Queen, or maybe a Valkyrie.

Kate had only the haziest notion of what a Valkyrie should look like, but whatever that was, Senta fit the bill. She could have been anywhere from thirty to fifty. She was six feet tall if she was an inch, with broad shoulders holding up very large, perfectly shaped breasts whose nipples jutted straight out in a manner that was vaguely threatening. She had a tiny waist, hips as wide as her shoulders and long, well-muscled legs. Her hair, makeup and nails looked as if she had come to camp straight from Elizabeth Arden. Like the men, she was dressed in khakis. Hers fit better.

Dieter was almost but not quite as tall as Senta, and Kate noticed that he took care not to stand next to her so as not to call attention to the difference. In his late forties or early fifties, Kate estimated, Dieter was all Teuton, a broad forehead, a square jaw, a thick neck, short, stiff blond hair and blue eyes so pale they were almost gray. His mouth was wide and fleshy, his chin prognathous and obstinate. His nose was oddly flattened and uptilted, the nostrils facing forward like a pig's. His chin hinted at arrogance, his belly at a lifelong fight with his weight, and his attitude was pompous, self-important and patronizing. The first thing he unpacked was his rifle. The first thing he said was, "How many can I kill?"

Not what, Kate thought, just how many. Okay. One of those kinds of hunts. She reminded herself of her generous wages and let it pass.

Everyone deferred to Dieter. They didn't defer to Eberhard; they stepped out of his way. They never looked directly at him if they could avoid it, either. First rule of the wilderness, Kate thought, never look a predator in the eye; he'll take it as an invitation to attack. He was taller than Senta, with a brush cut that had more gray than blond in it, more of an indication of his age than his face, which was clear and unlined except for two deep scars, one in each cheek. He looked as if he'd been sliced open with a carving knife and stitched together afterward with an eye toward preserving the marks.

Without thinking about what she was doing, her hand

went to her throat. The roped scar tissue there, extending almost ear to ear, had not healed as well.

Eberhard was agile in movement in spite of his bulk,
quick and sure on his feet. He looked up to see Kate watching, saw her fingering the scar at her neck. His eyes were flat
and impersonal. She felt a distinct chill and dropped her hand.

He stood at Dieter's shoulder, in Dieter's shadow. He made
no effort to help with the unloading, not even his own bags.

Muscle, Kate thought. Muscle, pure and simple. What
the hell does Dieter need with muscle out here? Maybe Eberhard'll wrestle a bear for him.

Gunther was about Kate's age, slim and muscular with
a round pink face, bright eyes, a quick handshake and an en-
gaging grin. "You are an Alaska Native," he said, proudly,
as if he had been the first person ever to discover this wonderful fact.

"That's right," Kate said, stifling a sigh. He was so good-
natured she couldn't snap at him.

"A Native guide, yes?" He laughed uproariously.

"That's right," Kate said grimly.

Klemens was the eldest of the bunch, Kate estimated in
his mid to late sixties. He was a thin man with a kindly smile
that deepened the wrinkles around his eyes and mouth. He
said gently, "Forgive him, he is very young. Is it true, there
are fish in the stream? I like fishing."

"Yes," she said. "There are rainbow trout and dolly var-
den, even some late silvers, although they're looking pretty
rough by now. Probably not very good eating, and certainly
no good for trophies. Unless you go for dark red monsters with
hooked snouts hanging on your wall."

He had trouble understanding this. He smoothed back a

glorious mane of pure white hair, carefully trimmed and styled, and said, "But there are fish, yes?"

"There are fish, yes," Kate said solemnly.

"Good." He nodded once, satisfied.

Hendrik and Fedor were so alike they seemed to be twins; in their mid thirties, they had dark blond hair, dark brown eyes, beautiful teeth and slim, graceful bodies. They asked no questions and took little interest in the proceedings except when Dieter's eye was upon them.

Hubert and Gregor were another set of near twins; stocky, stolid and sober, pants legs tucked neatly into their boots, boot strings carefully double-knotted. Hubert looked a little more upright, Gregor a little seedier. They'd helped with the luggage not out of a friendly spirit but because it was the socially accepted thing to do. They would have wives, 1.9 children each, paid-up life and medical insurance and a retirement plan that called for a vacation cruise to St. Croix every other year while they lived and adequate provision for their wives after their deaths. They looked like suburban characters out of a John Updike novel, minus the angst.

The final member of the party was Berg, who was tall and beefy and silent, blinking at the world through lenses so thick you could count his eyelashes from the other side. He spoke when he was spoken to. Kate saw him watching Senta when he thought no one was looking. He had a dog-like devotion in his eyes that was magnified by the lenses and uncomfortable to witness, and she turned her back on it in some embarrassment.

No one except Dieter seemed overly excited to be there. Was this hunt a command performance by the boss, perhaps? Kate wondered if any of them had had any experience on the trail. If not, it was going to be a long ten days. But the good weather was holding, and she and Jack could always sneak off once in a while, visit the beavers up at the top of the airstrip. She smiled to herself.

Her attention was drawn to the luggage pile, where some sort of confrontation appeared to be taking place.

"You will help with the luggage," Eberhard said. He picked up a very large suitcase in one hand without apparent effort, and handed it to Old Sam.

Old Sam accepted it, and then, deliberately, let it fall to the ground. It was heavy, and when it landed something inside broke.

There was an unpleasant pause.

"I didn't hire on to be a goddamn pack mule," Old Sam said. He was talking to George but he was looking at Eberhard. Eberhard stared stolidly back. Without any recollection of how she got there, Kate found herself standing at Old Sam's shoulder. Eberhard's flat gaze acknowledged her appearance without expression.

"I know," George agreed, at his most soothing.

"I ain't a goddamn coolie."

"You certainly aren't."

"You hired me as a guide, as I understood it."

"Yes, I did."

"I ain't humping no bags to no cabins, and while we're on the subject of humping, I ain't nobody's gun bearer, either, and I ain't packing out no meat I don't shoot or that I don't get to put in my own cache, neither."

"No."

"Glad you agree," Old Sam said. "Think I'll make some coffee. You want some, you come get it."

"We will."

Old Sam brushed by Kate on his way to the lodge.

George spoke to Dieter but he, too, looked at Eberhard as he spoke. "Dieter," George said, "you folks paid for a wilderness experience. This experience includes hauling your own bags and your own guns and your own game. I explained this to you when you called. You had the choice to sign up with an outfit that would butter your bread for you. I even gave you some names. You chose my outfit instead. You having a problem with that now?"

Eberhard outweighed George by about fifty pounds, and as George himself would explain to anyone who asked, "I'm in good enough shape to fly and fuck. What else is there?"

It seemed that Eberhard was right on the verge of showing him when Dieter said with false heartiness, "Come on, Eberhard. We're in Alaska now, not Munich. Let's get all this stuff into the cabins."

He gave Eberhard a comradely slap on the back and waited, confident, more so than Kate thought he had a right to be. Eberhard broke the stalemate by hefting two of the larger suitcases and turning to carry them to the cabins. Dieter reached for a carry-on and followed. The others fell in line.

Kate, not wishing to exacerbate the situation by watching, turned away and bumped into Jack. He stared over her head at the party straggling into the woods. "Yeah. Like I said, this is going to be one of the fun ones."

By evening, everyone had eaten heartily of Demetri's superb cooking and had subsequently mellowed out, at least on the surface. Kate herself, full of spaghetti and garlic bread, was charitably inclined to write Eberhard's attitude off to jet lag. She sat down next to Senta and George, who were sipping schnapps with their backs against the driftwood log. "Would you like some schnapps?" Senta inquired hospitably, holding up a bottle.

Kate shook her head. "No, thanks, I never drink on a hunt." Or ever, she could have added, but didn't because such a statement always required an explanation, which she didn't care to go into with strangers.

Up close Senta was even more awe-inspiring than she was at a distance. Her skin was flawless, her eyes a deep, oceanic blue, her hair glittered in the firelight like spun gold. Judging from his besotted expression, George was in love. Kate devoutly hoped that Senta was not on the verge of becoming wife number seven. "So, Senta," Kate said, partly in what she knew deep down was a vain attempt to deflect George, and partly doing the host thing, "tell me a little bit about your company."

"Certainly," Senta said, refilling George's glass and smiling at him over the rim. George quivered visibly. Senta's smile widened. Oh lord, Kate thought.

"Dieter is our CEO," Senta said. "You know what our company does?"

"Sure. You make computers."

"No, we make the operating systems that run the computers."

"Software, as opposed to hardware."

Senta's smile was bright and flashing. "Correct. Dieter is our president and chief executive officer. He is the hill from which all shit rolls down."

Kate laughed, surprised into it. "I see." She glanced across the circle at Dieter, absorbed in cleaning what looked like a shoulder-launched rocket.

"I will go around the circle," Senta said. Eberhard was sitting next to Dieter. "So next is Eberhard." He must have heard his name because he turned his head and met Senta's gaze full on. She went very still next to Kate.

"And what does Eberhard do?" Kate prodded.

Senta looked down into her glass and said, "Whatever he wants."

There was a faint tremble in her voice, or so it seemed to Kate. Something personal going on there. Sexual harassment, maybe? Or maybe Senta was just intimidated by the big man, as everyone else seemed to be. "What's his official job title?" Kate said.

Senta took a healthy swig from her glass. "He's the head of our legal department."

This was so far off from what Kate had imagined that only strong self-control kept her from sitting up with a jerk. "Eberhard's a lawyer?" She managed a chuckle. "What do you know, yet another partner of that well-known firm, Huckster, Shyster and Finagle."

Senta's smile flashed again, hard and bright. "Yes."

Kate still had a hard time believing it. "He's got a degree and everything?"

"Oh, yes. The University of Heidelberg. Where do you think he got the scars?"

Eberhard a lawyer. Muscle and brains. Kate appreciated that combination only when it was on her side, and it was obvious right up front that she couldn't afford Eberhard. "What's that about the scars?"

"Didn't I say that right? The marks on his face." Senta gestured with her glass. "Like the one on your neck. His are not so ugly," she said, so matter-of-factly that Kate could not take offense. "How did you get that?"

Kate ignored the question. "Yes, you said it right, but what have the scars got to do with Heidelberg?"

"They duel in Heidelberg."

"They what?"

"Fight. The students. With swords. You know." Senta demonstrated, crossing her index fingers in a mock salute. "Like knights in the Middle Ages." Senta snorted and held out her glass for a refill. "You have words for that in American which I like very much." She frowned at her drink, concentrating.

"Macho bullshit?" Kate suggested.

"That's it!" Senta toasted her and beamed. "So Herr Eberhard is a lawyer, with scars." She leaned forward and dropped her voice to what she must have imagined was a confidential level. "He has other scars, too. Not from swords."

Kate debated asking her how she knew, and decided it came under the heading of Too Much Information. "So Eberhard heads up Dieter's legal department. From what I read in the papers," she said mendaciously, "I imagine he's been busy lately."

"He is more than a lawyer, though," Senta said. "I was in Dieter's office one time when there was a demonstration in the lobby. Eberhard went down, and the demonstration went away." She drank. "Some of the demonstrators went away in ambulances."

"He's good, then," Kate said. "Eberhard."

"He's big," Senta said. "Sometimes that's better than being good."

There was an undertone to her voice that Kate could not interpret. Some corporate backbiting going on there, she thought comfortably, and decided it was time to move on. "How about Gunther?" Gunther was working the action of what looked like a brand-new rifle, face furrowed with concentration.

Senta gave the impression of just barely managing to refrain from a rich snicker. "Gunther is the head of security."

Kate frowned as if this puzzled her; in fact, it did. Most corporate heads of security were retired cops of some kind, vested in state or federal retirement funds and ready to begin building a second and infinitely more remunerative one in the private sector. Gunther, on the other hand, was a baby, a mere child. Dieter must have an abiding belief in on-the-job training. "Isn't he a little young for a job like that?"

"Yes, but he will grow into the job."

He'd better, Kate thought, and fast.

"Hendrik is in research and development. He thinks up all our wonderful products."

There was almost but not quite a sneer in Senta's voice. It was unpleasant and jarring, coming from the Ice Queen, who judging on looks alone should be icily regular and splendidly null.

"Hubert works with Hendrik. Between the two of them, there isn't anything they don't know about computer operating systems. Gregor heads up public relations, and Berg is head of quality control."

Kate nodded her head at the young man standing behind

Hendrik, one hand resting casually on his shoulder. "And Fedor?"

Again with the sneer. "Fedor works for Klemens."

"And what does Klemens do?"

Senta's voice was clipped. "He's the head of the finance department. He has been with the company the longest, even before Dieter."

"So, what do you do?"

"Human resources."

"Wow." Senta was well cast for her role; that hair and those eyes would look terrific on camera. "The CEO, legal affairs, security, finance, p.r. The whole management team. The gang's all here. You could run the company from Taiga Lodge if you wanted to."

Senta threw back her head and laughed, a deep, throaty sound. Kate saw Berg look across the fire at Senta with an expression in his eyes that made the fire look dim by comparison. "We could at that," Senta said. "We could at that."

"But you're here on vacation," George said, seizing his moment, as well as the schnapps bottle. He poured with a lavish hand, ignoring Kate's frown. Senta met his ardent gaze with a languorous look of her own, and Kate decided Senta was in no need of protection. Tactfully, she got to her feet and went into the lodge to help Jack clean up the dinner dishes.

Jack was washing and Kate was drying and putting them away when someone screamed in the yard. Kate dropped dishcloth and pan and ran outside, Jack right behind her.

Her first startled glance showed no one in immediate distress, with the exception of Mutt, who had been slumbering peacefully next to the fire. She shot to her feet, looked wildly in every direction, put her muzzle up in an emphatic and un-equivocal howl of protest and vanished into the brush.

Dieter had produced a boom box equipped with full stereo effects, bass and treble both cranked all the way over. Singing poured forth into the clearing and at that volume probably all the way to Denali, which was, after all, only about seventy-five miles to the northeast.

"What the hell is that?" Kate said, raising her voice.

"The Valkyries," Jack said. He didn't sound happy, or she didn't think so, what she could hear of his voice over the noise.

Involuntarily, Kate looked at Senta. Jack grinned. "It's an opera."

"Oh." Kate, after one performance of *Carmen* by the Fair-banks Opera Company during her college days, did not con-sider opera necessary.

She had company. Dieter's party looked either resigned or enthralled, probably depending on how sure they were of their jobs. Dieter stood where he was, one hand gently con-ducting the orchestra. He caught sight of Kate and Jack and smiled. "Wagner. Isn't he wonderful?"

He might have been, for all Kate knew, but not in the middle of nowhere in the Alaskan Bush, where people paid large sums to get away from the obscenities of modern life. Chief among these obscenities Kate numbered jet engines, cel-lular phones and nonstop noise being played at you, whether it was CNN in the airport, synthesized pop rock in restau-rants or hip-hop with the bass turned up loud enough to break the windows of a passing car.

Or Wagner in the Bush.

Dieter appeared to think he was playing music to clean guns by. He bustled over to a long, gray case and opened it.

Jack sucked in a breath. "Are those Purdeys?" He had to repeat the question in a louder voice.

"Here," Dieter said, and held one out with a lordly gesture. "Take a look."

Jack stepped forward to receive the shotgun as if he were Moses being handed commandments eleven through fifteen. He pulled the stock into his shoulder and sighted along the barrel. "Nice," he said, trying and failing for nonchalance. "Purdeys," he said to Kate.

"Uh-huh," she said.

"From England."

"Uh-huh," she said. "They shoot as well as a Remington twelve-gauge?"

Kate knew enough about guns to keep her own in serviceable condition and to shoot straight when required. She wasn't a gun fancier. An elaborately scrolled stock did not send her into raptures, she wouldn't think of loading her own ammunition, and she didn't own every copy of *The Shooter's Bible* ever published. A gun was a tool, one necessary to the Bush lifestyle. Gun nuts, on the other hand, spent thousands of dollars for something they'd never take down from the rack except to show off, as Dieter was showing off now. Kate wondered if the Purdeys had ever brought anything down more edible than a clay pigeon, or if they were merely toys bought specifically for this hunt, to be used once and then stored with the G.I. Joe doll his parents had given him when he was ten and which had bored him before his birthday was over.

Fortunately Wagner had drowned out her cavalier reply.

"If I might," Jack said, entirely too deferentially for Kate's taste, "may I ask how much they cost you?"

Dieter said something in German, and then apologized. "Excuse me. Sixteen thousand pounds British. What is that in American dollars, let me see. About thirty thousand dollars, I think."

Kate thought Wagner had done something to her eardrums. "Thirty thousand dollars for a couple of lousy shotguns?"

His smile was condescending. "No, Kate. Thirty thousand dollars each."

"You have to be fitted for them," Jack crooned, caressing the butt of the one he was holding with a reverence previously reserved for Kate's thigh. "They're made to order, like a suit. You have to fly to England for fittings."

Kate stared at Dieter, who looked insufferably smug. "Let me see that," she said to Jack.

He yielded it with reluctance. It felt good in her hands, she had to admit. It looked good, too, all shining metal and gleaming wood, carefully crafted down to the last tiny screw. She broke it open. It was empty. She looked at Dieter, whose indulgent smile waned a trifle.

"You want ammunition?" he said doubtfully. "Well, all right. You must be careful, though. It has a hair trigger."

Jack eyed Kate warily. He knew that look. Out of the corner of his mouth he muttered, "Kate, what are you up to?"

"Just looking at a gun." She gave him a sunny smile he instantly distrusted. "Maybe that bear that's been hanging around smelled the spaghetti. Can't hurt to throw a little scare into him."

Kate took the cartridges and slid them home. She walked around the circle, moving slowly, shotgun carried casually in her hooked arm, to all intents and purposes looking as if she were moving toward the creek, there to let off a few rounds. Dieter sensed no menace in this, and relaxed. Jack knew better, and didn't.

The cassette recorder was sitting on a round stump smoothed to a level finish to be used alternately as a chopping block, a table and a stepladder to the woodpile directly in back of it. The woodpile, three and a half cords of seasoned birch, was stacked in a rectangular wooden frame sheltered by a blue plastic tarpaulin.

Hendrik and Fedor sat on the left-hand curve of the circle, a little apart and heads close together, talking in low voices. The German gutturals reminded her of something. For a moment she couldn't think of what it was, and then it came to her. The gutturals, so thickly articulated, so deep in the throat, were like Aleut, the language of her grandparents, the language her parents had rejected for fear their daughter would be handicapped by it in an English-speaking world. As a result, the only Aleut she knew were a couple of swear words, ripe oaths that ripped out in satisfying growls, curses whose meanings she had long since forgotten.

They appeared to be arguing about something. As she strolled by, Hendrik's voice rose in protest. Fedor looked over his shoulder at Kate and put a soothing hand on Hendrik's arm. Hendrik shook it off but fell silent.

Hubert had forsaken the fire for the edge of the brush and stood shoulder deep in a patch of fireweed, examining the topped-out tufts with a notebook in one hand and a frown of concentration on his face. As she passed, he waded deeper into the brush, catching at a handful of highbush cranberries Kate had missed that afternoon, tasting one, making a face, spitting it out, jotting a note in his notebook. Hubert was into R&D of more than just computer operating systems.

A few feet beyond them, the firelit circle on her right, the woods on her left and the cassette player with its wood-pile backdrop ten feet in front of her, she stopped. She raised the shotgun, looking to Dieter's indulgent eye as if she were admiring its finish, and why not? It was a perfect example of the gunsmith's art. Hadn't he paid thirty thousand dollars to make sure it was?

Instead, Kate pulled the stock into her shoulder, laid her cheek to its smooth finish, sighted along the barrel and, almost as an afterthought, pulled the trigger.

The result was spectacular. There was a deafening boom, the cassette player leapt into the air and shattered into a hundred pieces, silencing the music in mid-shriek. Bodies dove for cover and German oaths filled the air.

There was a long, strained silence. Inevitably, heads popped up and turned Kate's way, eyes round with a growing comprehension and intensifying incredulity.

"Oops," Kate said.

She lowered the shotgun and smiled at Dieter. "You were right, Dieter. A very sensitive trigger. I didn't realize. You understand, I'm sure. It was an accident. I'm terribly sorry."

Demetri, whose natural expression was stoic in the extreme, became so impassive he looked like he'd been stuffed and mounted. George said, "I'd better go check on the planes," and headed off toward the airstrip at a smart clip. Jack made the mistake of catching Old Sam's wicked eye and had to turn away hastily, his shoulders shaking.

Dieter was engaged in picking little pieces of black plastic from the front of his shirt. When he looked up his face was very still.

"Not a problem," he said. He even smiled, a widening of his full lips to expose most of his square white teeth. The pale blue eyes met hers.

"An accident. I understand." The mirthless smile widened. "Oops."

THREE

*There ain't a damn bit of difference between
a bull moose in rut and a drunk chasing girls in a bar.*

The guests bedded down in the cabins, two to a cabin. Dieter shared with Eberhard, Gunther with Klemens, Hendrik with Fedor, Hubert with Gregor, and, in a pairing that caused no end of speculation among certain of the guides, Senta with Berg.

"Berg means mountain in German," Demetri observed in a rare burst of loquacity.

There followed more speculation in the lodge, where the guides were bunking. Demetri, Old Sam and George slept on fold-out cots placed on three sides of the enormous old wood stove that took up most of the west wall of the building. Jack and Kate, declared more or less unanimously to stand in no need of the warming influence of the stove, had been banished to the double bed tucked into a corner behind a three-quarter wall made of stacked Blazo boxes that doubled as pantry shelves.

"You think they got something going?" George wanted to know.

"Why, you interested?" Old Sam said.

"Of course he's interested," Kate said, snuggling backward into Jack's ready embrace. He was interested, too, and she smiled into her pillow. He couldn't do anything with three men in the room. She wriggled some more, to torture him.

"It's a funny group," George said thoughtfully. His cot creaked as he rolled to his back, staring at the shadows cast on the ceiling through the cracks in the stove's fire door. "Dieter's the only one who appears to have any real interest in hunting. The rest of them don't seem to care one way or the other. They aren't even urban warriors. I can't figure out why the bunch of them aren't at Club Med, laying around on a beach and knocking back mai tais."

Old Sam grunted. "I can. Dieter's the boss. He signs their paychecks. He wanted them to go skydiving on their vacation, they'd say how high you want us to jump from."

"You think any of them have shot a gun before now?" Demetri said.

Old Sam snorted. "Not hardly."

"Great," Jack grumbled, raising his voice to be heard above the partition. "So that means we're going to be giving shooting lessons along with everything else?"

"Looks like it," George said glumly. "Kate, I want you with Dieter and Eberhard when we go out."

"After what happened tonight?" Old Sam said. "Dieter's as likely to shoot Kate as he is a moose, George. Might want to rethink that."

"Dieter's looking like the only one with enough experience to hurt himself," George said.

"He'll probably show off all the more with a woman watching," Old Sam said. "He's the type."

"Not after tonight," George said. "Not in front of Kate. He knows he can't buffalo her now. Which is why I want her to keep her eye on him."

"Oh?" said Old Sam. "While you will be keeping an eye on who, exactly?"

"Why," said George, elaborately casual, "I think that Senta requires some hands-on supervision."

Old Sam snorted. "Imagine my surprise."

"We might as well split them between us the way they're split between the cabins," George said. "Kate'll take Dieter and Eberhard, Jack, Gunther and Klemens, Demetri, Hubert and Gregor, Old Sam, Fedor and Hendrik—"

Old Sam snorted again and made a production out of pulling all his blankets loose and rearranging them and himself on the cot.

"—and I'll take Senta."

"And the mountain," Demetri said demurely.

"And the mountain," George agreed.

The Great White Hunters straggled into breakfast one at a time, Senta first, to George's clearly demonstrated delight, Dieter second, Klemens third. Kate thought the lines of his face looked deeper than they had the day before. "Did you sleep well, Klemens?" she said, handing him a mug. The cabins were rudimentary affairs, with small wood stoves for heat and plywood bunks with thin pads for sleeping. An older man with less supple bones might find them less than comfortable.

He smiled at her with obvious effort. "I slept very well, Kate," he said. "This coffee is wonderful."

"Kaladi Brothers," Jack said cheerfully. "A local roaster. You can pick up some on your way back through Anchorage if you want to. Who's making breakfast this morning?"

Old Sam made breakfast, eggs, home fries, toast and caribou sausage, the latter because George wanted his hunters to see the proper outcome of a successful hunt. "Moose steak for dinner," he told Demetri, who had cooking duty that night. "And some of your chocolate chip cookies for dessert," he told Jack.

Since chocolate chip cookies were the beginning and the end of Jack's expertise in the kitchen, he was agreeable. He and Demetri cleared away the breakfast dishes while George explained the drill to the guests. "All right, folks, here's how it works. I'm going up in the Cub to take a look-see."

"An aerial survey," Dieter said, nodding.

"Er, yes," George said, "an aerial survey. No point in walking farther than we have to, right, guys?" There were emphatic nods all around. "Let's see, it's"— George looked at the calendar on the wall— "okay, it's Wednesday, September twenty-seventh. I'm sure Dieter passed on what I said before you left home, but just in case, let's go over it one more time."

He was on his feet, standing at the end of the table. A map of Alaska was taped to the wall in back of him, a window on either side. Kate looked at the assembled party and wondered what they made of the lodge. The linoleum underfoot was clean but worn and cracked and coming up in places. The planks lining the walls were painted white to reflect much needed light but they were rough and unfinished. The gas stove was utilitarian, and the sink drained down a rubber hose that led through the wall and into the row of pansies planted outside.

There was a wooden table and molded fiberglass chairs in the center of the room. A shelf full of tattered paperbacks hung on one wall, with copies of National Geographic, Aviation Week and Field & Stream stacked beneath. On another wall was a gun rack, full of rifles and shotguns and with knives in sheaths hanging from it. Boxes of ammunition were stacked on counter, table and floor.

Coleman lanterns hung from hooks on every wall, and an Aladdin lamp, its chimney immaculate, sat next to the stove. A length of pipe suspended from wires nailed to the ceiling served as a coat rack, and the Blazo boxes that did double duty as kitchen shelves and room divider were clean and neatly organized, but they were still Blazo boxes, proclaiming the fact in loud red letters on each exposed side. Every couple of years George married someone who took it into her head to dust.

The group didn't seem to be taking much notice one way or another. They gave a collective impression of patient endurance, which made Kate wonder how many times Dieter had shanghaied his staff on one of these so-called retreats. What was next? Diving the Great Barrier Reef? Climbing Everest? George was right about one thing, at least; they would have been more at home at Club Med.

Senta was smoking a thin, brown cigarette, Klemens a pipe, Dieter a cigar, naturally. The smoke met and mingled in the air, creating graceful swirls gilded by the sunlight now cascading through the windows like four individual cataracts. If George had known how it also lit up his scalp through his thinning hair, he would never have stood there.

Kate caught a whiff of cigar, nearly gagged and moved out of range.

"This is moose season," George said, standing very straight and sounding very stern. "Today, tomorrow, Friday and Saturday, we're hunting moose. Plus I see most of you are packing shotguns, so we can hunt some birds, too, if you like, spruce hen, ptarmigan, we'll probably run into some Canadian geese and maybe some wood ducks, too. Bear season, however, doesn't start until the first of October. That's Sunday."

George cocked an eyebrow and even went so far as to waggle a finger. "Now, that doesn't mean you won't see any bears between now and Sunday, that just means you're not supposed to shoot at them until Sunday. If they charge you, that's a different story, but half the time it'll be a false charge. Let your guide decide whether or not to shoot, okay?"

He leaned forward, both hands flat on the table for emphasis. Dieter started to smile, met George's flinty gaze and changed his mind.

"We've got some pretty strict laws in this state about what to shoot and when," George said, slowly and with deliberate emphasis. "You shoot something when or where you're not supposed to, and there's a state fish and wildlife protection officer watching, which they are more often than you know or like, then you're likely going to be fined, plus chances are pretty good you'll do some jail time, too."

"How much money?" Dieter said.

"How much jail?" Klemens said.

"For shooting an illegal moose, which is what we're hunting today, the maximum penalty is a five-thousand-dollar fine and a year in jail."

Dieter shrugged. Five thousand American was pocket change to Dieter, the shrug said; he probably tipped more than that on a night out. Or liked people to think he did.

Klemens frowned. "One year? That is a lot of prison time for shooting out of season. Our laws are not so strict."

Old Sam glared. "Probably not, since you people hunted your last bear along about the time of the Reformation."

Klemens looked startled at first, met Old Sam's fierce eyes and gave a sudden laugh. "You could be right," he admitted, and Kate liked him all the better for it. Judging from his expression, so did Old Sam, although he wouldn't have admitted it unless his fingernails were being ripped out by redhot pincers.

George ignored them both. "The sentence depends on the offense, what kind of game, what game management unit you're in, how cranky the agent who catches you is, what side of the bed the judge got up on that morning, like that." George straightened. "In case you think I might have some pull with the local authorities in these matters, let me tell you that it doesn't matter who you are or who you know. A while back, the director of the Division of Fish and Wildlife and an FBI agent buddy of his got liquored up and illegally shot a caribou in a closed area on the Glenn Highway. They were both arrested, convicted, fined and they both did time. As I'm your guide, if you screw up I'll be liable. I could lose my guide's license, my lodge. My planes."

He looked each of them in the eye, one by one. "I guarantee you, folks. You make that happen, you'll pray the state gets to you before I do."

There was a short silence. Kate watched everyone translate George's words into German and back again. They turned almost as one to Dieter, waiting for a response to this comprehensive and unsettling threat on their lives.

"I have told them this already," Dieter said.

George gave Dieter a cordial smack on the back that in no way diluted the menace of his warning. "Just a friendly reminder, Dieter, is all. Listen to your guides, let them estimate the width of the rack and count the brow tines. And don't shoot unless and until they give you the go-ahead. Now, anybody have any questions?"

No one did. "Okay, anybody else want to say anything?"

"I do," Old Sam said, and stood up to bend a severe eye on the gathering. "There ain't a damn bit of difference between a bull moose in rut and a drunk chasing girls in a bar."

Gunther's giggle was high-pitched and nervous.

Old Sam ignored him. "You people have chosen to hunt in the rut, fine. You don't care about meat, you're looking for racks, I understand that. Just you understand up front that moose are like people as soon as they get to chasing girls. They get to fighting and flexing their muscles and doing a lot of stamping and snorting and grunting and whoofing. They'll charge anything that doesn't get out of their way fast enough." He raised a pontifical finger. "Don't get in between a bull moose and his girlfriend. Don't get in between a bull moose and another bull moose who's in between the first bull and his girlfriend. The only time a moose should know you're there is the second after you shoot him, just before he falls down dead."

He paused, added with emphasis, "What I'm saying is this. You get your sorry ass stomped by a moose, I ain't packing you out."

There was a brief silence. Kate examined the upturned

faces, sternly repressing a grin. When was the last time this bunch of autonomous executives had had such a talking to? When was the last time anyone had dared?

Well, they had signed on for a wilderness experience, and Old Sam was doing his best to provide one. Most big-game guides did everything up to and including laying a red carpet from plane to lodge for their paying guests, pampering them with comfortable beds, gourmet meals, packing their rifles in and their meat out, and sometimes shooting for them. As George said, "They want a wilderness experience, I give 'em a wilderness experience. They want to be babied, they can take a cruise."

"Okay," George said now, and smiled widely for the first time that morning. "Now how 'bout I grab some air and go find us something to shoot at tomorrow?"

"Can I go?" Gunther said, so eager his tail was nearly wagging.

"Sure," George said, waving him on. "I can always use an extra pair of eyes."

"Wait a minute," Dieter said, sitting up. "We aren't hunting today?"

George shook his head and said firmly, "Remember what I told you, Dieter. No flying and shooting the same day. It was too close to dark when we finished flying everybody in yesterday for me to do an eyeball then. We'll go first thing tomorrow, though, so start getting your gear into shape. After that, you might want to get in a little fishing. I took a look this morning, and there's a mess of rainbows sitting under that log on the far side of the creek."

Klemens brightened and made a beeline for his rod case.

Shortly afterward the Cub rose off the strip and began

making lazy circles in the sky, sometimes where it could be seen from the lodge, sometimes where it could only be heard, and sometimes, ominously, where it could be neither. Kate resigned herself to a long and anything but leisurely journey bushwhacking through the dense undergrowth of the surrounding countryside in search of the elusive moose.

But that wasn't until tomorrow, and today the sun was shining and she didn't have to walk any farther than the creek if she didn't want to. She turned to Dieter. "There's stuff for lunch on the table in the lodge. Fill up on water or whatever you're drinking. Check your weapons, pack your ammunition."

"I take five rounds," Dieter stated.

He seemed to have decided to ignore what had happened the night before, and Kate, guiltily aware that she could have put George's hunting party and the assistant guides' paychecks in the toilet with one shot, strove for a tone of friendly inquiry. "Really? Five rounds of ammunition, total? Why is that, Dieter?"

"Capstick says he takes five rounds to hunt tigers. He says if you don't get what you're aiming at in five rounds, you don't deserve any more shots." Dieter challenged her with a look.

She kept her expression mild. "Fine, whatever you want, it's your hunt, after all." She had no idea who or what Capstick was. "You have no objection to my carrying an extra box of cartridges, I hope?"

He couldn't quite succeed in keeping the condescension, perhaps even the contempt, from showing on his face. "Of course not."

"Good." She gave him a cheerful smile, kissing her tip

good-bye, and Dieter would have been the type to tip big. Oh well. "You see, Dieter, I've been charged by a bear. A bear is a large and scary animal, with a lot of teeth and a ton of atti-tude. I'm going to be toting all the ammunition I can carry. I'd just as soon be safe than sorry, myself."

He didn't believe her, that was obvious, but he made a great effort not to show it. "Attitude?"

"Means the bear is pissed off most of the time," Jack said, adjusting the straps of a packboard to fit his large frame.

"What is that for?"

"It's what we pack out the meat on," Jack said.

Hubert gave Dieter a sideways look. "We are bringing the meat back? Why? We want the horns, not the meat."

"We want the horns and the meat, as long as the meat isn't too rank from the rut," Jack said patiently. "And even if it is, we'd be breaking the law if we let it lay."

He exchanged a glance with Kate. It continually amazed them how you could tell a cheechako something three times over and he still didn't hear it. "If it is, we'll turn it over to a couple of mushers we know for dog meat. The rule is, we can't waste it. Come on, pick one out and try it on, I'll help you cinch it up. You next, Dieter."

Dieter said nothing, and after a moment's pause Hubert allowed himself to be fitted with a packboard.

To Kate, Dieter said, "Where are your weapons?"

Kate, wondering if Dieter was going to want to fire a test round at, say, her feet, fetched her Remington bolt-action .30-06 and her Browning single-barreled pump-action twelve gauge.

Dieter jerked his chin at the shotgun. "How many does the magazine hold?"

"Five," Kate said. "And one in the chamber. Six, altogether."

He looked down at his breaktop Purdey. "How much did they cost?"

"A little over six hundred each," Kate said.

"Six hundred dollars?" Dieter's voice scaled up in a disbelief parodying Kate's of the night before.

"Uh-huh." She loaded the rifle and leaned it against a tree trunk close to hand.

"You're not loading the shotgun?" Dieter said, watching her.

"No need. Tomorrow I'm the guide, not the hunter. The rifle's plenty, should I need to back you up."

She looked at Eberhard's weapon and her eyes widened. Hers weren't the only ones. "Goddamn!" Old Sam said. He stepped lively across the clearing. "Jesus, son, what is that cannon you're carrying? You must have thought we were gonna be hunting humpback whales." He held out a hand, and after a moment of hesitation Eberhard handed his rifle over.

Old Sam probably had about thirty-five, forty years on Eberhard. He didn't quite come up to Eberhard's shoulder, and Eberhard outweighed him by a hundred pounds. Nonetheless, Old Sam tossed Eberhard's artillery around like it was a toy pistol and kept up a running commentary besides. "I'll be dipped and fried, a Weatherby Magnum .378. Don't think I've ever seen one outside the *Gun Digest*. Bubba, this will sure as hell ring your bell every time it goes off. You get a head shot with that thing, we won't have to pack the rack back."

He strong-armed a toss at Eberhard and the Weatherby

smacked solidly into Eberhard's hands. "You get a body shot," Old Sam added, "and we won't have to worry about packing out much in the way of meat, either."

Eberhard didn't smile. He finished loading the Weatherby with quick, practiced movements. The Weatherby, Kate noticed, was the only weapon in sight besides her own that didn't look brand new.

Mutt had observed the ongoing preparations, identified them for what they were from prior experience and correctly deduced that she was about to be left behind. Mutt never took kindly to being left behind, and from breakfast on had been shadowing Kate with all the efficiency of a continental op. With her shoulder pressed against Kate's knee, she watched Eberhard closely out of intent yellow eyes.

Eberhard looked up and saw the big gray half-wolf, half-husky whose head passed Kate's elbow even when they were both on their feet. Man and dog exchanged a long, unsmiling look, and Kate was suddenly struck by their likeness. Watchful, efficient, predatory. They looked like they were both from the same litter.

And then Mutt looked up and caught Kate's eye and dropped her jaw in a wide, lupine grin, and the similarity vanished as if it had never been.

Dieter made a fuss over producing his rifle, which he introduced to the group as if he were presenting a family member of whom he was particularly proud. According to Dieter, it was a Gebruder Merkel Model 90 Drilling, an over-under job, two shotgun barrels with a rifle barrel mounted beneath, which seemed something like overkill given the brace of Purdeys in the gray case. It looked, as one might expect, brand new, very heavy, and right out of Kate's price range.

"Eight thousand dollars American," Dieter volunteered proudly, displaying the weapon while at the same time keeping it carefully out of Kate's reach. He might never forgive her for the slaughter of his tape deck but he couldn't help showing off. "More for the engraving and the custom wood. Notice the teak inlay."

She hid a grin. "I notice."

He held out a small box of twenty rounds. "Ammunition from RWS, TUGs, 293 grain." He ran a swift internal calculation. "For you, eighty dollars American per box."

"Uh-huh." Kate ran her own calculation. Dieter's ammo was running him about four bucks a bullet. A box of twenty rounds of Winchester 180-grain .30-06 cartridges cost between sixteen and eighteen bucks, or an average seventy-five cents a bullet, and you didn't have to fly them in from Munich, either. Kate decided she'd stick to the homegrown.

She stood up and cast a quick eye around the rest of the group, who had been armed with duplicate automatic rifles, .30 calibers at a guess, and duplicate twelve-gauge shotguns, all of some unfamiliar and probably European brand. Kate would bet her homestead that they were half the caliber and a quarter the price of Dieter's arsenal, which was probably just as well, given the beating they were about to take in inexperienced hands.

"No, like this," Old Sam told Hubert, and slammed the rifle in poor Hubert's shoulder harder than the recoil of a shot would.

Demetri watched silently as Fedor tried to load his rifle with the bullets backward.

They traveled in a group down to the firing range George had set up at the foot of the runway. Targets were concentric circles drawn on sheets of typing paper tacked to plywood backboards standing on the edge of the Kichatna. Eberhard declined to take a practice shot, Dieter's first knocked his target off its two-by-four legs, and Berg flinched just as much from his tenth shot as he did his first.

The rest of them were similarly skilled, with the exception of Klemens, who was competent if a little rusty. He caught Kate's eye and gave her an apologetic smile. "It's been a long time since I shot a rifle."

Kate wondered when and where that had been. Klemens looked old enough to have served in World War II. At that moment the Cub was heard on final, and they trooped up the airstrip to meet it. Gunther looked a little green around the gills, but from George's expression the news was good, and his words confirmed it. "Found us two nice big bulls about three miles up the creek."

"How many can I shoot?" Dieter demanded.

George looked at him sternly. "One. You've all got one moose tag, Dieter. You get one moose each, and that's it."

Dieter's expression came perilously close to a sulk.

"Unless," George added, "you can talk one of your people into giving up their tag to you."

"Is that legal?" Klemens said in surprise.

"Well." George scratched his chin. "It isn't if you tell someone about it. Don't."

"Okay." Klemens smiled. "You can have my tag, Dieter."

Dieter began to expostulate. Klemens raised one hand, palm out. "Oh, I'll go, I'll go, if only to walk around the country a bit. But I've done all the killing I need to. You can have my tag, Dieter."

Dieter shook his head firmly. "Everyone gets a shot at a moose, Klemens. That's what we came for, and that's what we are all going to do." His tone was final, and Klemens subsided.

Dieter, having got his way, beamed.

That afternoon everyone scattered along the Nakochna with rod and reel, mostly light tackle on ten-pound test. There was a lot of snagging at first, of humpies too tired to resist, of deadfall trailing limbs in the water, but after a while Gregor caught and by a miracle landed a two-pound rainbow and everyone began fishing in earnest.

The guides took turns keeping watch. At four o'clock it was Kate's turn, and she shouldered her rifle and ambled down to the creek. She found Klemens around the first bend, tucked cozily into a niche made between a couple of boulders.

He was sleeping, his mouth open, a gentle, inoffensive snore issuing forth in a steady purr of sound swallowed up by the sound of the creek. Rod and reel lay discarded at his feet, and a book lay open on his chest. She rested a hand on one of the boulders and felt the stone warm to the touch. She tried to read the title of the book but he stirred and opened his eyes.

She smiled down at him. "Hi. Guess you didn't find any fish."

He yawned and stretched, bones popping. "I didn't look for any. The sun is too hot."

"Umm." Kate turned her face into it. "We've got company." She pointed without looking.

Klemens raised his head to follow her finger and sat up with a jerk.

"Shhhh," she said. She had already unslung her rifle but she didn't think she was going to need it.

The grizzly coalesced out of the brush like a great brown ghost made manifest, an immense creature with a silver snout and little pig eyes. As always, Kate marveled at how silently something that large could move when it wanted to.

"A bear," he breathed, his eyes enormous.

"A grizzly," she agreed, keeping her voice low.

He wasn't twenty-five feet from where they sat, and he'd had a good summer, attested to by the rolls of fat sliding around beneath his thick coat of golden brown fur. He ambled out into midstream and took a halfhearted swipe at a dog salmon. Claws scooped and lifted and the dog smacked onto the bank. Weary from its long journey from ocean to birth waters, it flopped once and gave up. The grizzly sauntered out, brown fur tipped with drops of water gleaming crystal in the sun, picked the fish up with his teeth and seemed once more to vanish, leaving nothing behind but the print of a paw in a patch of sand, filling rapidly with water and soon washed downstream with the current.

Klemens, still sitting bolt upright, said, "I should have brought my rifle."

"You always should," Kate agreed. She looked down with a smile. "I thought we told you that."

Klemens gave a grave nod. "You did. I will remember next time."

"Good," Kate said, equally grave.

Klemens looked across the creek. "He won't come back?"

"He'll eat his fish and take a nap," Kate said, and closed her eyes against the sun. "We're okay. For now."

There followed a few moments of silence broken only by the lazy gurgle of water flowing next to them. "You were always a guide?" Klemens said eventually.

Kate smiled without opening her eyes, hearing in Klemens's words the echo of Jack's question about the Bush word for Renaissance woman. She liked this old man, who had done all the killing he wanted to and who was now content to laze in the sun with a book, who took the occasional wandering grizzly in his stride. "I was always a lot of things, and still am, but I hunted with my father from the time I was able to walk."

"What did you hunt?"

"Deer, mostly. In the islands in Prince William Sound. And moose." She opened her eyes, feeling like a lizard as she blinked. "Whatever we could find to put on the table."

"So you hunted to eat?"

"Yes."

Klemens was silent for a moment. "A good reason to hunt," he said at last.

The only reason, Kate thought.

He looked at her and she had an uneasy feeling that he could read her thought in her face. She got to her feet. "I'd better check on the rest of the crew. See you later, Klemens."

He smiled, it seemed to her, a little sadly. "See you later, Katerina." At her surprise, he added, "Kate is for Katherine, yes? Katherine is Katerina in German."

"Ekaterina," Kate said.

"Ah, Russian." He nodded. "From the Russian Alaskan Company, yes?"

She smiled. "More or less."

He seemed to relax, as if he had regained her favor some-how.

Klemens was too old and too successful to need the ap-proval of strangers thirty years his junior, Kate thought. Dieter must do one hell of a number on his employees' egos.

FOUR

Just try to make sure nobody shoots anybody else in the ass, okay?

The next morning George convened the guides in the lodge for a brief meeting. His manner was brisk and businesslike as he pointed out their various routes on a U.S.G.S. map of the area mounted on cardboard. "Demetri, Jack and Old Sam, you take your people up the road to Blueberry Ridge. If you decide to overnight it, remember there's a spike camp on the point of the ridge overlooking the creek where it forks, right side. If you get into trouble and need help, fire three shots, bang, one-one thousand—"

"Bang, two-one thousand—" Old Sam said.

"Bang," said Jack.

"—and we'll come on the run," George said, unperturbed. "Same here." He dropped his voice. "I don't know that we're going to bag anything first day, not with this bunch. Just try to make sure nobody shoots anybody else in the ass, okay?"

"Okay," Demetri said, stolid as always. Jack nodded and shouldered his rifle. Old Sam grunted and spat.

George turned to Kate and grinned. Kate braced herself for the worst. "You and I, dear heart, are heading east. You know that little pear-shaped lake about four miles thataway?"

Kate sighed. There were about fifty lakes between the camp and the Yentna River, but, unfortunately, they'd been to this lake on previous hunts and she knew where it was. "You mean the one on the other side of Backbreak Ridge? The one across Mud Ass Swamp? The one just this side of the Youngstown Bend? That lake?"

George's laugh had a distinctly sadistic flavor to it. "That's the one. I found us a nice big fat bull grazing on the diamond willow growing next to the creek feeding into that lake."

"Oh, joy," Kate said.

The screen door banged as George stepped into the yard. "Come on, folks, get your gear on. We've got a ways to walk today."

Senta paused in the act of buckling her packboard on. "You mean we have to walk the whole way? No flying?"

"No flying," Dieter said, boisterous and beaming and brimming with macho. "This is Alaska! The Last Frontier! I wanted us to have the true wilderness experience!"

From the expressions on a few faces, it wasn't a desire shared wholeheartedly by his employees, but although Dieter's face bore nothing but good humor, there was no give in it. No one said anything and there was no outward mutiny. Kate wondered what would have happened if they'd been on a spring hunt, complete with thigh-deep slush and mosquitoes fresh out of their larvae and ravenous for their first meal.

Old Sam and Demetri got the four-wheelers out of the garage, two Honda FourTrax Foremans with four-wheel drive and towing capacity. The four-wheelers alone would have set George back six grand each; fortunately, the previous spring a couple of bear hunters from Anchorage got liquored up and went hoorahing across country with Park ranger Dan O'Brian in hot pursuit. They'd wound up in Kate's front yard, the fashion of their arrival bringing irresistibly to mind that immortal stage direction by Shakespeare, "Exit, pursued by a bear."

Dan had hauled them off to the pokey, abandoning the four-wheelers to Kate's tender mercies. She had sold them to George for a thousand each, who, after he bought two new trailers seating six each, was out less than the price of one Foreman new. Everybody was happy, except maybe the original owners, and they were still in jail, so it didn't matter.

Jack hopped on board the second trailer as it rolled past, and grinned at Kate. "Don't worry, Kate, I'll give you a foot rub when we get back."

That's not all you'll be rubbing, buddy, Kate thought.

He read her mind as he often unnervingly did, and flashed a grin. "Hold that thought."

The two-vehicle convoy purred up the airstrip. Jack waved a smug good-bye as the second trailer vanished into the undergrowth as surely as the bear by the creek had the day before.

"Okay, let's move like we got a purpose," George said, shouldering pack and rifle.

They moved like they had a purpose. Mutt, left behind on guard duty, sat sulking at the edge of the yard as they crossed the strip and entered the trees on the other side.

They were over Backbreak Ridge before they realized they'd lost Berg. "Well, shit," George said. "How the hell'd he do that? I been hiking drag ever since we left camp."

They'd been following an overgrown game trail down the far side of the ridge, and it didn't take any encouragement at all to get the party to stop for a breather. The brush, after thinning out over the top of the knoll, had begun to thicken again, and since most of the alders were hanging grimly on to their leaves in spite of the season, there were places where they couldn't even see the sky, let alone each other. It was dark and sweaty going in the undergrowth, sometimes with only the sound of brush breaking ahead to guide you down the track. And it was steep going, up and down over a razor's edge of rock thrust upward by a geologic strength of will that had defeated even time's efforts to wear it into a gentler slope. Even Kate's thigh muscles were protesting.

"I'd better go back and roust him out," George said in disgust. "Sorry, Kate. Don't know how I got to be so sloppy."

"Not your fault," Senta said. "Berg is always wandering off. Sometimes in body, sometimes in mind. Always in spirit. Not what you would expect from someone who heads up quality control, but there you are." She smiled, a light film of perspiration giving her already flawless skin a rosy glow. The effect was dazzling enough to require sunglasses, which George was not wearing. George and Senta had been trailing the rest of them, lagging farther behind with every turn of the trail, and Kate had heard Senta laughing a lot. It could be just her suspicious mind, but that might have had something to do with George not noticing Berg's disappearance.

George shed his packboard. "What do you do again, Senta?"

The smile became even more dazzling. "I'm the head of human resources for all of DRG."

"All of DRG's resourceful humans are damn lucky." He reshouldered his rifle. "Want to backtrail with me?"

Kate waited confidently for Senta to tell George in no uncertain terms that there was no way this three-piece suit was going up and down that ridge one more time than necessary, no matter what her boss said.

Senta smiled again. "Sure." She doffed her packboard and readjusted her fanny pack.

"Great," George said, a matching smile spreading across his face. Kate thought sourly that he might trip over his tongue if he wasn't careful. "Kate, take Dieter and Eberhard on to the lake. Don't want to let that big fat bull get away now, do we?"

"What do you mean we, white man," Kate muttered.

George didn't hear her or pretended he didn't, and started back up the ridge with Senta in tow. Ten steps up the trail he stopped and turned. "And Kate, if you run into Crazy Emmett, just move on, okay? Don't say hi, don't look at him, just pretend you don't even see him. He hates being noticed. He'll leave you alone if you leave him alone."

"Yeah, yeah," Kate said, and waved Dieter and Eberhard on as Senta and George started back up the ridge.

"This Crazy Emmett," Eberhard said, speaking for the first time that morning. "Who is he?"

Kate nodded in the direction of the horizon. "He lives on a lake over there. Kind of a hermit. Likes his privacy. He's harmless. Let's get a move on, shall we?"

They followed the game trail into Mud Ass Swamp and walked for what seemed like forever to Kate, who didn't like getting her feet wet and who spent the entire time sending out feelers to her toes to see if the waterproof job on her boots was holding. They emerged eventually on a low, rocky knoll covered with lichen and blueberry bushes. About a quarter mile distant they could see the lake glinting through a stand of white spruce. Kate checked the wind. What there was of it was in their faces.

She looked back at the ridge and didn't see anyone coming their way. She hadn't really expected to; she had a feeling George and Senta were experiencing a close encounter of the third kind, and taking their time over it. She only hoped Berg hadn't had a close encounter of his own with a bear in the meanwhile. He had a rifle, of course; they all had, but that didn't mean he had either the skill or the presence of mind to use it.

"Okay, guys," she said. "Looks like you get first crack at that bull. We're downwind of him, so if we take it slow and quiet he shouldn't hear us coming. Let's have some lunch first, though."

"No, let's go," Dieter said, shifting his rifle from one shoulder to the other. "Maybe he'll get away."

Kate shook her head. "He'll be there, and we haven't had anything to eat in four hours. A shaky hand isn't going to do your aim any good. Come on, sit down." She met his glare with a steady, implacable gaze.

Eberhard touched Dieter's shoulder and murmured something in German. Dieter's face cleared and he laughed. It was an unpleasant laugh in any language, and so was the look he ran over Kate. "Yeah, okay, we eat." He made it sound like a command, and as if on cue, Eberhard dumped his packboard and opened his fanny pack.

Kate sat a little apart from them and ate her sandwich,

apple and cookies, with her rifle on her knees. She hadn't seen any sign of bears but it never hurt to stay alert. She'd known those who hadn't, but the friendships were never of a very long duration.

Dieter completed his meal by crumpling up the Saran wrap his sandwiches had come in and tossing it over his shoulder.

Kate took a deep breath, held it, and let it out again. "Dieter," she said, "pick that up."

Dieter appeared genuinely confused. "What?"

She pointed at the wrapper. "Pick that up."

"What, the wrapper?" He looked from her to the wrapper, and added something else in German, something that sounded less than complimentary, and again she was reminded of Aleut. It might as well have been Greek; for all she knew, Dieter could have been thanking her for reminding him of his duty as a visitor to the Alaskan Bush. From the look on his face she didn't think so, though.

Patience was a virtue Kate neither had in quantity nor particularly admired. "The rule is, leave it how you found it. You pack it in, you pack it out. We don't leave trash behind on our hunts, Dieter. Pick up the wrapper." She thought it over, and added—he was a paying customer, after all— "Please."

His fair skin flushed a dull red. "You pick it up."

Kate didn't move. "I'm your guide," she said flatly, "not the garbage man. Pick it up yourself." Almost casually, she shifted her rifle so that the muzzle was pointing between his feet.

There was a strained silence. Dieter glared at Kate, face turning even redder. Either he didn't like women, didn't like people of color or didn't like anybody who didn't have as much money as he had, or maybe it was all three and nobody told him what to do besides. Take a number, Dieter, she thought.

Eberhard broke the impasse by leaning over and picking up the wrapper. He stuffed it in his fanny pack and buckled the pack around his waist. "Those moose don't stay around forever, do they?" he said. "We'd better get going." He cradled his Weatherby in his arms, and its muzzle came to rest pointed in Kate's general direction.

She laughed. He didn't like it, and neither did Dieter. She managed to control her amusement and jerked her chin in the direction of the lake. "Let's take it slow and easy, boys. Quiet as you can, okay?"

They took it slow and easy down to the lake, although the strain of carrying fourteen pounds of Merkel at present arms for three hours was beginning to show in Dieter's face and shoulders. He called for a rest often. Eberhard continued to manage his Weatherby like he would a toothpick.

They crouched in a stand of diamond willow, peering through the thicket to the water on the other side.

"My feet are getting wet," Dieter said, too loudly.

"Quiet," Kate said, without heat. Dieter was wearing hiking boots that laced as high as the ankle and no higher, not a lot of support over rough ground and no protection at all in the swamps that grew the best moose browse. She had no sympathy for him; George sent out a list of equipment to each of his hunting parties, including specific instructions about footwear. It wasn't her fault if Dieter chose not to follow them, although the hike home, particularly if they got their moose, was not looking like a fun time.

The lake was half a mile across, a limpid pool with the barest ripples showing in a silver surface that reflected every needle and leaf and branch of the trees that grew at its edge and the blue sky above. The diamond willow stood twelve feet deep in places around the edge, guaranteeing this lake would be first in the chow line for the local moose.

Since the day before George's bull had been joined by a second. Kate groaned to herself. Dieter would probably want both.

The first bull was directly across from them, broad butt planted in the lake, head buried in a thicket of diamond willow. He was on the scrawny side, though, and his rack was a little droopy around the edges, giving him the look of a character who just wandered out of a Disney cartoon.

About a hundred yards on their left, the second bull, nice and firm and fat, was planted with all four knees deep in water, a hundred percent of his attention focused on systematically stripping the bark from a stand of alders clustered at the edge of the lake, one branch at a time, making a leisurely journey around the clump, which direction was moving him slowly but steadily to dry ground. Perfect.

"Nice," Kate said in a voice barely above a whisper. It was an understatement. She estimated a good nine hundred pounds of meat dressed. "He'll fill up somebody's cache for the winter." Neither one of the bulls looked twitchy, so they might have yet to go into rut, which meant the meat might even be edible.

She looked at Eberhard and Dieter and for once was not disappointed.

It was impossible to realize the sheer bulk of *Alces gigas*, genus *Alces*, family Cervidae, order Artiodactyla without going into the wild, although there was a stuffed, mounted specimen of this ungulate ruminant antler bearer in the Anchorage International Airport, which made a living out of stopping tourists in their tracks. While ambassador to France, Thomas Jefferson had been laughed at when he spoke of the size and weight of the North American moose, and had had one stuffed and shipped to the French court to prove he wasn't just telling tales.

But this bull was very much alive, living, breathing, the sound of branches snapping between his jaws audible across the still water of the lake. He stood seven feet at the shoulder and measured at least nine feet nose to tail, with great humped shoulders, a long, heavy snout and a broad rack of antlers seventy, maybe seventy-two inches wide.

He was mature, about six or seven years old from the size and number of his brow tines, four on each side and similar in length and evenly spaced. It was a handsome rack, broadly and evenly palmed, which was just as well since it was destined to grace the wall of the board room at DRG. Kate felt a pang of regret that he was not long for this world and hoped fervently that he had gotten lucky on multiple occasions every year of his adult life and had many offspring scattered between here and Beluga.

"Look at those horns!" Dieter said.

"Quiet," Kate said.

"Are those horns a record?" Dieter demanded in a lower voice.

"No," Kate said without expression, but Eberhard gave her a sharp glance. "I'd guess about a seventy-inch spread, maybe a little more. It's well shaped, though, nice and even."

"It'll look good on the wall of the office," Eberhard said.

Dieter was not to be placated. "What's the record?"

"A little over eighty inches, tip to tip," Kate said, "according to Boone and Crockett."

Dieter crouched over his Merkel, hands clenched on the stock, face flushed with excitement, and worked this into centimeters. He swore. "A third of a meter short of the record."

One of the bull's ears twitched. "Quiet, Dieter. You don't really want to have to chase him through the bush, do you?"

"I wanted a record," Dieter said stubbornly.

Kate, crouching with her elbows on her knees, rifle held easily in her hands, said with great patience, "I don't think George puts any guarantees of record kills in his contracts, Dieter. You want this bull or not?"

Dieter flashed her a look of irritation, and looked back at the bull. "I want him," he said, and raised the Merkel to his shoulder.

"No, not yet!" Kate said urgently, but it was too late. The Merkel boomed in her ear.

Kate, quite forgetting who she was speaking to, said, "You stupid bastard!" and knocked the barrel of the Merkel upward as it boomed a second time.

Dieter leapt to his feet and yelled at her in German, face red with fury. Across the lake, the first bull bolted. As the ringing cleared from Kate's ears she could hear his frantic crashing through the undergrowth growing steadily more distant.

She got to her feet, ignoring Dieter, intent on the second bull, which was her mistake. He raised the Merkel, butt toward her, and pulled back as if to strike. She caught the movement from the corner of her eye and turned on her heel to face him directly, rifle held horizontally across her chest. As the butt came toward her, she used her rifle like Little John's quarterstaff, jerking it sharply upward. The swift, abrupt contact of barrel to stock jarred the Merkel out of Dieter's hands and it flew over his head and fell into the lake.

Eberhard's rifle was coming around and up. "Don't," Kate said. The bolt of the Remington shot home with a heartening sound.

There was a brief, tense silence, broken only by the frenzied splashing sounds Dieter made as he waded into the lake to search for his beloved Merkel. He found it and pulled it up, covered with muck and bracken. He wasn't happy, and he said so.

Kate didn't move. All of her attention was focused on the big man opposite her with the big rifle in his hands. Eberhard took a quick look at Dieter. He relaxed visibly, standing down, as it were, and actually bent his head, a warrior's recognition of his equal. "I won't underestimate you again," he said.

"Oh please," she said, impatiently. "Spare me the Marine's Hymn." She looked across the lake.

Dieter hadn't missed, but it hadn't been a clean hit, either. The second bull was lying half on the bank, half off it, surrounded by a widening pool of dark red. As she watched, he thrashed feebly, tangling his rack in the alders. She raised the .30-06 to her shoulder, flipping up the sights and bringing the bead to bear on the moose's head. He thrashed once again, before lying back against the bank, flanks heaving. Kate let out a breath, held it and sighted on the moose's left eye. Before the shot finished echoing across the lake, the bull was still.

She ejected the spent shell and picked it up. She was as short on diplomacy as she was on patience and only the fact that George Perry was a sometime employer and longtime friend kept her from giving forth with her unvarnished opinion of Dieter, his character, his ancestors and his associates. She pocketed the shell and shouldered the rifle. "Let's go," she said and walked around Eberhard in the direction of the dead moose.

There was a mutter of German behind her. She ignored it, forcing her way through the undergrowth. It caught at her braid and her clothes until she managed to shove head and shoulders through the alders lining the edge of the lake where the moose was.

There was nothing to show for Kate's shot but a missing left eye. The Merkel, on the other hand, had taken half a shoulder with it. Broken bones gleamed whitely through red meat, and Kate caught a whiff of something unpleasant. Dieter's slug had clipped an intestine. Goody.

Dieter fought his way through the brush and pounced. The next ten minutes were fully occupied with picture taking, Eberhard producing a small but undoubtedly expensive Leica and shooting a roll of film with Dieter in various poses.

The camera came to the end of the roll and started rewinding. "Okay," Kate said, pulling a knife.

There was a startled exclamation from Dieter and Eberhard almost dropped the camera going for his Weatherby. Kate kept her face straight and extended the knife to Dieter, hilt first. "Time to start skinning."

He took the knife automatically. It was a slender eight-inch blade with a wickedly sharp edge. "To take the head off?"

"Among other things," Kate murmured, and stood and

watched him hack off the head with clumsy enthusiasm. It would have been easier for him if she'd produced the hatchet from her pack, but she didn't, and he was panting and covered with blood and moose hair by the time the head broke free from the body. He went to lift it up and was surprised by the weight, as well he should be. The rack alone probably weighed fifty pounds.

Wet to the knees with swamp water, stained to the waist with moose blood, red rage replaced with a pink and gratified pride, Dieter displayed his trophy. Eberhard's attaboys were as flattering as one of his phlegmatic nature could produce. Kate waited. Dieter finally remembered her presence, and turned to hand her the knife.

"Not so fast," she said. "Finish skinning him out."

"What?"

"Finish skinning him out," she repeated. "You'll have to haul him from the water first."

Dieter gaped at her for a moment, then recovered. "We got what we wanted," he said, indicating the head.

"We take the meat, too."

He looked baffled. "But—" He looked around at the surrounding brush and brightened. "There are other animals who will eat the meat." Inspired, he stuck one finger in the air like Christ pointing the One Way. "Wolves! There are wolves in Alaska! They will eat the meat!"

Kate shook her head. "Not this moose. You shot this moose, you recover the meat, we'll hang what we can't pack back to camp and come back for it tomorrow."

He was starting to get red again. What the heck, he'd match his shirt. "We're leaving," he said shortly.

"Fine," she said equably. She turned and surveyed the

area. There was a tiny clearing to the left and she squeezed
into it, bent a few branches back to let in more light, and sat
down with her back to a trunk.

All this was watched in perplexed silence by the two
men. "What are you doing?" Dieter said, finally.

She smiled at him. "Taking a nap," she said. "You boys
go on, head back to camp." She leaned her head against the
bark and closed her eyes. "You get lost, you remember the signal. Three shots, fired a second apart. I'll come running."

There was silence on the other side of the bushes, followed by some conversation in German, Dieter's voice rising
with wrath, Eberhard's calmer and less voluble.

Now, Kate was totally out of line here. State law required that the moose be gutted as soon as possible and all the
meat recovered, but it was the guide on the hunt who was responsible for doing this. It was also the guide who would suffer the consequences of the wanton waste law if he or she
didn't, which consequences as George had pointed out included large fines and confiscation of personal property such
as private aircraft, not to mention jail time.

Furthermore, drop-off hunters packed their meat out.
Guided hunters did not. Dieter and Eberhard were indu-
bitably guided.

On the other hand, she'd seen George Perry's standard
contract and the clause that guaranteed a "true Alaskan
wilderness experience." George provided packboards for all
his hunters, taking their willingness to pack as understood.

And Kate was pissed off by the way Dieter and Eberhard were behaving, irritated that they had evidently had
wax in their ears when George had instructed them the previous morning on the recovery of game, and was subsequently

disinclined to volunteer any advice or help, or to be conciliatory or coaxing in any way.

All she had to worry about was the Fish and Game showing up unexpectedly. Her luck was the local fish hawk was probably overhead this minute, alert for wrong-doing on his turf.

Or George would arrive and carve out her liver with a dull knife when he found out what she was up to.

The voices stopped. Kate stayed where she was.

Dieter's voice said, "You'll help us." It wasn't a request.

She opened her eyes and looked Dieter right in the eye. "The best way to go about it is for one of you to hold the rear legs apart while the other uses the knife to open him up. Start at the anus, one cut straight up the belly to the throat, and let the guts fall out. Don't nick any of the internal organs—" or any more than you already have, she thought "—or you'll taint the meat." She paused. "Of course, you'll have to haul him to dry ground first. Might have avoided that if you waited until he'd worked his way on shore, which was where he was heading when you shot him."

"We're not taking the meat," Eberhard said, his deep voice quietly menacing.

"Then we're not going back to camp," Kate said, just as quietly.

If Dieter's face had been red before it was purple now. "You can't talk to me like this! No one talks to me like this!"

"Then you're about due, aren't you?" Kate said coolly. She looked up at the sky. "Better get a move on, guys. Sun's headed down, and we haven't got much time left to butcher and get back to camp before dark."

Exit, pursued by a bear.

They retreated a few feet and Kate heard the murmur of German, Dieter's voice louder and more insistent, Eberhard's calmer and less ruffled. There was some movement and Kate opened her eyes to see Dieter shoulder the packboard and Eberhard hand him his rifle. They waded into the brush, the sounds of breaking branches interspersed with muttered curses.

Well, shit. Kate sighed. Looked like the boys had called her bluff and decided to head back for camp on their own.

She got up and eeled her way through the trees to the moose's body, lying where they'd left it, beheaded, half in and half out of the water. The blood was still oozing from the jagged flesh of the neck, the bony spine protruding from the skin and hair of the nape.

There was a rustle in the brush behind her. It was a small

rustle so she didn't turn around. The smell of blood had had enough time to spread; an aroma that said "Dinner is served!" to every omnivore for miles around. It was a small lake without much flow-through, or in other words not much of a built-in mechanism for self-cleaning, and probably not filled with flesh-eating fish, either. She didn't have much choice and sighed again. Maybe she should have batted her eyes at the guys, just once. Oh well. No help for it now.

She had a length of line in her pack; she rigged a noose and tossed it over the branch of a nearby cottonwood. The noose tightened around the moose's rear left foot, and after much straining and swearing he rolled toward her, coming to rest on his left side, mostly on the bank and out of the water, where at least he wouldn't foul the lake. She left the line hooked to his foot and took a half-hitch around the trunk of the tree with the free end, and then with one swift stroke of her skinning knife opened the moose up, as Abel would have said, "from asshole to appetite." The guts spilled out on the ground, the moose between them and the water and a nice, full-bodied stink rising up to perfume the air and entice the clean-up crew.

There was a squawk above her head and she looked up to see a seagull, no, two, gliding by with a critical eye to assess the possibilities of the situation. There was another rustle in the brush and Kate looked around, expecting to see a fox, or even a wolf.

Instead a man who looked like one of the lead singers for ZZ Top stepped into the tiny clearing.

He was thin to the point of emaciation, with hollow, pock-marked cheeks. His jeans were patched at the knee over storklike legs, and held up by a wide, worn leather belt. His shirt was a plaid flannel so faded the checks were indistinguishable, and his beard was long enough to be tucked into his belt with the shirt. He was close enough for Kate to smell how long it had been since his last bath, and it was too late to take those teeth to the dentist.

His eyes were dark and watchful. Right then, they were fixed unwaveringly on her.

Without consciously deciding to Kate reached for her rifle. The stock felt infinitely reassuring as it slid into her hands and she felt marginally safer.

George had said not to talk to Crazy Emmett, not even to look at him, but he hadn't envisioned this scenario. "I'm Kate Shugak," she said, keeping her voice as neutral as possible. "I work for George Perry, the pilot who owns the hunting lodge west of here. You must be Cr—you must be Emmett. Cabin on the lake a mile or so that way?"

He nodded at the moose. "Yours?"

Evidently Crazy Emmett did not believe that introductions were necessary. "Belongs to one of the hunters I was guiding."

"You going to pack him out? If you're not, I'll take him."

From all reports, that was a long speech for Crazy Emmett, who had had his fill of teaching teenagers who didn't listen, and before he got to the end of it Kate had decided. She hadn't been looking forward to coming back tomorrow and finishing the butchering and packing out the meat, and she didn't feel under any particular obligation to mind Dieter and Eberhard's meat for them. "Sure," she said. "He's all yours. You want some help?"

"No." Crazy Emmett looked at her again. It was a slow

and thorough inspection and at the end of it Kate felt as if she had been stripped naked. "I haven't had a woman in a while."

The contrast between his precise diction and his *Deliverance* appearance was disconcerting. Her .30-06 had never felt so comforting in her hands. She met his eyes steadily. Never let them see you sweat.

"You aren't going to have one today, either," she said, fighting the urge to take a step back. Retreat to Crazy Emmett would look like surrender and an invitation to attack.

He gave her a long, assessing look, estimating his chances of getting the rifle away from her before she shot him. He shifted where he stood and her eyes dropped involuntarily to see his erection strain at the front of his faded jeans. Is that a gun in your pocket or are you just glad to see me, she thought, and slid her right forefinger oh so casually inside the trigger guard of the .30-06. The safety was already off.

They stared at each other for what felt to Kate like a very long time. Crazy Emmett broke first, setting his rifle against a tree to unshoulder a small pack. He pulled out a long and extremely sharp skinning knife.

Kate backed up, one careful step at a time. Crazy Emmett, in an about-face that was disconcerting, acted as though she were no longer there. His indifference was not reassuring; she had the feeling that if she tripped he'd be on her before she hit the ground. She took the utmost care not to.

When enough brush was between her and him she turned and moved smartly up the trail, ears tuned for any pursuit. Mercifully, there wasn't any. There were other rustles in the brush going the opposite direction, though. Crazy Emmett wasn't going to have any problem disposing of scraps.

Somehow Kate didn't think there would be all that many.

She had to hand it to Dieter and Eberhard; they'd made it a whole three hundred yards before losing the trail. Their revised course would have had them stumbling into Anchorage in three or four weeks. She was interested to see that Dieter, not Eberhard, was carrying the trophy. Hanging from the back of a packboard, insecurely fastened with loose-fitting and ill-tied rope, the moose looked as disgusted as Kate felt.

As she came up on them, Dieter was loosening the straps of the board, trying to shift the load in what appeared to be an attempt to ease a twinge in his back. He'd set his rifle down, butt to the ground, and then one of the brow tines got caught in his pants pocket. He turned and another brow tine caught the Merkel's trigger.

Of course the Merkel's safety was off. The rifle boomed. Dieter spun around like a top. A bullet sang over Kate's head and instinctively she ducked. So did Eberhard, hauling his Weatherby up in a defensive stance.

Dieter stopped spinning. He staggered a few steps in Kate's direction and then stood where he was, staring down at his upper arm, a white, shocked look on his face as rich red blood welled from a neat crease bisecting his right bicep. He said something in German, his voice dazed.

Kate got slowly to her feet, feeling a little light-headed herself.

Dieter blinked at her. "I shot myself," he said, enunciating each word with studied care.

"You sure did," Kate said, and she wasn't smiling.

"I—I shot myself," he repeated. He touched the blood

with one finger and stared at it. "But how? The safety, I know I put the safety on."

Yeah, right, Kate thought. "You'd better let me take a look." Eberhard made as if to get in the way and she halted him with a glare. "I used to be an EMT, an emergency medical technician. It's just a crease, Eberhard, I think I can handle it."

She had a first aid kit in her pack, which included a packet of gauze, and she wrapped this around Dieter's arm and knotted the ends. He was swearing in German by the time she was done. There was aspirin in the kit, too, and Kate shook out two tablets and handed them over. "We've got something stronger at camp," she said, "but first we have to get there. Can you make it?"

He nodded, washing the pills back with water from the bottle of Evian he pulled from a pocket attached to his belt. Next to it was a pocket for a Swiss army knife. Another larger knife with an ebony handle protruded from a leather sheath on the other side of his waist. A compass dangled from one belt loop and a thermometer from another. Kate squinted. It was fifty-three degrees Fahrenheit. Not bad for an afternoon in late September.

"Okay, let's go," she said. "We've got plenty of time, we'll take it slow and easy."

Eberhard shouldered the trophy, and neither man said anything when Kate turned and headed back in the direction from which they had come. Neither did they say anything when she found the correct trail and headed west.

They gained the top of the ridge two hours later. There was no sign of Berg, Senta or George. "Wait here," she said to Dieter and Eberhard, and went in search.

Berg was easy to find. He was a big man and unskilled in wilderness navigation; he'd left a trail through the brush three moose wide. He was lying in the middle of a blueberry patch, fingers and mouth stained blue, a deep, phlegmy snore issuing forth, thick-lensed glasses folded neatly and protruding from his pocket protector, along with a couple of pens and a ruler marked in centimeters. His rifle was leaning against the fork of a small alder some twenty feet away, the stock barely discernible between the leaves.

Kate kicked his foot gently. He woke with a snort and gawped up at her.

"Enjoying the blueberries?" Kate said.

Berg sat up, brushing the twigs from his hair and shirt, face serene. He didn't appear to realize that he'd been lost up until a couple of minutes ago. "Yes," he said. "The berries are very good."

"Yes," Kate agreed. "He thinks so, too." She pointed.

Berg couldn't see what she was pointing at so he lumbered to his feet and craned his neck around a small stand of mountain hemlock. A stick broke with a sharp crack beneath his foot, flushing a group of ptarmigan, noted blueberry aficionados, into startled flight. In the same moment Kate heard footsteps coming up the path behind her.

Berg met the startled eyes of a half-grown black bear picking berries not ten feet from where he was sitting. They regarded each other for a split second, and then the man let out a yell and the cub let out a squall and the big man galloped off in one direction and the little bear in another.

"Exit, pursued by a bear," Kate said, unable to stop herself, and burst out laughing. Seconds later Dieter came around her with his Merkel clutched in his hands. Evidently the as-pirin had taken effect.

Kate stopped laughing and said severely, "Put that down, Dieter, that little cub didn't do you any harm. There isn't enough meat on him to feed a mouse and what there is will taste like fish anyway at this time of year." Her voice rose as he galloped by. "He's not big enough for a rug or a trophy, dammit, and it's not bear season yet anyway!"

Eberhard followed, Weatherby at the ready. Kate swore and lit out in pursuit. The two men sounded like a couple of water buffalo crashing through the brush and the cub's fright-ened squalls must have been audible for ten miles. Kate hoped most sincerely that the cub was on his own.

She caught up with the three of them in a small clearing. The bear cub was frantically scrabbling up a knobby young cottonwood with Dieter, red-faced, sweating and determined, close behind. The Merkel had been cast off and Dieter now had the ebony-handled knife clenched between his teeth. Eberhard watched from the ground, Weatherby held at the ready in case the vicious animal attacked his boss, who prob-ably outweighed the poor little bear by fifty pounds.

"Oh for crying out loud," Kate said, disgusted, and kept a weather eye peeled for the bear's mama. He looked even younger up a tree, and he was letting the world know of his distress.

The cottonwood wobbled back and forth across the sky with the howling cub clutching to the trunk twenty feet in the air. Dieter was shinnying up from below, looking like a pirate who had lost his ship. The cub looked over his shoul-der and beheld Long John Silver at his heels. He'd been in the berry patch for the same reason Berg and the ptarmigan had, and it was all too much for him; with one terrified bawl his sphincter muscle gave out and he cut loose with about a gallon of half-digested berries that engulfed Dieter in a reeking flood of dark bluish brown. Dieter gave a cry of outrage, a mistake, let go of the tree to paw at his mouth, and slid ignominiously down the trunk to land hard on his fanny. He threw up immediately, and kept on retching, until the cub's blueberries and that morning's breakfast and that afternoon's sandwiches had all landed in his lap, until there couldn't be so much as a teaspoonful of fluid left in his stomach.

By then, the cub was long gone, having dropped to the ground and lit out for points vaguely southeast, assisted on his way by a shot from Eberhard's Weatherby that narrowly missed him, the report of which made Kate's ears ring for some thirty seconds afterward. At the rate he was going, Kate estimated the little cub would be in Tyonek before dark.

Kate was laughing so hard she couldn't speak. Dieter was swearing in German again, and from the tone of his voice and the fire in what you could see of his eye, Kate thought a momentary retreat the wisest course of action. She choked back her laughter, although irrepressible little giggles kept surfacing inadvertently. "Get yourself cleaned up," she said. She dug in her pack and tossed him a box of Wash'n Dri towels. "I'll see if I can't find George and Senta. We'll wait for you by the spike camp."

She beat feet back to where the trail crossed the ridge, marked by the three fifty-five-gallon drums that constituted the spike camp. Each contained the bare essentials for a couple of hunters caught outside overnight on a hike: a tent, two sleeping bags and a store of freeze-dried food with a small set of cooking utensils and a Sterno stove. There was a wrench taped to the side of the barrel to open it up, judged too complicated for a grizzly to understand and employ.

Berg was standing nearby, licking berry juice from his fingers. "You shouldn't have lit out like that," Kate told him, "you missed all the fun."

Berg looked startled, as if unaccustomed to being directly addressed in civil tones. "Please excuse me," he said, and sidled over to stand behind a tree, presumably out of range. It must be unfortunate to be that large and to live a life in the preeminent desire to avoid all attention.

Footsteps thudded up the path, and Kate turned to see George and Senta running the last few feet to the top of the ridge. "What was that?" George said breathlessly, skidding to a halt. "We heard something screaming—was it a bear?—and a shot. Did you get charged?"

"Not exactly," Kate said.

George looked baffled. "What, then?"

"It was kind of the other way around," Kate said. Senta's long blond hair had come free of its intricate knot and now tumbled in glorious disarray around a glowing face. She hadn't bothered to tuck her shirt back into her belt or her cuffs into her boots. As for George, he virtually radiated that purring gratification specific to the male of the species immediately following a score in the sack.

Both of them carried rifles in one hand and fanny packs and packboards by their straps in the other. Kate raised an eyebrow, and said in her blandest voice, "So, did you manage to find Berg?"

"Berg?" George said in a blank voice, and then had the grace to look a little guilty, just a little, not a lot. He exchanged a furtive look with Senta and said, "Uh, no, we didn't." He looked at the sun, seemed to realize how much time had passed and checked his watch. "Christ! I mean, he's still lost? You haven't found him either?"

"I was minding my own hunters," Kate said virtuously, "and Berg's name was not included on that list."

George shouldered his rifle. "Well, let's leave our gear here and go—"

Hearing his name, Berg stepped reluctantly into the open. "Here I am."

George looked from him to Kate. "So you did find him."

"Yup."

"Well then, why—" The words trailed off as George looked over Kate's shoulder. His jaw dropped. "What the hell?"

Even Kate, who knew what she was going to see when she turned, was impressed by the view.

Dieter was a marvelous sight. He was scraped cleaner than he had been when he slid down the tree but face and shirt were nonetheless dyed an arresting shade of deep blue, with here and there an interesting streak of moose blood, slowly going brown. The colors complemented the dark red stain on the gauze binding his upper arm, which had started to bleed again.

Eberhard trailed a very distant second, the moose rack bobbing on his pack. Even absolute loyalty went only so far.

George drew in a breath of pure enjoyment before recollecting who and what Dieter was. "Jesus, Kate," he said in a low voice as Dieter approached, "what the hell did you do to him? I know the guy's an asshole, but he is a paying customer."

"I didn't do anything," Kate replied with perfect truth. "Dieter hunts his own dogs, don't you, Dieter? Or in this case, bears."

Dieter caught only the tail end of this remark, and by the unfriendly look he shot Kate it wouldn't have mattered if he'd heard it all. She had made the cardinal error of being present during two episodes in which he had not appeared to advantage, and he would never forgive her for it.

"Bears?" George said ominously.

Kate raised a hand. "Let it be, George. The bear managed to save itself."

Dieter caught sight of Senta, refastening her belt buckle after tucking in her shirt, and his face hardened. She returned his look with a long, cool stare of her own, entirely unintimidated. Her eyes drifted down over his body, lingering on the bandaged arm, an eyebrow lifting over the stain, nostrils forming an aristocratic wrinkle when they caught a whiff of the smell. Ice Queen, 1, Dieter, zip. Kate gave a silent cheer.

They stood staring at each other, blue eyes into blue eyes, identical expressions of obstinacy on identically square-jawed faces. Dieter broke first. "We're going back to camp," he said. "Now."

It was an order, not a question.

George looked at the rack bobbing off the back of Eberhard's packboard, and said, "I see you got one, guys, good for you." He looked at Kate's empty packboard, at Dieter's. "Where's the rest of it?" Kate could see the alarm, followed by a slow burn. "Kate? Where's the rest of it?"

Kate was saved from answering by the distant report of a rifle shot. George spun on his heel to face toward camp, but Kate was before him, hand cautioning silence.

It seemed more like ten seconds before the second shot came. Another pause, followed by a third.

"Shit," George said with emphasis.

"From camp, do you think?" Kate said.

"Sounded like it," George said shortly. "All right, we've got trouble, everybody back to camp on the double. Get your gear on and let's get going. Move, move, move!"

As they assembled and donned their gear, George drew Kate to one side. "Where's the rest of the moose, Kate?"

"I gave it to Crazy Emmett."

George paled beneath his tan. "You saw Emmett?"

"Yeah. Right after the guys took off up the trail with the trophy."

"The guys took off?"

"Yeah, they decided they didn't want the meat."

"Goddammit, I—" George's skin went whiter. "Wait a minute. You were alone when you met up with Emmett?"

"Yeah," she said, "you might have told me how needy he is."

He grabbed her arm. "Are you all right? He didn't hurt you, did he?"

She shook her head. "No. I'm glad I had my rifle, though. He didn't look to me like a man who'd take no for an answer."

"He isn't," George said with emphasis. "Remind me to tell you about a little encounter Emmett had with Ramona a while back. All right, people," he said, shouldering his rifle and moving to stand at the head of the group, "are we ready?"

There were nods, a curt one from Dieter, a sheepish one from Berg, no response from Senta and Eberhard. "Okay. I'll take point, Kate, you take drag. The rest of you, keep up." He directed an unsmiling look at Berg, who blushed and shuffled his feet. He also, Kate noticed as she fell in behind him, had his packboard on backward.

During the ninety minutes of the forced march back to camp, she wondered what Berg was doing in the Alaskan Bush, on a hunting trip for which it was painfully obvious he lacked inclination, aptitude and skills, or even a basic sense of survival for that matter. Baby bear could have brought mama along to share the blueberries, and Berg had left his rifle twenty feet away from him when he went for his snack and a nap.

Between Berg and Dieter, they'd been damn lucky they hadn't been the ones who'd had to fire the trouble signal.

I'm going to move. Really. Eventually.

When they got close enough to the lodge that the trail was clearly marked, Kate and George trotted ahead, leaving the others to follow in their own time. Jack was waiting for them on the airstrip, his face drawn into stern lines but otherwise looking whole and blessedly healthy. The knot in Kate's stomach relaxed. Mutt, standing at Jack's knee, saw Kate first and bounded forward, all irritation gone at being left behind. "Hey, girl," Kate said.

Mutt leapt up, front paws on Kate's shoulders, and anointed Kate lavishly with her tongue. "All right, all right," Kate said. "Enough. I'm okay."

Mutt looked her over critically, decided she was telling the truth and dropped down to all fours with a satisfied "Whuff." She fell in next to Kate as they trotted after George, all three heading for Jack, who was standing next to a mound covered with a blue plastic tarp.

"Who?" George said, voice tight.

"Fedor."

"One of the kids?"

Jack nodded. George swore, long and fluently, but swearing didn't make it not so.

"Was he shot here?" Kate said.

"No. Up the creek. We brought him in."

"You moved him?" Kate said. "You moved him, Jack? What, are you out of your mind? You wish to experience first-hand the effective methods of rehabilitation as practiced by the Alaska Department of Corrections, is that it?"

"I didn't move him," Jack said shortly, and Kate shut up. It was obvious he was restraining his temper and that the effort was taking considerable control. "They had him in a makeshift sling made out of some tree branches and their coats and were halfway home by the time Gunther and I caught up with them."

"Oh my," Kate murmured, "the troopers are going to just love this."

"Tell me something I don't know," Jack said glumly. "The other hunters told me where they found Fedor; I can probably find it again. I tried to get Klemens to show me where he was shooting from so I could at least mark the area, but he can hardly talk, he's so broken up. Poor bastard."

"Not Klemens," Kate said, dismayed. "It wasn't Klemens, Jack, was it?"

He took a deep breath, let it out. "Yeah. It was Klemens."

"Damn." Kate thought of yesterday afternoon, and Klemens dozing contentedly in the sun on the banks of the creek. "Poor Klemens."

"Correct me if I'm wrong," George said with mounting fury, emphasized by his extreme care with his words, "but I believe you were supposed to be with Gunther and Klemens?"

"I was," Jack agreed. "I don't have any excuse, George. He got away from me. I was setting Gunther up for a shot at one of those bulls, and when I looked around Klemens wasn't there. I didn't even hear him leave. I figured he'd stepped behind some bushes to take a leak or something, that he'd be right back. Only he wasn't." He looked George straight in the eye. "I screwed up. I'm sorry, George."

George, about to reply with even more care, caught Kate's eye and was put forcibly in mind of other events that had taken place that afternoon. It took a visible effort but he swallowed what he had been about to say.

Pulled back, the tarp revealed the pallid face of Fedor, the life drained out of him like wine from a bottle, leaving only the hollow vessel behind. His fair lashes lay thick upon his cheeks, an innocently incongruous contrast to the bullet hole in his forehead, just beneath his hairline and slightly off-center. He was lying on another tarp, and without moving his head Kate could see that most of the back of his skull was gone.

George tossed back the tarp. "I don't get it. Klemens and Eberhard are the only two nimrods in this bunch who know one end of a rifle from the other."

"He said he saw the brush rustle, a flash of brown. He thought it was a moose and shot."

George flicked up the tarp again. Over his safari suit Fedor had zipped the fluorescent orange vest that George demanded all his hunters wear before he'd take them out on the trail, especially in a group this large. "Who was supposed to be watching Fedor? Old Sam?"

"Yes."

"Well, why wasn't he!"

"George," Jack said. "You know it happens."

Kate gave him a sharp look. Who was he trying to convince, himself or George?

"It doesn't happen on my hunts," George snapped. He ran his hands through his hair. "Oh, hell."

Berg, Senta, Eberhard and Dieter were approaching. Jack looked around at the sound of their footsteps and saw Dieter. "Jesus, what happened to Dieter?" He looked down at Kate. "What did you do to him?"

"I didn't do anything to him," Kate snapped. "Why does everyone keep asking me that?"

Senta was a little ahead of the three men. She saw the group standing around the blue plastic mound and the blond eyebrows on the lovely brow creased. "What is it?"

"Someone's been shot," George said bluntly.

She gasped, one hand going to her mouth. "What? Who? One of us? Who is it, George?"

"Fedor."

"Fedor?" Senta stood very still, her face blank. "Fedor has been shot? Dead?"

"See for yourself," George said, all trace of lover banished for the moment.

Eberhard walked around Senta and raised the tarp. He and Dieter looked in silence on Fedor's still face. Senta fell back a step, said something in a shaken voice that Kate couldn't catch and whirled to come face to face with Dieter. For a moment nobody moved. Then Senta broke and ran for the lodge.

Berg took one look and fainted dead away, landing full

length on his back on the gravel with a thump that raised a small dust cloud. No one rushed to his aid.

Eberhard let fall the tarp and exchanged a glance with Dieter. Dieter said something in German. Kate thought she heard Klemens' name. But Eberhard and Dieter hadn't been anywhere near them when Jack had told them who had done the shooting; they couldn't have heard that Klemens had pulled the trigger.

Eberhard saw Kate watching them. He gave her a long, unsmiling look, and took Dieter's elbow to move him out of earshot.

"Goddammit anyway." George gave a heavy sigh. "Okay, I'll fire up the radio, see if I can reach anybody, get a call into the troopers."

"Troopers?" Eberhard said sharply, halting. "That is like the police, yes?"

"Yes," George said shortly.

Eberhard opened his mouth. Dieter said, "*Nein.*" Eberhard looked at him and Dieter rattled off some more German.

"Dieter," Kate said. "Dieter!"

Dieter broke off in midstream and looked around. "Something you wanted to share with the rest of us?" she said.

He stared at her for a moment. "*Nein.*"

"Dieter," George said, "you might want to do some thinking here."

"About what?"

"About whether you want to continue this hunt."

Dieter stared. "What?"

George nodded at the blue mound. "We've lost a man,

your man. You want to pack it in? It's up to you, you're pay-ing the freight."

"Pack it in? Is that like quit?"

George nodded. Dieter's face flushed a deep red Kate had seen before, and he said with a force filled with the kind of heavy-handed menace typical of most bullies, "We are not quitting this hunt. You signed a contract. You guaranteed this hunt. I pay, we stay, we hunt."

"Is there a penalty clause in that contract, George?" Jack said. Dieter glared at him. Jack didn't appear noticeably ter-rified. Poor Dieter, Kate thought dispassionately, there just wasn't enough cower in the Alaskans he'd met so far.

"No, but if I break the contract by quitting early he could turn me into the Fish and Game if he wanted," George said glumly. "And it looks like he'd want to."

Berg stirred and opened his eyes. He stared at the sky for a few mystified moments before sitting up and blinking around him. When he saw the tarpaulin-covered mound, his face went white and Kate thought he might faint again. In-stead, he got unsteadily to his feet and staggered off to camp.

"You want to talk this over with the others first?" George said to Dieter. "They might not want to stay after this."

"They do what I say," Dieter snapped.

George shrugged. "Okay. But tomorrow you don't hunt. Or all of you don't."

Dieter bristled. "Why?"

"Because I say so," George said evenly. "Second because I'm flying Fedor's body into Anchorage tomorrow morning, and you'll be one guide short."

"The other hunter can go with one of the other guides."

"No, they can't," George said flatly. "Two hunters per guide is the best and safest ratio. Although," he muttered, "so far this hunt's looking like it should have been one on one."

"Say amen somebody," Kate murmured.

"Anyway," George said, "tomorrow morning I'll be flying the body to town and bringing a trooper back with me."

Dieter, predictably, began to sputter. George cut him off with one horizontal slice of his hand. "That's the way it's going to be." He turned and stalked off toward the lodge, ending the argument by refusing to participate in it. Any one of George's ex-wives could have told Dieter how effective a tactic it was.

Dieter charged off up the strip, Eberhard following. Jack moved closer to Kate and raised a hand to her face. She rubbed her cheek against his palm and then, as natural as breathing, stepped forward into his embrace. "Are you all right?" she said, voice muffled in his chest.

"I am now," he said, mouth against her hair, arms tight around her. "I am now." He pulled back and looked down at her, framing her face with both hands. "My light bright shining."

"What?"

"A line from a poem. You're my light bright shining, Kate."

"Don't be so mushy," she said, but she blushed and had to fight back a smile. "What happened, Jack?"

Jack looked around. Dieter and Eberhard had walked up the runway a hundred yards and paused to converse in low-voiced, rapid German. As they watched, Dieter gave a sudden laugh, a braying, almost triumphant sound that echoed down the gravel strip.

"I guess it is pretty funny," Jack observed, "losing one of your top employees like that."

"A barrel of laughs," Kate agreed.

Jack was silent for a moment, still watching the two Germans, who were strolling back in their direction now, attitudes indicating not a care in the world to be shared between them.

"Come on," Kate said. Taking him by the hand, she led him down the strip and through a scattering of alders to the base of a tall, square steel tank with a ladder up one side.

"What is this? Oh, a fuel tank."

"Yeah," Kate said. "Back when this was a gold mine and needed diesel to run the generators, tankers would fly in and fill it up. George doesn't use it." She climbed up, Jack following. The top of the tank sank to echo hollowly beneath their feet, giving off faint booms reminiscent of Dieter's Merkel with every step. There was a wooden bench perched at the edge of the tank facing northeast. Jack sat down and pulled Kate into his lap. "Man, I was glad to see you, girl."

"Me, too," she said, looping her arms around his neck. "What happened, Jack?"

He kissed her in lieu of an answer, and she kissed him back, long, slow, sweet kisses that comforted and soothed and aroused. He responded with increasing urgency, pulling her shirt free to cup and caress her breasts, unfastening her braid to spread her hair over her shoulders, tugging at her belt and pulling at her zipper to slide his fingers between her legs and into her flesh.

"Jack—"

"Shut up. Just shut up. God, you're wet."

She arched her back to receive him with a gasping sigh,

the power and purity of his need purging the memory of Crazy Emmett's brutish stare. They tumbled off the bench, falling to the top of the empty fuel tank with a thud that echoed like a bass drum and landing in a tangle of limbs and clothes. She tried to remove her boots but he was so frantic for her that she gave up and let him tug her jeans over them. He cradled her hips in his hands and set his mouth to her, suckling greedily. She arched upward in surprise and plea-sure, hurled right over the summit without warning, and without giving her a chance to slide safely down the other side he rose up and kneed her legs farther apart and came into her.

He was forceful and demanding and wholly concerned with his own need but she came again anyway, and this time she couldn't stop the cry that ripped from her throat. She raked her fingernails down his spine and that was all it took to push him over the edge, the husky, inarticulate growling sound from deep in his throat almost taking her with him a third time.

They lay there in a jumble of denim and flannel and a hundred percent cotton, breathing hard, heat radiating off them in waves. Kate couldn't hear over the thudding of blood in her ears, and opened her eyes to see nothing but stars. She blinked. There were stars overhead, emerging one by one in the twilight sky.

The sun was setting in a blush of glory, the moon rising over the opposite horizon, almost full and softly radiant. The tips of Foraker, Hunter and Denali rose like ghosts against the northern horizon, hinting at the force and fold of geologic age beyond, whose names murmured a litany of beauty and chal-lenge, Pioneer Ridge, Silverthrone, Mount Deception, Ragged Peak. The air was calm and still warm from the day, and everything would have been simply perfect if it hadn't been for the blue-shrouded mound at the edge of the airstrip.

Finally Jack stirred and mumbled something. "What?" Kate said muzzily. "What did you say?"

Jack took a deep breath, tapped into his reserve and shifted maybe an inch. Obligingly, she matched his movements, not ready to give him up. He settled down again and sighed his content. "You know," he said lazily, "a friend of Damon Runyon's used to say that the only time a man was sane was the first ten minutes after orgasm. Empirical evidence here recently obtained may have proved his thesis to be one hundred percent correct."

Kate discovered she had just enough energy left to smile. "I feel kind of like the sack of Troy, myself."

"Umm." He nuzzled into her neck. "Have I ever told you how much I love your hair?"

"Yes, but tell me again."

"I love your hair," he replied obediently.

"Thank you."

"You're welcome." Another slow, luxurious sigh. Minutes passed. "I'm going to move. Really. Eventually."

"No hurry."

"Good. Because I can't."

"Me neither."

"Not yet anyway."

"Nope."

They dozed a little, and woke to the sounds of George and Demetri moving Fedor's body into one of the planes for the night.

Footsteps came close to the tank. There was a deliberate and ostentatious clearing of throat. "Jack? Kate?"

Jack raised his head. "Yeah?"

"Dieter's still insisting on staying the full time. If it wasn't for him and his hired muscle"—without difficulty Kate identified the "hired muscle" as Eberhard—"I think the rest of them would be ready to go tonight. Might be a little in-surrection brewing. Just so you know. Could be trouble when I take off tomorrow."

"Okay."

"Demetri's cooking dinner." They could hear the smile in George's voice. "You want it served out here?"

"Smartass," Jack mumbled, and George laughed and moved away. Jack waited until he was out of range before looking down at Kate. What she could see of his expression in the dim light looked sheepish.

"What's wrong?"

"I don't know, I guess I'm kind of embarrassed. I didn't hurt you, did I? I mean I did sort of—I mean I was kind of—"

"Determined?" she suggested demurely. "Forceful? Overpowering? We might even say, possessing all the finesse of a rampaging bull?"

He floundered. "Well, I—"

The bubble of laughter escaped. She pushed him over on his back and rolled on top of him. "Thank you," she said, and kissed away anything else he might have had to say.

"Oh," he said. A smile crept across his face. "Okay, then."

His hands slid beneath her shirt, and she snuggled her head into his shoulder. "What happened, Jack?" she said for the fourth time.

"No," he said. "I've got something I want to say first. Something I need to say."

There was a note in his voice she had not heard before. Her heart gave an uncomfortable thump somewhere high up under her breast bone. "You sound serious," she said.

"I am serious," he said. "We're both alive, and here, and the stars are out and the moon is full and there's no one around and I want you to listen to me. No cracks, no getting up and walking away. Just listen."

"All right," she said, uncertain, nervous without knowing why. He looked so serious, his eyes level and almost stern, belying the tangle of hair above, tousled from her hands.

"Light bright shining," he said.

"What?"

"Shut up," he said. "That's what you are. My light bright shining. It's from a poem by Mary TallMountain, an Athabascan from Nulato."

"A poem?" Kate said doubtfully. This was beginning to sound dangerously romantic and potentially sentimental. Kate, who prided herself on the hardness of her head, didn't do sentimental.

"No," he said quickly. "Don't say anything. Please don't. Just listen. Listen, Kate."

He feared mockery, anticipated ridicule, dreaded her scorn. She saw all that in his face and more, and she knew a sudden shame that he would expect such a reaction from her. The realization silenced her as nothing else would have.

He took a deep breath and closed his eyes for a moment. When he opened them to see her wary expression, his mouth twisted up in a wry smile. "I memorized it, word for word."

He waved a vague hand at their position, the top of the empty fuel tank. "This wasn't quite how I pictured saying it to you. But here goes."

He took a deep breath. His voice was clear and deep, letting the words speak for themselves.

> *Companion to me in every place*
> *You stretch your hand: I see*
> *Majesties of mountains*
> *Crowned with living light.*
>
> *Your arm flings wide: I see*
> *Wild little islands wrapt in fog*
> *Grey luminous: hidden folds*
> *Of emerald and ermine earth.*
>
> *I fly free clean through glowing*
> *Cat's eye aquamarine*
> *Filled with light air breath*
>
> *Swaddled in this cocoon*
> *this dense and lifeless mass*
> *Yet weightless I*
> *soaring with it shall be for you*
>
> *Light bright shining*

The poem, the words and the meaning behind them were so overwhelming and so unexpected that the breath left her body and she couldn't seem to find it again.

He saw her expression and his own relaxed. "Don't, Kate. Don't look so scared. It's just the way I feel. It's the way it is for me." His smile was crooked. "Light bright shining."

She opened her mouth and nothing came out. Again, he filled the gap. "I'm thinking of retiring."

She gaped at him. "What?"

"I'm thinking of retiring," he repeated. "I've got over twenty in, I'm eligible, and as you know the state is trying right, left and center to cut the budget. They're offering a good buyout to unload a few of us older employees, so they can hire someone in our place at half the salary and a quarter of the benefits."

She was still staring. "What would you do instead? You're only forty-five, Jack. Not quite time to put yourself out to pasture."

He knotted his hands over his head and stretched, comfortable now with the poem out of the way. Romantic gestures did not come easily to Jack Morgan, especially when they came from the heart. "I don't know yet."

Around the sudden lump in her throat she managed to say, "Were you thinking of moving?"

"Yes."

"Oh." The lump grew bigger.

His voice came as if from a great distance. "I was thinking I might try the Bush lifestyle for a while, see how I liked it year-round."

She stopped breathing. "Bush lifestyle?"

"Uh-huh." He met her eyes. "I know someone with a cabin. It's one-room, might be a little cramped for the three of us, but if she was willing we could always add on."

"You mean my cabin?" Her voice scaled up in disbelief.

"Yes." Jack was watching Kate very carefully, alert to every change of expression.

She stared back at him. "I—I—I don't know what to

say. What about Johnny?" Johnny was Jack's twelve-year-old son, currently bunking with his best friend's family in Anchorage and greatly miffed at having to go to school instead of being allowed to come on the hunt. He had his father's dark blue eyes, which also like his father's saw too much, and an impish charm all his own. "How does he feel about this? There aren't any video arcades on my homestead, or in Niniltna, either, for that matter. The last I saw, anyway."

"We've talked about it some." Jack grinned. "After this summer, up the creek with your aunties, picking fish with Mary Balashoff and out on the *Freya* with Old Sam, he's looking at Bush life through rose-colored glasses. And of course he's more in love with you than I am, always has been. Johnny won't be a problem."

She was mute. He gave a sudden laugh. Bristling was an easy response for her and so she went with it. "What? What's so funny?"

Still laughing, he said, choking over the words, "You should see your face. You look like a deer caught in the headlights. Jesus!"

Defensive, now that she knew what she was supposed to be reacting to, she said, "Can you blame me? Jack, I've never shared living space before, not with you, not with anyone, not since I was a little girl. I haven't had a roommate since I was in college. I just—I don't—"

He waved her to silence with one hand while he tried to bring himself back under control. Knuckling an eye, he said, "Look, Kate. I've pretty much made up my mind to take that retirement package. I've given some thought to starting up as a contractor, offering training and investigative services." He gave her what he obviously thought was a reassuring smile. "That part of it has nothing to do with you."

The smile faded. "This does. You're my light bright shining, Kate. I love you. When we were apart those eighteen months, I tried like hell to get over you, between most of the clean sheets in town and a few others besides. It didn't work. I've made you a part of my life, a necessary part."

He paused. She was back to staring, dumb, paralyzed, and he nearly started laughing again. It would be fatal to his cause if he did and he knew it, so he choked it back and said, "It doesn't mean I can't live without you. It doesn't mean I can't go on seeing you while not living with you." He spread his hands. "But I want more if I can get it."

He let his hands drop and regarded her steadily.

"Can I?" He raised one hand up, palm out. "Don't answer me now. Just think about it, okay?"

"Okay," she said numbly, for lack of inspiration.

He leaned forward to kiss her. "Good girl."

SEVEN

You get a bunch of nimrods like this out in
the Bush and you figure you're going to have
people popping off when they shouldn't.

He lay back down, to all appearances dismissing the subject
from his mind. Rough fingers traced the length of her spine.
"Is that what they call a hunter's moon?" he said.

"I don't know," she said, willing to go along with the
change of subject. In truth, her thoughts were so fragmented
she'd have a hard time coming up with anything to say for
herself, and was grateful for the lead he gave her. "It's a full
moon, or almost full. What's a hunter's moon?"

"The first full moon after the harvest moon."

She smiled without opening her eyes. "You sound like
the encyclopedia. What's the harvest moon?"

"I don't know, but it has something to do with the
equinox."

His fingers flexed, and she sighed her pleasure. "Sounds
like it's tied up with the old hunting and gathering seasons.
Or gathering and hunting. Or something. Um, right there,

yes. That's what Old Sam says, did you know?" She turned and crossed her hands on his chest and propped her chin on them, smiling down at Jack. "When we're on the tender at the beginning of salmon season and we're getting ready to pick up the first load. 'Time to hunt and gather, girl,' he says, and we go to work."

"I always knew Old Sam harbored a dangerous partiality for the Pleistocene. I'm surprised he doesn't wear bearskin and carry a spear."

"You ever see him when he's at home?"

Jack laughed.

There was silence. The moon seemed to grow in size and beauty as it rose higher in the sky. "What happened, Jack?"

He sighed, and his hand dropped away. "Pretty much like I told it to George." He sat up and began adjusting his clothes. "We found the moose, right where George said they were. You remember that little bend in the creek, before it heads up Blueberry Ridge? That stand of mountain ash that marks the turn?"

"Yes." She began buttoning her shirt. He brushed her hands away and did it for her.

"There were three big bulls, two of them looking pretty ratty and smelling to high heaven and grunting and snorting to beat the band." He gave a quiet chuckle. "Old Sam is right. There ain't a damn bit of difference between a drunk chasing girls in a bar and a bull moose in rut."

"Did you see the cows?"

He shook his head. "We heard some rustles off in the brush but we didn't see any of them. The way the bulls were behaving, they were there somewhere. Anyway, the biggest bull of the three hadn't come into rut yet, he was chowing down on the mountain ash like he'd never eaten before in his life, and I figured, as long as we were there, we might as well take the one who was going to give us the best meat. George makes such a point of his hunters eating as much of what they shoot as he can stuff down them."

"I know, all part of the George Perry Wilderness Adventure Guides, Inc., experience." She combed her hair back with her fingers. Again he brushed them aside and began braiding her hair himself. He was more acquainted in theory than in practice with French braiding, and the process involved much combing out and starting over. Again, Kate closed her eyes and leaned into it.

"And then there was always the little matter of my freezer and your cache."

She smiled without opening her eyes. "Thinking with your stomach again, Jack. It's what I've always loved most about you."

His hands checked a moment, and they were both put forcibly in mind of Jack's declaration moments before, lending weight to Kate's light-hearted words.

Jack's hands resumed braiding. "So, the guides flipped for first shot and I won, and Klemens and Gunther flipped for first shot and Gunther won. We spread out, my group on the left, Demetri's in the middle, Old Sam's on the right. The bull was eating his way around the willow, and we were waiting for him to climb up on dry ground when we heard a rifle go off. I looked around and Klemens wasn't there. Where's your rubber band?"

"Wherever you threw it, would be my guess. Here." She fished for one of the backups she carried in her pocket. It was tangled around the little drawstring bag holding the ivory otter she habitually carried as a pocket piece. He was part talisman, part amulet and part good luck charm, and she didn't feel dressed without him.

"Let me see." She handed rubber band and otter back. The bag's strings were knotted tight and Jack's big hands worked patiently to free them. The little creature, so sturdy of form yet so delicately made, sat back on his thick ivory tail, ivory fur soaked and ruffled with water, black baleen eyes bright with curiosity. "Why do you carry him with you, Kate? He's a piece of art. He could be damaged, banging against your knife or something."

She shrugged, and stuffed the otter back in the bag and the bag back in her pocket. "I like having him around."

Made of ivory taken from an Inupiaq-killed walrus, carved by a Yupik artist, representing an animal into whose body was reborn Aleut souls, the otter in some curious way formed a link to her ancestors, to the people who had come before. The Great Land, the Aleuts called it, *alyeska*, so as to distinguish the large body of the mainland from the islands of the Aleutian Chain. The otter connected her to them and to all the people who came after and who with them formed part of her ancestry, Aleut hunter and gatherer, British explorer, Russian trapper, New England whaler, miners and soldiers and sailors and airmen and farmers and fishermen from all over the globe. Somehow they were all encompassed in the tiny ivory figure of the otter, one paw raised as if to run or fight, ears cocked for any warning sounds, a study in survival and a tribute to evolution.

She could have told Jack this. He would have understood, and even if he hadn't, he could be trusted neither to laugh nor to scoff. Instead she said, "What did you do when you saw that Klemens was missing?"

He fastened the rubber band around the end of her braid and admired the result. "At first I thought he'd ducked out to take a leak."

"How long had it been since you'd seen him last?"

He shrugged. "I don't know. Gunther and I were watching the moose, waiting. Gunther was excited and I was afraid he'd shoot before he should. You know how I hate to drag a moose out of wherever he's not supposed to have fallen into."

"Don't we all," Kate said with feeling.

"Klemens was to my right and a little behind. He was supposed to be ready to take the second shot if Gunther missed. I got the impression he wasn't all that hot to shoot something, that he was glad he'd lost the toss."

"He tried to give Dieter his moose tag. Said he'd done all the killing he needed to."

"Yeah? That'd fit, I guess. Poor bastard." He paused, thinking. "I remember, I was glad he was there, because it was obvious he'd had some experience shooting. You sure as hell can't say that about the rest of this crew."

"Excepting Eberhard," Kate agreed.

"Yeah. Maybe. I haven't seen him shoot yet. Anyway. The moose heard the shot, too, of course, and naturally he spooked and ran for it. Gunther jumped to his feet and popped off a shot, and then another. Missed, of course, and the moose took off, and up river we could hear brush crashing around like the other two were beating feet, too. You could hear the cows taking off through the brush, then, all right, sounded like a herd of elephants."

He closed his fist around her braid and gave it a gentle

tug. She lay back against him and felt as much as heard his voice rumble up from his chest. "Well, I was sore, all that backstrap and tenderloin getting away like that, and I may have yelled a few things in the heat of the moment."

Jack was the original slow-talking, slow-walking guy, with a slow smile and an even slower temper, but there had been a few cherished occasions when Kate had experienced Jack "yelling a few things in the heat of the moment," and she could well imagine what his language had been like that afternoon. An immersion course in Alaskan invective, with some new and better words made up right on the spot, was her guess.

"It was quiet for a few minutes after that," he said pensively.

I'll just bet it was, Kate thought.

"Then I heard Old Sam yelling, and he was pissed, too." Old Sam pissed wasn't a guess, it was a given. "He was too far away for me to make out what he was saying. I told Gunther we better backtrack, but he was all hot to go after the moose. Well, like George always says, these are paying customers, and Kate, I just wasn't expecting any trouble. You get a bunch of nimrods like this out in the Bush and you figure you're going to have people popping off when they shouldn't. That's why we—Old Sam, Demetri and me, I mean—why we lined up in a row all facing the same direction, no circling around so we could get ourselves in a crossfire or some other nonsense."

"So you crossed the creek after Gunther."

"Yeah." His chest rose and fell with a deep, heavy sigh. "We're fighting our way through the brush—that was fun—and then we heard three shots. I told Gunther the hunt was off, we were going back now. He didn't want to, still wanted to hightail it after that damn moose. I had to persuade him."

"Um." Kate wondered how. "And then?"

"And then we forded the creek and hiked up the opposite bank. And that was where we ran into Hubert and Gregor and Hendrik and Old Sam and Demetri carrying Fedor in that makeshift stretcher, with Klemens bringing up the rear. It was like a goddamn funeral cortege. Spooky."

She leaned forward to relace her boots. "How long was it, between the time you heard the shot, and when you heard the next three?"

He thought. "Thirty, thirty-five minutes?" He showed her a bare wrist. "You know I never wear a watch in the Bush."

He got to his feet and stretched out a hand to pull her up next to him. She slid her arms around his neck. "Another of those reasons I love you the mostest."

His arms tightened. "Kate—"

"Come on," she said, pulling free. "Let's go eat. I'm starving, for some reason." Her grin flashed through the dark.

Mutt, wearing an expression of saintly resignation, waited for them at the foot of the ladder. She examined her two dependents with a critical eye, gave a vigorous sneeze and led the way back to camp, tail held at a tolerant angle as if to say, Well, and what could you expect from humans, who hadn't the sense to confine affairs of the heart to a window of opportunity lasting a few weeks once every year, the way more sensible mammals did?

Demetri cooked, New York steaks on the charcoal grill and potatoes wrapped in tinfoil and baked in the coals of the fire.

A tossed green salad with one of Demetri's special olive oil and raspberry vinegar dressings rounded out the meal. Everything looked and smelled wonderful. It was a pity, since no one had much of an appetite.

Kate ate enough to keep Demetri from pouting and disposed of the remainder behind a providentially placed cranberry bush, where Mutt discreetly polished the plate almost to its original high gloss, or as glossy as Melamine gets. In the meantime, Kate began a covert examination of the party. She didn't really know why, except that she felt a sense of unease that she could not trace to its source.

The group was uniformly blond and blue-eyed and tall, or tall compared to herself, at any rate. At five feet nothing, Kate had spent most of her life looking up into people's faces and she had never learned to like it. At first glance there had been a surface similarity to this group, one to the other, and since they would be out of her life in ten days she hadn't looked beyond it.

Now she took a second look, seeing past her preconceptions with an eye sharpened for detail. They sat quietly this evening, in direct contrast to the chatter and laughter of the night before. Gunther, sitting outside the light cast by the campfire but not far enough to hide the spectacular shiner ornamenting his left eye, picked at his food and avoided looking directly at anyone, disappearing into his cabin as soon as he had finished. He was so very young, his skin pink and smooth from lack of age and experience. She remembered his enthusiasm the previous morning, ready to jump in the plane with George, and upon his airsick return still eager for the chase. He had stamina, at least.

Senta turned up her nose at the steak, ate her potato with

a lot of salt, and sat very near George, who ate stolidly from start to finish. George never let anything get in the way of his food.

Senta had a hard and well-polished surface. She was an enthusiastic practitioner of big hair. She'd even worn makeup on the hunt that day, including bright red lipstick that Kate was sure Senta felt made her pout even more irresistible. Human resources was a natural for Senta; it was obvious she was bent on making the best of her own. Dieter probably put her out front as bait when he was recruiting for top-level jobs.

Which either did or did not explain why Dieter glared at Senta from time to time. She ignored him with supreme indifference. Kate wondered if one of Dieter's toys had had the unmitigated gall to allow itself to be played with by someone else.

Dieter was a bull, all huff and puff and pawing the ground and shaking his horns. John King of RPetCo Oil was just such a man, and a similar bullishness had pushed him to the top of his particular food chain, even if he had had to do some fancy stepping to stay out of jail on a conspiracy to murder charge along the way. Square-headed, square-jawed, Dieter was bluff and blustering and boisterous, but those traits didn't necessarily preclude intelligence. His most dangerous trait was his arrogance, the inner conviction that his opinion was the only opinion and his way of doing things the only way.

Since Kate enjoyed a certain measure of these qualities herself, they were easy to recognize in Dieter.

She wished she knew more about computers. She also wished she could speak German. She checked behind the bush. Her plate was clean. She picked it up and carried it to

the lodge, where Demetri and Old Sam were washing the dinner dishes. "Demetri," she said in a low voice, "keep your
ears open, okay?"

Old Sam gave her a sharp look. Demetri finished rinsing
a handful of silverware and picked up a towel. "What for?"

"Anything," she said. "When these nimrods start talking, listen in. Do they know you speak German?"

"I think George told them so."

"Hell. Well, pick up what you can."

Demetri and Old Sam exchanged glances. "Why?"

Her slight smile was a little shamefaced. "I'm not sure,
exactly. I've got the heebie-jeebies about this bunch."

"Fedor's death got you spooked, girl?" For once, Old
Sam's voice wasn't jeering.

"I don't know. It won't hurt us to be careful, though."

He winked at her. "I'm always careful, girl."

Popping the top on a can of Diet 7Up, she stood in the
doorway for a moment, watching the people around the campfire over the top of the can.

Hubert and Gregor, Demetri's hunters and the two Kate
was least familiar with, sat close together, murmuring in low
voices. She was close enough to make out the name of Fedor
and something that sounded like Microsoft. Gregor jerked
back from Hubert, his expression stunned, and Hubert, seeing Kate standing almost directly behind them, shook his head
in warning. They waited until she returned to her seat on the
log before making their goodnights and heading for bed. Gregor looked like a veteran of many a convention, who would
be much more at home in the hotel bar with a scotch in one
hand, alert for any lone female to make the mistake of being
in the same city with him. He had a wide wedding band on

his left hand that looked loose, all the better for removing when expedient. He had an incipient bay window pushing at the waist of his pants, and the pouched, red-veined eyes of the heavy drinker.

Hubert looked marginally fitter, but his shoulders had the faint stoop of someone who spent most of his days hunched over a computer. His glasses were thicker even than Berg's. His hair was so thin on top it looked like he'd had a tonsure, which matched the vaguely ascetic cast of his face and the inward look of his eye, as if on one level he were always absorbed in some ongoing internal debate between himself and—who? Or what? Kate had no idea. This evening he was regarding a plant held in one hand. On closer inspection Kate saw that it was the limb of a soapberry bush, half a dozen berries ranging in color from red to yellow depending from stems. Hubert was sketching it in a notebook, high on the corner of one page, the rest of which was filled with cramped writing.

Klemens was the *eminence grise* of the group and Kate would have said the steadiest of the lot. He seemed secure in himself, with a latent twinkle in his eye that invited one to enjoy the joke, whatever it was. He also had an erect carriage that smacked of long practice in marching in step. You could always tell an old soldier; they never slumped, and their clothes were usually perfectly ironed, too, even, in Kate's experience, the clothes of old soldiers in the Alaskan Bush, where irons and the electricity to power them were often hard to come by.

Her father had been such a man. Drunk or sober, his shirts had been ironed, his shoepaks shined. He'd been a soldier, too.

Tall, spare, long of jaw, Klemens had big hands and fin-gers with knuckles so large Kate wondered how they fit through the trigger guard. They had today. Too bad Klemens hadn't insisted on staying in camp and doing the fishing he would have preferred. She thought of him by the creek the day before, content to laze in the sun, taking the odd grizzly in stride. After today, that man would never return to this world, and she was sorry for it.

Dieter seemed less than downcast. One might even say, judging from his frequent brays of laughter, that he was pos-itively jubilant. He'd scrubbed off in the creek and arrived at dinner in a fresh set of immaculate khakis, his cuffs unbut-toned so he could roll up his sleeve and display his wound at a moment's notice, which he did a minimum of four times while Kate was watching. Somehow, without actually saying so in so many words, Dieter managed to convey the impres-sion that he'd received the wound in hand-to-hand combat with his moose, the head of which was propped up against the log to stare out over the campsite with a vacant look in its glassy eyes.

Eberhard, sitting next to Dieter, was as enigmatic as al-ways, calmly eating through his meal and responding when necessary to Dieter's conversation. Because he didn't feed into it, Dieter's good spirits were muted. Kate wondered if it was deliberate. She would guess so, and wondered why Eberhard wasn't running the company.

But then, maybe he was. It wouldn't be the first time someone pulled the strings on a figurehead. And if Kate had ever seen someone who could pull strings, Eberhard was it. Eberhard was a big man, as tall as Jack, slow without being clumsy, certain without being arrogant. The scars, one on each cheek, had healed cleanly, unlike the scar on Kate's throat, but they formed deep creases that would never go away. If he ever smiled, they would be even deeper. His eyes were so light a blue they were almost colorless, and he had a habit of staring that could indicate either myopia or a need to intimidate. Either way, it was unnerving. He was a hard man to figure. He was a man to watch.

Berg alone went back for seconds. Kate noticed the others avoided sitting next to him. It didn't seem to bother him. During the after-dinner coffee his glasses steamed up, until he looked like a character from a Little Orphan Annie cartoon. He ate well, concentrating on what was on his plate and how fast he could get it down. He hadn't worked hard enough during the day to justify that much of an appetite, so he was probably just greedy. Greed would explain his size; Kate figured he weighed in at 275, if not 300: a big barrel of a man. She wondered what quality control involved when you were working on computers. Berg looked as if he'd be more at home swinging an ax.

Dieter laughed again. Kate was watching Hendrik at the time and saw a look of pure hatred pass swiftly across his face. She didn't blame him. Young Hendrik had spent the meal in shocked silence, white of face, staring of eye, his plate of food untouched in his lap. He moved like a dancer, and he had hands down the nicest buns of the bunch. Kate admired them as he leaned against a tree, staring out at the wilderness. She remembered Hendrik and Fedor sitting closely together the last two nights, the conspiratorial whisperings, the intimate laughter, and wondered.

George and Senta had their backs to the log and their feet stretched out to the fire. Kate took her can of pop and went to sit down next to Senta. "Nice evening," Kate said, looking up at the stars.

Hendrik heard her and stirred from his misery to say loudly, "I bet Fedor would have thought so." His face started to crumple, and he fought to bring himself back under control. "If that Nazi hadn't shot him he might have had a chance to see it!"

Dieter barked a command in German.

"I called him a *Gottverdammt* Nazi!" Hendrik said loudly. "He learned his shooting in the Wehrmacht in World War Two, the miserable son of a bitch. He was the one of all of us who should have known what he was doing in the *verdammt Wald!*"

There was a crackle of twigs where Klemens had been sitting in the dark at the edge of the circle. "You're right, Hendrik," he said, his voice strained. "I should have. But I didn't."

There followed a strained silence. With dignity, Klemens walked to the trestle table that did duty as serving line, ammo dump and garbage collector and picked up a plate. He loaded it with cold steak and potatoes, one item at a time, with everyone watching his every move.

He took his plate to his cabin. No one tried to stop him.

EIGHT

Damn, why does all the fun stuff
happen when I'm not there?

"I don't like this," Kate said.

"Don't like what?" Jack said without looking up from
his cards.

The screen door closed behind Kate with a faint rattle.
"Any of it. I don't like Fedor dying, I don't like Dieter's rape,
ruin and run attitude, I don't like the feelings I'm getting from
this bunch."

"Fifteen-two, fifteen-four, fifteen-six, fifteen-eight, and
eight are sixteen," Old Sam said, and pegged with relish.
"Much as I hate to admit it, you got a point, girl. What the
hell are they doing here, anyway? Bunch of goddamn city
slickers, don't know one end of a gun from the other. They
already shot one of their own stone dead, who's to say when
we take 'em out again they don't shoot one of us next time?
If it were up to me, I'd run the bastards back to town at first

light, and come back and do some real hunting, fill up the cache for the winter."

Jack looked glumly at the cribbage board. Old Sam was an entire loop ahead of him and coming down the home stretch. Skunked again. "So would I. Unfortunately, it's not up to us, it's up to George."

"And George says it's up to Dieter, and of course Dieter is hot to shoot anything that doesn't move or fly out of range in the time it takes him to aim that elephant gun of his," Kate said.

"Be fair, Kate," Jack said. "George signed a contract to provide a ten-day hunt. If he breaks that contract, Dieter could make trouble big time for him with the Fish and Game."

"Not to mention the money he'd be out," Old Sam said, an eternal capitalist, always ready to consider the financial downside of any situation. "What's he get for a moose hunt nowadays, anyway?"

"For the full ten days?" Kate said. "Somewhere between five and eight thousand per person."

"Uh-huh," Old Sam said. "For a caribou hunt, it's something like thirty-five hundred to five thousand apiece for ten days. And a bear hunt runs what? Twelve thousand a head? Fifteen? And these folks are here for all three and whatever else they can get. From their outfits I'd say they're pretty well heeled. George isn't the man I know he is if he isn't charging them the red-shift limit. With or without the dead kid, I'd be a mite reluctant to turn my back on that kind of money myself."

Demetri came in.

"So," Kate said, "you hear anything?"

Demetri shook his head. "They see me, they shut up."

"Really," Kate said slowly. "That's almost as interesting as what you're not hearing."

"Our resident conspiracy theorist," Old Sam told Jack in a not-so-confidential tone of voice.

"All right, all right, it's my imagination. Maybe I am spooked by Fedor's death."

Jack was more understanding. "No, Kate, you just want there to be a reason for his death, and there isn't one, and it bothers you." He gathered the cards together. "It bothers me, too."

"And me," Demetri said unexpectedly. "There is something wrong with these people."

"I say it's a wild hair up their collective ass, and I say the hell with it," Old Sam said definitively, and closed the subject for the night.

Kate stoked the stove with a couple of logs. Demetri retired to a chair to disassemble and clean an already immaculate Remington .30-06. Jack shuffled three times. Old Sam declined to cut, and Jack dealt six cards each. Old Sam turned up a jack and got an extra point. "Why do I bother?" Jack asked the ceiling and went on to be skunked again.

Kate swiped Jack's copy of Mary TallMountain's *The Light on the Tent Wall*. Careful to avoid "Light Bright Shining" as an emotional hotbed seething with sinkholes ready to swallow her up whole, she had very nearly committed "Good Grease" to memory by the time Jack gave up trying to beat Old Sam. Old Sam, cackling his triumph, raked in his winnings, which amounted to every spare penny Jack had on him, in addition to five dollars of Kate's and another five of Demetri's.

"Where's George?" Jack said, pushing back his chair.

Old Sam cackled again. "If that big old gal let the schnapps do the talking, probably with her."

"She's got a roommate."

"Tonight I'm betting that roommate is commiserating with Hendrik on the loss of his roommate," Old Sam said. Even Demetri smiled.

Jack got to his feet. "Let's take a walk," he said to Kate.

"Ain't love grand," Old Sam said.

They strolled up the airstrip, hand in hand, Mutt trotting a little ahead of them, nose to the ground. Once she stopped in her tracks, looking off to the right. Following her gaze, they saw a pair of moonlit green eyes staring at them unblinkingly from the undergrowth. Jack adjusted the .357 riding on his hip and they paced slowly on. Mutt waited until they were ten feet away before breaking off the staring match and running to catch up.

It was a over a mile from the camp to the dam George had built to divert the wayward trickle of water whose original stream bed formed the basis and provided much of the gravel and rock base for the airstrip. The dam was fifteen feet high, a curve of solidly packed dirt with a conveniently placed boulder at the top of the curve.

"Could have been made for couples to lean against," Jack said.

"Who says it wasn't?" Kate said. "This is George we're talking about here."

Jack laughed and pulled her closer. There was a sudden squawk and thrashing of brush from somewhere behind them, followed by a splash and then, silence. "Dinnertime," Kate said.

"Mutt never was one to eat too soon of an evening," Jack agreed, pulling Kate's thick braid through a lazy hand. "She might wake up hungry."

"That would never do," Kate agreed. Jack's shoulder was very comfortable, and the moon was being very obliging in rising straight up the runway, face forward. "Can you see Copernicus?"

"Where?"

"Right there, that big meteor crater."

"Oh, yeah," Jack lied. He was more interested in things earthly than lunar this evening. "You been thinking about it, Kate?"

"I've been thinking about almost nothing else," Kate said readily. "This whole business smells, and I don't mean Dieter. Senta walked me around the circle that first night and she said Fedor worked for Klemens. Do you think—" His chest shook with laughter and she tipped her head back. "What? What's so funny?"

Unsteadily, he said, "What I meant was, have you been thinking about the possibility of cohabitation? Cabin in the Park? You, me, the kid and the mutt?"

"Oh," Kate said weakly.

They both started to laugh at the same time. "Jesus," Jack wheezed, "I trained you and I still can't believe how single-minded you are. You're worse than a ferret at a hole, woman."

Mutt reappeared, a satisfied look on her face, and arranged herself in an elegant curl, tucked her tail beneath her nose and to all appearances went soundly to sleep.

Kate watched her and knew a flash of envy. Life was so

much simpler for Mutt. A full stomach, a dry bed, get laid once a year. At the moment it seemed to Kate like the perfect life. "Yeah," she said slowly. "I've been thinking about it."

"And?"

She was silent for a long time, long enough for him to think that was her last word, but it wasn't. She sat up and laced her fingers around her knees. The moonlight turned her skin to cream silk, her hair to black rain. She closed her eyes and he could see the tiny shadows her lashes cast on her cheeks, the bones beneath high and slanting up.

"When I was at school in Fairbanks," Kate said slowly, "I remember one time these two girls on fourth floor—Lathrop, my dorm, I lived on the fourth floor—anyway, these two girls got into a fight. I don't remember what it was about, nothing, probably, but it ended when one of the girls shouted at the other, 'At least I've got a man!' " She glanced around at Jack, a faint, wry smile on her face. "That was it. The other girl burst into tears and stumbled back to her room, humiliated. The first girl had won whatever the argument was, just because she had a man."

She looked up, and he followed her gaze. The stars were brilliant in the autumn sky; Orion, the Dippers, Big and Little, the Pleides, Cassiopea, all the easily recognized constellations standing out in bold relief against a sky filled with other, lesser stars.

Kate's voice was naturally low and made huskier by the scar tissue bisecting her throat. Her words were deliberate and precise, allowing no room for misinterpretation. Jack understood, and waited patiently, attentive, alert to every subtlety, every nuance.

"I made up my mind then and there that I would never

be defined by a man, made right by a man, given validity as a woman just because I had a man in my life." She turned to face him, dark of hair, tilt of eye, bone of cheek, curve of breast and hip all lit in tantalizing outline by the moon.

"It was a pretty easy vow to make. Look at my life. I lost both my parents before I was out of grade school. My grandfather was long dead by the time I was born, and Emaa never talked about him. Then, because I kept running away from Emaa's house, back to the homestead, she agreed to let Abel take me, and Abel, other than seeing to it that I could take care of myself, my weapons and the homestead, in that order . . . well, none of us, not me, not his own kids, got much affection. Inga died giving him his youngest son, so it was just him and the boys. I loved him, as much as I would any other childhood god, and I was grateful as hell, because him taking me on meant I could stay home. Home with my ghosts. But I didn't have any urge to go out and find someone just like him."

Her face seemed somehow more in shadow. "There were a few men in college. I pretty much decided to lose my virginity there, because I figured it had to happen sometime, and because I sure as hell wasn't going to sleep with some second cousin once removed back home who would have the news all over the Park by noon the next day."

She gave a faint sigh and shook her head, her smile rueful. "So I let myself be seduced by this guy who knew as much about it as I did, which was nothing. It wasn't a great success. Later on, I found someone who did know all about it." She grinned.

"I am forever in his debt," Jack said courteously. He was lying through his teeth, and they both knew it.

"There was a guy at Quantico, a few others. You know

about Bobby." She looked at him with a sudden smile, and his heart turned over. "And then I came to Anchorage, and there was you."

"I remember," he said.

He did, he could remember that day as if it had happened five minutes before. She had walked into his office and he had been struck with a need so sharp, so intense, so great it had caused an immediate physical reaction he had to stay seated to hide. It didn't help when he looked up to see her eyes fixed on him in recognition, alarm and, above all, a reflection of his own hunger.

Fresh out of a hellish marriage, struggling to stay close to his only child, mindful of the necessity for professional distance between supervisor and employee, he managed to stay out of her bed for ten of the longest days of his life. It helped that her first day on the job a particularly nasty child abuse case had fallen apart in mid-trial due to negligence on the part of the arresting officer. The judge had granted the DA a one-week extension with the caustic admonition that the case would be summarily dismissed if at that time probative, as opposed to prejudicial, evidence was not produced. The assistant district attorney assigned to the case had been demanding results of Jack's office as in yesterday, or his job as in tomorrow.

Working together only strengthened the attraction. He was very good at what he did, and she was a natural born snoop with an uncanny ability to get anyone to talk. They found their probative evidence and better, an eyewitness the police had missed, and the jury was out of the room for approximately nine minutes. The investigator's office celebrated the conviction that evening at the Fly-By-Night Club, where

Kate and Jack discovered a mutual devotion to Jimmy Buffett. There was no going back after that.

The truth was, Jack reflected, that Kate was a little too good at what she did, and had burned out on the sex crimes cases that invariably came her way. Her conviction rate was over ninety percent, a statistic she wasn't proud of because she thought it should have been a hundred. Yes, when Kate was good, she was very, very good, and when she wasn't, she quit. It had led to an eighteen-month hiatus in their relationship, during which time they had both experimented elsewhere, pallid flickers that only mimicked the incendiary blaze that resulted when they came together.

And now here they were, ten years later, still together, although he lived in Anchorage and she lived in the Park, hundreds of miles apart. He'd learned to fly, he'd bought a Cessna 172 so he could fly into the Park to spend weekends and vacations on her homestead. If she'd lived in Atlantis, he would have become a submariner.

"I guess what I'm trying to say," Kate said, bringing him back to the present, "is that I haven't had a lot of object lessons in . . . well, in coupling."

He grinned at her, and she had to laugh. "I didn't mean that, idiot. I mean I haven't seen a lot of relationships that made me think, Hey, I want something like that."

He knew a sinking feeling. "So? What's the verdict?"

"I don't know," she repeated. Screwing up every ounce of courage she had and reaching for more, she took a deep breath, let it out and said with a rush, "Maybe I won't know until and unless we try it."

Jack appeared to cease breathing. The next moment Kate

found herself snatched up and nose to nose with him. "You mean it?"

She wasn't sure she did, but she made another terrific effort. "I think so."

He kissed her then. He'd had a lot of practice and he was very good at it, and by the time he was done they were missing most of their clothes and breathing hard.

"Yeah," Kate wheezed, "I'm real sure I mean it now."

He laughed, a deep rumble full of happiness and satisfaction. "I take it that was my rent?"

"Let's call it the first installment." She smiled up at the moon. "Although I have had other offers."

He raised up on his elbows and inspected her face. "What's this, I'm involved in a bidding war?"

"Not exactly." She told him about Crazy Emmett.

Displaying a complete lack of the manly man's need to defend his own, not to mention the law enforcement officer's sworn duty to protect, he laughed so hard he came out of her. "Damn," he choked, "why does all the fun stuff happen when I'm not there?"

"I'm nearly raped and you think it's funny?" She shoved him and he rolled off her.

She pulled her clothes on, smoothing her hair back and assuming an expression of wounded dignity, which wasn't easy because Jack was still laughing. "Yuk it up, jerk," she said, and marched off down the runway, or she did until he grabbed her hand and yanked her into his arms.

He grinned down at her. "Crazy Emmett must really be crazy," he observed. "You'd have had his balls for breakfast."

Because it was true, she relented. Seizing the moment,

Jack yanked on his clothes with hasty hands and they walked back down the runway, Jack almost skipping with joy, Kate already wondering if she'd done the right thing. But she could always kick him out again, couldn't she?

Nobody said this had to be permanent. He was so big he was bound to fill up the cabin more than she liked.

And then there was Johnny. Any teenager took up all the space they occupied, ask any parent.

But as Jack had pointed out, they could always build on an extension. She'd been thinking of adding on a bathroom anyway, with running water and maybe even a water heater she could run off the generator.

But what if they wouldn't let her read in peace? What if Johnny insisted on listening to, what, Aerosmith or Kiss or some band of heavier metal at all hours? At least Jack liked Jimmy Buffett.

His cooking skills were rudimentary at best. But he did have the endearing habit of cleaning up after she cooked, and unlike other men of her acquaintance the dishes were actually clean when she went to get them out of the cupboard again. Johnny was house-trained, too.

He used her hand to pull her to a halt. "I can hear you thinking," he said. "Stop it."

"I don't know what you're talking about," she said.

He threw back his head and laughed so loudly Mutt came trotting up to see what was going on. "Don't bullshit me, Shugak, you're practically fossilized with fear." He wrapped an arm around her waist and raised her up so that they were eye to eye. "Don't even think about taking it back. We're going to do this, and we're going to make it work."

Sez you, Kate thought.

"Says me," Jack agreed, and she gaped at him. He laughed again. "Don't you know everything you think is written all over your face? Don't worry," he added as he set her back down on her feet, "the only other person besides me who could read your face is dead."

"Good," Kate said. "I mean—"

He laughed again, and Mutt sneezed once and trotted off, shaking her head. "Don't strain yourself. I know what you mean, and so would she." He grinned down at her. "And I guarantee you, your grandmother would be laughing her ass off, too."

Back at the lodge, Kate made up an excuse to make a pit stop in the outhouse. In truth, for some reason she could not specify, she was shy about climbing into bed next to Jack this evening. Something in their relationship seemed to have passed out of her control and into his, and she knew a sudden strange skittishness in his company. Over what, she couldn't precisely say.

She covered it up with a matter-of-fact gruffness that, if his wide grin were anything to go by, didn't fool him for a New York minute. She stamped off to the outhouse, grumbling to herself. She didn't walk in and out of his mind like it was her backyard; how dare he do it to her? "A woman," she informed Mutt, "is entitled to some privacy, at the very least between her ears."

Mutt gave her a quizzical look. She escorted Kate to the outhouse and then vanished silently into the brush—raiding the refrigerator for a midnight snack.

Kate meditated with the door open for a while, looking at the stars tangled in the treetops, listening to the night sounds. For a moment she thought she heard voices, one male, one female, but it was only the murmur of water running downhill all the way from Denali.

When she had achieved once more her normal state of placid serenity she congratulated herself, pulled up her jeans and picked up the .357 Jack had handed to her before going off to the main lodge. She stepped outside and nearly jumped out of her skin when a voice said, "Hello?"

She had the gun out of the holster and the hammer back before she saw that it was only Hendrik. "Christ!"

"It's okay, it's only me," Hendrik said meekly.

At that moment Mutt crashed out of the brush and streaked to stand on tiptoe in front of Kate, head down, haunches quivering, lips curled back and teeth gleaming in the moonlight. She didn't look friendly.

"It's okay!" Hendrik said hoarsely. "It's only me!"

It took Kate two tries to get the pistol back in the holster. She snapped the flap and gave Hendrik a stern look that belied the knocking of her knees. "Don't sneak up on people like that, Hendrik. It isn't safe, not in the Bush, and especially not at night in the Bush."

"I'm sorry." The moon turned his face a sickly white. His eyes were swollen from weeping. "It's only me," he repeated forlornly.

Kate pressed the heel of her hand against her thumping heart. "Yeah, yeah, it's okay. Mutt, it's all right, relax."

If she didn't quite relax, Mutt did retire a few steps to stand next to Kate, her eyes fixed on Hendrik in a yellow, unwinking stare.

"Did you want to use the head?" Kate said, waving a hand. "I'm all done."

"No," Hendrik said. He was whispering, his voice husky, Kate thought also from crying. "I saw you come back with Jack. I was waiting to talk with you." He looked around furtively. "Can we go somewhere else?"

Going somewhere else in the middle of the night in a grizzly bear habitat did not sound like a good idea. Kate humored Hendrik by leading him behind the garage. Mutt, curious, tagged along. Hendrik gave the big gray half-husky half-wolf as much room as she wanted, and she grinned at Kate, tongue lolling out between sharp incisors. There was nothing Mutt enjoyed more than putting the fear of beast into a cheechako.

Kate swallowed a return grin and said, "Okay, Hendrik, what's up?" When he was silent she said impatiently, "Come on, it's late, I want to hit the sack. What do you want?"

He swallowed hard. "I loved him."

Oh no, it was going to be that kind of conversation. Kate stifled a groan. "Who?"

"Fedor."

"That was kind of obvious, Hendrik," Kate said, raising a hand to hide a yawn. Jack's attentions, while ranging anywhere from ten to ten and a half on the applause-o-meter, did tend to leave one with a lack of enthusiasm for anything but a full night's sleep. "I'm very sorry for your loss."

Hendrik pitched forward so suddenly that Kate had no choice but to grab him, staggering slightly beneath his weight, as the whole story of his lost love was sobbed out against her shoulder.

They had met at work, he said, and it had been love at

first sight. They had tried to take their time, to be responsible in their work and in their personal lives, but they were in bed together within the week—in spite of herself, Kate was put forcibly in mind of those first days with Jack—and living together within the month. They would have married if they could have, but in Germany—

"Alaska, too," Kate said, moved, albeit reluctantly, to sympathy by the intensity of the man's grief.

They had kept it as quiet as they could at work, but "Everyone knew," Hendrik said, tears soaking through Kate's shirt. "Fedor was scared we would lose our jobs. But Dieter, he said nothing, and no one else said anything, and we think, Okay, we're safe."

And you were until you went wandering around in the Alaskan Bush without a clue as to what you were doing, Kate thought. He mumbled something she could barely understand into her shoulder. With less than motherly concern she shoved him upright and away from her. "Hendrik, look, I'm sorry for your loss—" those awful, standard-issue law enforcement professional words "—but there isn't anything we can do about it now. Fedor is dead, and—"

"And Dieter killed him," Hendrik said, wiping his nose on his sleeve.

Kate looked at him and said patiently, "Hendrik, Dieter was eight or ten miles in the other direction at the time Fedor was shot, reducing the Alaska moose population by one. I know because I was with him. Besides, Klemens has already admitted to doing the shooting."

"Dieter had him killed," Hendrik said stubbornly. "He told Klemens to kill him."

Kate studied him. His eyes were swollen to slits but his

mouth was set in a determined line. "You mean Dieter had Klemens kill Fedor?" He nodded violently. "Why? Why did Dieter have him killed?"

"Because of the international lawsuits. DRG is under investigation, and someone is giving information to the investigators. Dieter thought it was Fedor. But it wasn't."

He was absolutely sincere and deadly serious, willing her to believe, as he believed, that his lover's death wasn't just a terrible accident, that it had served some purpose, however sinister. Useless, accidental death was something with which it was very difficult for anyone who loved to come to terms with. It hit the young hardest of all. The young were convinced that they were immortal, invincible, unstoppable. Kate had been young and immortal once herself, and she remembered how resentful she had felt when life had showed her otherwise.

Hendrik swiped his sleeve across his nose, gulped and took a step back. Mutt relaxed. Kate belonged to Mutt, and Mutt was nice enough to share her with Jack. She didn't like it when anyone else got too close.

The moon streamed down the way the sun had during the day, casting velvety shadows in every direction. The night looked amorphous and somehow suddenly menacing. Suppose this poor little lovesick boy was telling the truth? Suppose Fedor's death had been deliberate? Kate remembered the triumph in Dieter's bray after he had seen Fedor's body. He certainly hadn't been unhappy over Fedor's passing, but it didn't necessarily follow that he had arranged the boy's death.

What was it Jack had said, something about DRG being involved in legal action of some kind? Mention had been made of the FBI and SEC, she remembered that much, and American assets being frozen by the IRS. That would certainly clear sinuses at the executive level but it wasn't especially a novelty, or even something to be overly concerned about. Big corporations had entire law firms on retainer for the purpose of fending off legal attacks of one kind or another; look at RJR Nabisco, or RPetCo Oil after the oil spill in Prince William Sound. Generally speaking corporate executives didn't murder to make those kinds of problems go away, not because they lacked the basic amorality to commission such a task but because of the difficulty in justifying the expense of a hit man before the annual stockholders meeting. In corporate life, bookkeeping was all.

Bookkeeping. Finance. Senta had said that Fedor worked for Klemens in finance. "Hendrik," Kate said, "why tell me? What do you want me to do about it? Why don't you just wait until we get back to town and tell the police?"

His voice rose. "Because he will kill me next! Fedor and I, we lived together, we worked together, we talked. Dieter will know what Fedor told me."

"What did he tell you?"

He remained silent. Kate sighed. "Surely you're safe enough until we get back to Anchorage. Then you can tell your story to the police."

"Why should Dieter wait? He's already gotten away with it once. And there are so many guns here, so many." He clutched her with grasping hands. "And just now, down by the creek, I heard the others talking. They will kill me, Kate. I know too much. They won't let me get back home alive."

"What others?" Kate said sharply, remembering the

voices she thought she'd heard. "Was someone down by the creek just now?"

"You must help me," he babbled, "you must or—" His head swiveled around, his eyes gleaming whitely in the moonlight. "What is that?"

She had heard it, too, a sound like clothing brushing and catching against wood. So had Mutt, who growled, low in her throat. Kate held up a silencing hand, and moved carefully to the corner of the garage, waiting for a moment before looking around it, back toward camp.

There was a sudden rustle at her feet and she took an involuntary leap backward.

It was the porcupine, his quills rattling an indignant protest. The night was his, to seek out nice salty things like fan belts, and what did they mean by disturbing his regular rounds?

Kate felt an insane giggle rise to the back of her throat and swallowed it down. "It's all right," she said, turning. "It's just the porcupine who lives under the garage. Now what were you saying about—"

She stopped.

Hendrik was gone.

NINE

Dieter likes to party with large quantities of money and nubile and preferably famous young women.

"Jack," she said as they were getting dressed the next morning, "tell me again what you know about DRG."

He grinned. "You're worse than a ferret at a hole."

"This is a hole I want to go down," she said pointedly. "Preferably sometime in this century."

He raised his hands in mock surrender. "Fine, fine, I've always been one for a quiet life." A bald-faced lie for anyone who would willingly tie themselves to Kate Shugak's tail. "DRG stands for Deutches Radio Gessellschaft."

"I remember that much," Kate said. "Radio like our radio?"

"Yeah, I think it means the same in both languages."

Kate looked around for Demetri but he had already gone out. Old Sam scowled at her through the neck opening of a very ratty University of Alaska, Fairbanks, sweatshirt that Kate distinctly remembered buying as an undergraduate. It had gone missing after last summer on the *Freya*, Old Sam's seventy-five-foot fish tender. "Okay. Tell me about them."

Jack finished tying his shoes and went to pour coffee, which George had made before going to the strip to do a pre-flight inspection. "I only know what I read in the papers."

"Then tell me what you read," Kate said, accepting a mug. "After all, if you read it in the papers, it must be true, right?" She added Carnation evaporated milk straight from the can with a lavish hand.

Jack, watching, shuddered. "Yeah, right. DRG is in the computer business. From what it sounds like, they write the programs that make computers run."

"Like Steven Jobs of revered memory," Kate said, think-ing nostalgically of her first on-the-job Mac. No electricity at the cabin, of course, so no computer.

"I don't think Steven Jobs is dead yet," Jack said. "Although he just went into partnership with Bill Gates, so he probably is well on his way to being eaten alive."

"Whatever," Kate said. "Tell me about DRG."

"Okay," Jack said obediently. "Where was I? Oh yeah, they write the programs that make computers run. They are, according to the Associated Press, the only European computer company that has the talent and the capital to give Microsoft a run for its money, in the European Community, that is. I forget how much of the market in operating systems they've managed to capture, but I remember the writer compared them to Airbus Industries, and how Airbus stacks up to Boeing."

"Small but talented, capable and energetic?" Kate sug-gested.

Jack grinned and said smoothly, "Are we drawing com-parisons to anything else here?"

It took her a minute to get it. When she did, she blushed and said crossly, "Yeah, yeah." His grin widened. Old Sam snorted, stamped his foot down into his boot and slammed out the door, disgusted by the excess of sentiment. "So," Kate said in a monitory tone, "DRG has a lot of European customers?"

"And Asian," Jack said, "according to the articles I read, anyway. Plus it is said they are beginning to carve out a sizable niche in Canada, which, as you may or may not know, is right across the border from the U.S." He drank coffee, ignoring the face she made at him. "And what with that new North American Free Trade Agreement, maybe you don't get to market under your own name, but I bet you could market under someone else's if you found a Canadian distributor willing to shift your product. Which they did. Before you ask, I don't remember the name of the Canadian company. DRG bought a controlling interest in the stock of some distributor or other, and they started selling across the border." He paused. "Yeah, and I think there was something about them beating everyone else into Russia, some government contract to do with monitoring oil exploration, or maybe it was gold production. It was something to do with minerals in Siberia."

The coffee settled into her stomach and produced a warm and comforting glow. "Interesting to see how well Russia and Germany are getting along after the Germans starved everyone to death in Stalingrad and the Russians raped everyone in Berlin."

Jack shrugged. "'When war is over, it's over forever. When it's over, it's as if it has never been.' Baron Wharton," he added at Kate's quizzical expression. "One of Elizabeth the Great's advisors. Or maybe Henry the Eighth's. And I probably misquoted anyway."

"So, ancient enemies are new pals and everything's coming up roses," Kate said. "What's wrong with this picture?"

"Maybe nothing. Nothing that has been proved so far, at any rate. The U.S. government, which as you know is never, ever wrong—kind of like the newspapers—has accused DRG of—horrors!—bribing American officials to allow DRG to dump their product at vastly inferior prices to gain a foothold in the American market and has brought suit before the World Trade Commission. This, of course, has opened the door for various American makers of computer operating systems to charge DRG with industrial espionage and patent infringement. This was naturally followed by a statement from the IRS announcing its own investigation into the taxes paid by overseas corporations doing business in the U.S., and in particular corporations whose home offices were in the European Community."

Thirsty, Jack drained his mug and went back for more. Kate accepted a warmup. "What about Dieter? What about his crew?"

Jack brightened perceptibly. "Ah, Dieter, now, that lovely lad. Dieter likes to party with large quantities of money and nubile and preferably famous young women."

"Is he married?"

"He's European," Jack said superbly. "Being married in Europe isn't the same as being married in America." He thought about that for a moment, and added, "Sometimes even being married in America isn't like being married in America. It's probably all Norman Rockwell's fault."

"Right," Kate said faintly. She rallied. "And Dieter?"

"Dieter also likes to have his picture taken. Barely a month goes by without an episode of *Entertainment Tonight* featuring footage with him frolicking on the beach in Cannes with Julia Roberts, or a front page of the *National Enquirer* given over to the tragic but absolutely true story of how he fathered a three-hearted, two-headed, one-legged son on the Princess of Scienfictia, third planet out from Rigel."

"What's *Entertainment Tonight?*" Kate said.

Jack looked at her, saw that she was serious, and said with becoming gravity, "This, Kate, is why I love you."

"But what is it?"

"It's better you should not know," Jack said, still grave.

He wasn't going to tell her, so Kate left it for another day. "So Dieter's a publicity whore." She reviewed what she had seen of the man so far, and it seemed to fit. Dieter liked being the center of attention, and if the reactions of his people were any indication, didn't like it when that attention wandered. Even Eberhard didn't make the mistake of ignoring Dieter when Dieter was performing, and Eberhard didn't seem like that kind of guy. Kate wondered what happened if someone didn't say "How high?" when Dieter said "Jump!" "Do you know anything about any of the rest of them?"

Jack shook his head. "Dieter's the CEO, he gets all the press."

"Did he buy or build?"

"Neither. He inherited, from his father, who manufactured transistors for radios and who by all accounts was one of those Germans who managed to sail close enough to the

Nazi wind to coast by most of the nastier squalls of World War Two, and at the end of the war have enough breeze left in the luff to land softly on the Allied shore."

"Nicely put," Kate said, admiring. "And very illustrative."

Jack inclined his head in gracious acceptance of praise earned and duly received. "Thank you. Anyway, he left all to his only son."

"Dieter."

"Dieter," Jack said, nodding, "who sniffed out the trend of, well, hell, the world and everything in it toward computers, and shifted the focus of the company there."

"So it's partly his creation and partly his birthright," Kate said.

"Yes."

"He'd be doubly determined to protect it."

"Kate," Jack said dryly, "on a bad year DRG grosses enough to fund the yearly budget of the state of Alaska."

"Wow," Kate said, impressed.

"So don't kid yourself. Dieter will be keeping very close tabs on his assets." Jack raised his second cup and paused to regard her over the rim. "So? Why do you want to know?"

"Because last night, on the way back from the outhouse, Hendrik buttonholed me and told me that Dieter—"

The screen door slammed and they turned to see Berg standing there, blinking like an owl through his glasses. "George is about to take off. He would like to talk to you first, Frau Shugak."

Frau, Kate thought. What, it was written on her forehead that she was about to take a permanent live-in mate? "It's Kate, Berg," she said.

Berg held the door open for her with a quaint little bow that spoke of early and intensive training on the part of a pair of very old-fashioned parents.

"You're taking the Cessna?" Kate said in surprise.

"It's faster," George said. "I'll be back that much quicker. And Demetri can do any spotting you need done better in the Cub."

"True enough," Kate said, but still, she wondered. It wasn't like George to burn gas that fast for the benefit of a dead man, especially when it would have been so easy to pull the rear seat from the Cub and fit Fedor's body into the vacant space remaining with his legs extending into the tail, or under the front seat for that matter.

Instead, George had taken the shotgun seat and the seat behind it out of the Cessna and strapped Fedor, the blue tarp duct taped around him now, to the floor in the vacant space.

Of course, it could mean only that George was anxious to get back to Senta as fast as possible, but he put that thought to rest with his next words. "Turbulence," he said, nodding at the horizon. "I want all the power I can get."

Kate looked, and was not pleased at what she saw. A thick band of gray was lying on the southeast horizon, investing the otherwise limpid blue sky with an air of approaching menace. She was even less pleased to realize that she had been so preoccupied she hadn't noticed it first.

George climbed into the Cessna and paused, one hand on the open door. "I'm going to take off and circle overhead while I call Flight Service in Kenai for a forecast. You fire up the radio on the Cub and I'll relay it to you."

"Okay."

George slammed the door and started the engine. Kate stepped back, almost bumping into Gunther, and behind him, Berg and Senta, all with wistful expressions on their faces. The wistfulness was more for the fact that they weren't on the plane going back to Anchorage than for Fedor's death, or so Kate thought. And wasn't it interesting who hadn't shown up to see Fedor off? Not Hendrik, not Klemens, not even a cer-emonial appearance by his boss, Dieter, who evidently didn't give a damn what anyone thought, he wasn't rolling out of bed at this hour for anyone.

The propeller roared into life and the Cessna taxied down to the foot of the runway and turned. Kate went to the Cub and climbed in as the Cessna took off behind her. The radio came immediately to life, and in a few minutes George was relaying the forecast. It wasn't good. Kate signed off and climbed out. "Okay, guys, let's head back to camp."

She led the way into the yard, Mutt trotting ahead. "Folks? Folks, could you listen up, please?" She waited until they had gathered around, all of them keeping a safe distance from Mutt.

Kate looked for Hendrik but he wasn't there. "Some-body go get Hendrik," she said. "What cabin was he in last night?" She knew better than to look at Berg or Senta, but from the corner of her eye she saw Berg blush. Senta looked supremely unconscious, a layer of invisible, impermeable armor between her and everyone else there, possibly between her and everyone else in the world. The reason she and Dieter disliked each other so much, Kate thought, was because they shared the same brand of arrogance, although Senta just might have an edge. Kate was reminded of a line from an old blues song: "ain't nobody's business but my own." Something like that. Senta said all that and more without once opening her mouth.

"Come on, folks, this is no time to be shy. Where did Hendrik sleep last night?"

Berg mumbled something that could have been, "He was with me."

No one very carefully looked at Senta. "Gunther?" Kate said. "Go find Hendrik."

Gunther, still young enough to take orders without question, all but saluted and trotted off to find Hendrik. They waited, listening to him bang on doors and call Hendrik's name. Ten minutes later he panted up, breathless. "He's not in camp," he said. He looked worried.

Kate remembered Hendrik's swollen eyes from the night before, his air of barely restrained panic and above all his fear, and knew a cold feeling in the pit of her stomach. "Anybody see him this morning?" She looked from face to face, Dieter polishing his Merkel, Eberhard cleaning his Weatherby, Berg wolfing down a second heaping plate of scrambled eggs. Hubert and Gregor were helping Demetri clean up, although they both seemed to be more hindrance than help around even a camp kitchen. Gunther stood almost at attention, as if waiting for more orders. Klemens sat apart, avoiding eye contact, nursing a mug of coffee. Senta was filing her nails, two-inch talons enameled a brilliant red the same shade as her lipstick.

No one said anything, and the pit in Kate's stomach grew colder. "This is not good, people. We're going to have to go look for him."

"Why?" Dieter demanded with what looked like genuine impatience. "We want to hunt. Hendrik is lost, so what? Let him find himself. Let's go."

"Not until the whole party is present and accounted for," Kate said. She would deal with George's hunting ban after Hendrik had been found. She watched with detached interest as his face turned a brick red. No, Dieter wasn't used to being contradicted, and he didn't take it well when he was.

Well, hell, as George and Jack and even Old Sam had pointed out, he was a paying customer. "Look, Dieter, I'm not saying this out of capriciousness, this is something we have to do."

Dieter looked confused.

"She's not saying we need to do this just to piss you off," Jack translated. His tone was deceptively amiable.

"This is something we have to do," Kate repeated. "Hendrik doesn't know his way around the Bush any better than you do. Maybe he went exploring. Fine. But he didn't tell anyone where he was going, when he left or when he'd be back. He could be lost. He could be hurt. We—" she indicated the guides "—are responsible for his safety, the same way we are responsible for yours."

The same way we were responsible for Fedor's, they were all thinking.

"We have to find Hendrik, and we have to find him now, before he gets into trouble. You can help, or you can stay here in camp. I'd prefer that you help, because the more pairs of eyes on the job the better chance we have of finding Hendrik fast." Also, she thought, because if even one of them decided not to help, one of the guides would have to stay with them to see that they didn't wander off in their turn, and that was one less experienced tracker on the trail.

To Kate's surprise, everyone volunteered. They had a search party organized in half an hour, each group led again by a guide. Dieter and Eberhard were with Kate, Hubert and Gregor with Old Sam, Gunther and Klemens with Jack and Senta and Berg with Demetri. They split into two groups, one walking up the runway and the other up the creek bank, spread out but no one out of earshot of anyone else. They began their search at the foot of the airstrip, where the Nakochna flowed into the Kichatna, and walked toward the distant outline of Blueberry Ridge.

They found Hendrik in less than twenty minutes, but by then he was already far beyond any help they could give him.

Impaled on the bare limb of a fallen cottonwood spanning the creek, he was very, very dead.

TEN

I'm starting to feel like
we're marooned on Ship-Trap Island.

Kate's party had been toiling up the runway. Jack's shout brought them crashing through the undergrowth that lined the bank of the creek, to skid to a halt on the loose gravel of the creek bed itself. In the water a few late humpies switched their scraggly tails in a feeble attempt to move upstream. They wouldn't make it. They would die here, and wash up on the bank, fodder for the eagles roosting overhead.

Two of the eagles were immature, brown in color, slightly smaller in size than the two roosting above them, whose white heads gleamed in the sunlight and who were probably the parents. All four had their chins tucked into their feathery chests, great yellow beaks matching the talons clutching the limbs of the trees. Motionless, too far away to see if their eyes were open, they could have been asleep. They probably weren't.

Kate let her eyes travel slowly back down, until they

rested on Hendrik. He had fallen backward on the trunk of the cottonwood, which was polished smooth and white from the water of the creek. The limb that pierced his heart was three feet long, slender and sharp.

Too sharp, Kate thought on first sight.

Jack, who was nearer the body, came to the same conclusion, and swung around, blocking the view. "Demetri, Old Sam, take these folks back to camp. Kate, you stay."

"He is my employee," Dieter said, shaken but determined to establish his authority. "I'm staying."

"Nope, Dieter, you're going," Old Sam said, and grabbed the president and chief executive officer of the multinational corporation known as DRG by the upper arm and hustled him willy-nilly up the bank and into the bushes.

Demetri looked at Eberhard. Eberhard met Demetri's eyes, turned to see Kate and Jack watching the two of them, gave a small shrug and followed Dieter and Old Sam up the bank.

The rest of the group complied without demur, pale faces and wide eyes indicating a haste to put the dreadful scene behind them. Kate turned her back on them; later, when she wanted to know where everyone was and what they had been doing and when they had been doing it, she would be watching them very closely indeed. But not now.

"Guard," she told Mutt. She didn't want anyone sneaking up behind her.

Mutt's ears went up, and in a graceful leap she gained the bank of the creek and slid into the underbrush, her dappled gray coat blending seamlessly with the branches and leaves, invisible except to someone who knew she was there. Mutt was better than a security camera and an alarm system any day.

"Actually," Jack said, "the real reason I want to move in with you is that I want the dog and I don't think I can get her any other way."

They turned to face the creek and regarded the body in silence for some minutes. Finally Jack stirred and said, "I'm starting to feel like we're marooned on Ship-Trap Island."

"Huh?"

He sighed. "Never mind. Just call me Rainsford."

It took her a minute. "Oh. *The Most Dangerous Game?*" He nodded. "So who's Colonel Zaroff?"

"We'd better find out," he said, his voice bleak. "Fast."

"Agreed," she said. "You see anything in the way of tracks?"

He shook his head. "The gravel's all churned up from my search party. It's been dry lately, so as long as you didn't wade in the creek you weren't going to track a lot of mud around."

"Let's look at his feet."

"Okay."

They squatted, looking at the bottoms of Hendrik's shoes—thick-soled hiking boots, so new the spaces between the treads were still relatively free of sand and dirt. "Pretty clean," Jack said.

They stood up again. "You think that point was sharpened?" she said.

"It's possible. First thing I thought when I saw it."

"Me, too."

He sighed. "You want to finish that story you started to tell me this morning? Something about bumping into Hendrik on the way back from the john last night?"

"Yeah." Kate leaned forward and tried to flex Hendrik's

foot. It wouldn't budge. "Rigor's fully developed." She looked at her watch. "So, what, six to twelve hours ago."

Jack raised Hendrik's foot and pushed back the cuff of his pants. "Lividity's fully developed, too. What time is it?"

"Ten o'clock."

Jack pulled the pants leg back into place and set Hendrik's leg down gently. "What is it, fourteen hours before the body temp falls to the ambient temperature?"

"More like eighteen to twenty."

"Well, he's cool, but not cold yet. It hasn't frozen overnight yet, has it?"

Kate shook her head. "Not even close. It's been an unusually warm fall." She looked to the west. The bank of gray had crept higher in the sky, high enough to be seen, barely, over the treetops. "That could change with the storm."

"Uh-huh." Jack followed her eyes. "Nasty." He looked back at the body. "So, we've got a time of death roughly anywhere between ten last night and four this morning."

"Yeah. I was probably the last one to see him alive."

"Next to last."

"Right."

"What did he say?"

"Not much," Kate said. "We heard a noise. It was only the porcupine that lives under the garage, but it spooked Hendrik and he took off."

"What did he want to tell you?"

"He said Dieter had Klemens kill Fedor because of the lawsuits."

"The lawsuits?" Jack's brow creased. "You mean the legal action being taken against DRG for unfair trade practices?"

"He didn't elaborate. He didn't have time. We can't leave him here, Jack."

He looked at her, an eyebrow raised. "And this from the woman who reamed me out for letting Fedor be moved?"

Kate pointed. "There are four eagles sitting in that cottonwood, just waiting for us to walk away. They must be too stuffed with salmon to fly or they would have been on him already. I haven't seen a bear yet but I'd bet everything I own there is one inbound right now."

"And the troopers?"

"There's a pad of paper back at the lodge. We'll write everything down." She snapped her fingers. "I'm an idiot. Every one of those Germans has his own personal Leica. Gunther's is a little automatic, isn't it? I'll be right back."

She headed down the trail to the lodge, where she found everyone sitting around the dead campfire in morose silence. When asked, Gunther produced his camera and voluntarily offered extra film. She took both, along with a handful of gallon Ziploc bags.

She found Jack standing on the bank where the top of the cottonwood deadfall had landed, scrutinizing the ground. At her look he shook his head. "No. Some impressions of footprints, but nothing definite, and we've all been doing a lot of walking up and down this trail. You get it?"

She held up the camera. "And extra film."

"Is it a point and shooter, or do we have to fiddle with f-stops?"

"Point and shooter with a built-in flash."

"Better and better. Shoot some from down there first. You got anything for scale, for closeups of the wound?"

Kate pulled out her trusty Swiss army knife. "Here. Try this. It's almost exactly three and a half inches long."

"And bright red," Jack said approvingly. "It'll show up well. I believe you've done this before, Kate."

"I believe I have," Kate said.

"You're lighter, you get up here on the trunk and take the pictures of the body."

"I've always loved how you save the best jobs for me."

"It's nice working with you again, too, Shugak."

It didn't matter that the creek was no longer very full or very wide. Kate hated getting her feet wet. She stepped very carefully onto the log.

Hendrik lay in a splayed position, his head lolling back, his sightless eyes staring at the sky, mouth open, arms extended, fingers slightly curled, legs spread. All his body weight was suspended from the tree limb driven through his body, although he had not slid all the way down the limb to the trunk, giving the eerie impression that he was floating a foot above the log. "The count, with a stake through his heart," Kate said. "Who saw him first, Jack?"

"I did," Jack said.

She looked at him. "Poor baby."

He managed a smile, faint but there. "I did kinda clutch for some garlic, there at first."

"Must be a knot or something holding him up."

"I thought that myself," Jack said. "We'll see when we get him off it."

"Goody," Kate said. She took a delicate step forward, another, until Hendrik's crotch impeded her forward movement. She leaned down to place her knife next to the wound, leaning precariously to one side to avoid poking herself in the

eye with the pointed end of the stick impaling Hendrik. The
blood on it was dried brown. So was the blood staining his
wound and shirt. She stepped back and began shooting again,
using up the roll of film in the camera and a second roll as
well. When she was done, she pocketed her knife once more,
removed the second roll of film from the camera and handed
both to Jack.

"A big man could do it," Jack said, buttoning a vest
pocket over the rolls of film and frowning at the scene.
"Look." Jack demonstrated with his hands on Kate's shoulders. "They're walking along the bank, Hendrik in front,
whoever behind. They get to the log, with the branch. Whoever says something to make Hendrik turn to face him, Whoever shoves Hendrik backward and the sharp end of the stick
pierces Hendrik's torso."

Kate, dangling from his hands, said, "I get it, I get it."

He raised her upright. "Sorry. A big man could do it
easily. A smaller man could do it, too, but his timing would
have to be just right."

"Or a woman," Kate said.

"Or a woman," Jack agreed.

"Or it could have been an accident," Kate said. "He
could have tripped and fell."

Jack considered. "He could have. Most trippers and fall-
ers I know fall forward, but it could have happened. He could
have gone out for a midnight walk, he could have wanted to
commune with the moon from the middle of the log, he could
have tripped and fallen backward on that tree limb on his way
back."

They looked at each other. "Okay," Jack said, "I was willing, even eager, to call Fedor's death accidental. Hendrik's,

now, makes me look at Fedor again. What's that great line Auric Goldfinger gave James Bond? Goes something like, 'Once is happenstance, twice is coincidence, three times is enemy action.' You take a look at that stick while you were up there?"

Kate nodded. "You think it was sharpened?"

"Do you?"

"We'll never be able to raise the body high enough to get it loose," Kate said. "There's a saw on my knife, we'll use that to take the stake off first."

"The all-purpose, super-duper, utility knife," Jack said. "It slices, it dices. Don't mess with the wound."

"Did you want to do this, Jack?" she said sweetly.

"No," he said, "no, indeed, you may have that little task all to yourself. Just don't slip or you'll become one of Dracula's brides."

It wasn't funny, none of it, but humor, however dark, was the only thing that stood between sanity and madness in the face of violent death. Law enforcement officers were especially adept at this honorable craft, and Jack was a master practitioner. He kept up a steady patter of nonsense as Kate kneeled gingerly between Hendrik's legs, placed a steadying hand on one of his hips and began to saw at the protruding tree limb. It had been dead a lot longer than Hendrik and was dry as a bone, and it did not yield easily to the tiny saw. Besides, Hendrik's body, suspended as it was from that one focal point, had a tendency to rotate, and Kate was sweating by the time the branch finally snapped in two. Jack was standing ready with a Ziploc bag on the gravel below, water running freely over his boots. He didn't mind wet feet.

Carefully, Kate backed down the log to the bank and mopped her face with the arm of her sleeve. "That was fun."

"Yeah," Jack said, "and this is going to be even more fun. But I promise, you don't have to get your feet wet."

"For the first time in my life, I'm glad I'm short."

Standing in water up to his knees, Jack boosted Kate to a section of the log beyond Hendrik's head. There were plenty of branches to grab onto and she scrambled up without difficulty. She took Hendrik's shoulders, Jack took the legs of his pants and they managed with a maximum of concerted effort to lift the dead weight straight up enough to free Hendrik's body of the spike.

"Keep going," Kate said, panting.

"I'm going, I'm going." Jack backed off the log, Kate following, and when they were both safely on the bank, Hendrik's body was laid down with possibly less ceremonious dignity than the occasion required.

"Let's not do that again," Kate said, puffing.

Jack waved a hand. "Deal."

"Look," Kate said, pointing. "It wasn't a knot, it was a bend in the branch."

Jack squinted up. "Used to be two branches. The other one either broke off or was cut away."

Kate looked at him.

"Oh hell," he said heavily. He took the knife she held out and slogged back up the bank. He edged out onto the tree trunk, grasped the branch where it had sprouted from the trunk and sawed laboriously.

Kate went back down to the creek to splash some water on her face. It was past eleven and the sun glittered off the water drops on her eyelashes. Something else was glittering, too, winking up at her from beneath the rippling stream.

"Jack?" she said.

"What?"

"Come here."

"In a minute," he said testily. The log was only eight feet up but that was about seven feet too high for Jack, who didn't care for heights. It added enthusiasm to his efforts with the saw. It cut through the branch, the branch toppled and Jack caught it just before it fell into the creek, and himself just before he was about to follow it. Muttering curses, he backed off the log, snatching up a Ziploc bag and shoved the length of wood inside.

When he got to her she was holding it up, a cartridge, its nickel-plated case gleaming wetly in the sun. They had both seen more exactly like it the day before, being loaded into a Gebruder Merkel rifle.

"Well, well," Jack said. "I believe what we have here is a clue. A 293-grain RWS clue, to be exact."

Kate held the bullet up. "Awfully convenient, finding it right here. Real close in to shore, too, where you can't miss it."

"Uh-huh," Jack said thoughtfully. "Especially when he made such a point of taking only five on the hunt." He scratched his chin. "Tell me, Kate. What do you need for a lawsuit?"

"Evidence," Kate said.

"And where do you get evidence?"

Kate thought this over. "You think one of Dieter's employees was going to rat him out?"

"Why not?"

"That's why not," Kate said grimly, nodding at what was left of Hendrik.

"Every time you turn around," Jack said, "somebody at the White House is swearing to something or other in front of a congressional committee or a special prosecutor. The easiest way to keep yourself out of jail is to put your boss there instead. They got Al Capone through his bookkeeper." Her expression changed. "What?" he said. "What, Kate?"

She met his eyes. "Fedor and Hendrik were lovers."

"That was obvious and is not news. So what?"

"We can assume a fair amount of pillow talk."

"Right again."

"Fedor worked for Klemens."

"Really? And what does Klemens do?"

"He's the head of the finance department," Kate said.

"Is he," Jack said slowly. "Is he indeed. Isn't that interesting."

"Almost as interesting as Klemens's being the one to shoot Fedor."

He nodded. "Which would make this—" a jerk of the chin indicated Hendrik "—more understandable. If Whoever is still thinking they can get away with this, Whoever has to know that you could only get away with one accidental shooting on a hunting trip."

Kate's lips quirked. "I think George has it in the contract."

His grin was quick and brief. "I wouldn't doubt it."

Kate slipped the bullet into her shirt pocket, where residual traces of water soaked through and chilled her breast.

There was a rustle of brush and a warning growl. They looked up to see Senta standing on the edge of the bank, nose to nose with Mutt.

Kate had to hand it to her; Mutt was on full alert, teeth bared, a steady growl issuing from her throat, and Senta didn't turn a hair.

"I thought I told you to go back to the camp with Old Sam and Demetri," Jack said shortly.

"I did," she said. "I came back. Can you shut up this dog?"

The first trace of nerves she had displayed, Kate thought. "Mutt. Off."

The growl shut down and the fangs disappeared but Mutt stayed where she was, between Senta and Kate.

"You are wrong," Senta said. "Dieter has bought his way out of much worse trouble than this. He would not risk his inheritance over a little legal matter. Lawyers are for sale. Dieter buys them. Beginning with Eberhard." Her eyes were like blue diamonds, and her voice had an edge of contempt sharp enough to cut glass. "Klemens shot Fedor. Maybe that wasn't an accident. Klemens was in the Wehrmacht. He knows his way around a rifle. Maybe Hendrik saw or heard something to prove it wasn't an accident, and maybe that's why he's dead now, too."

She turned and walked back up the trail. They watched until she was out of sight.

"What do you think?" Jack said.

"She makes a certain amount of sense," Kate said slowly. "I suppose Fedor getting killed and Hendrik dying because he knew why Fedor died is the most reasonable explanation. They were sharing a cabin. Fedor didn't have to tell Hendrik anything. Hendrik could have seen something."

Jack stared after Senta. "Maybe."

Kate nodded. "Maybe. And maybe she wants us to think it's Dieter."

"How so?"

Kate shrugged. "Notice how she slid in that business

about Dieter always buying his way out of trouble. Makes you wonder what kind of trouble Dieter gets himself into, doesn't it?"

"That's too Byzantine even for you, Shugak."

They stood in silence for a few moments, contemplating Hendrik's body as they listened to water gurgle lazily down the creek.

"Jack?"

"What?"

"When we get back, I think we need to seize all the weapons and lock them up."

"Agreed," he said. "And then I think Demetri or I need to climb in the Cub and get enough altitude to send a message to George, telling him we've got another body and to come a running, with help. Lots of help."

"Works for me." She looked down at Hendrik. Jack had closed his eyes, and his lashes lay like thick blond fans on his cheeks, cheeks that had faded from a healthy pink to a waxen white. "Poor little boy. Poor little lovesick boy."

ELEVEN

Feeding someone peanut butter on pilot bread
isn't just manslaughter, it's premeditated murder.

Old Sam grinned his evil grin. "I get to play detective again, do I, girl?"

"Why?" Demetri said, stolid as ever.

"For the hell of it!" Old Sam said. "For the fun of it, dammit!"

Kate, interpreting for a baffled Jack, said, "Demetri doesn't understand why we don't just lay low and wait for the cavalry to arrive."

"Oh," Jack said. "Because," he told Demetri, "we've got two dead guys on our hands, and their deaths might be related. Plus, we don't know what the weather is like in Anchorage, or how many hoops the troopers are going to make George jump through before they get the lead out, so we don't know when he'll get back."

"Accidents," Demetri said. At times he rivaled Berg for loquacity.

"Maybe," Jack said. "I sure as hell hope so. But we're marooned here—"

"On Ship-Trap Island," Kate murmured.

"—we're marooned here with what may be at least one big-time loony on the loose, and I want us to take every precaution. That means trying to figure out for ourselves what's going on."

Demetri thought it over. "Okay," he said finally.

"Okay," Jack said, relieved. "We know DRG has big-time legal problems and is being investigated for fraud. Any idiot investigator knows to follow the money, and we're talking seven or eight and maybe nine zeroes here, so the logical place to start is with an audit of the numbers coming out of DRG. Klemens is the head of finance for DRG. Fedor worked for Klemens and he slept with Hendrik. Klemens works for Dieter and Klemens used to be in the army, according to Senta."

"Which means he knows how to use a rifle," Old Sam said, echoing Senta's words. "Eberhard and Klemens are the only two of this bunch who do."

"Dieter?" Demetri said.

"Dieter has read way too much Robert Ruark," Kate said. "He knows which bells to push and which whistles to blow, but if I had to bet, I'd say this is his first shot—you should pardon the expression—at hunting. He gut-shot that moose yesterday."

"That don't count, girl." Old Sam curled his lip. "Dieter isn't a hunter, he's a collector. He wasn't going to mess up his trophy. He wants to hang it on the wall of the boardroom for all his flunkies to admire. He probably hit right what he was aiming at."

"You could be right, uncle," Kate said. "I think we can safely say we shouldn't turn our back on any of them. Now, can any of you remember if Klemens helped arrange things so that Jack's and Old Sam's groups would be hunting side by side? Specifically, to arrange it so he'd be hunting next to Fedor?"

The three men looked at each other. "I don't remember anything definite," Jack said. "Klemens did disappear on me, like I told you."

Demetri shook his head. Old Sam shrugged. "If he did, I didn't hear him."

"Hell," Kate said. "Okay, how do we get them out of camp?"

"I'm going to go out there," Jack said, "and suggest that we take the four-wheelers up the trail to the ridge. We've got, what, eight passengers, four each in the trailers."

"Who's gonna drive 'em?" Old Sam demanded.

"You and Demetri."

"While you and Kate will be doing what, exactly?" Old Sam inquired suspiciously.

For the first time Jack grinned. "I wish. Get your mind out of the gutter, old man. Kate and I will be rounding up the weapons and locking them down."

"Oh," Old Sam said, his sarcasm elaborate, "we're going to tell them their weapons are not needed, headed up into bear country?"

"We're going to tell them it's a sight-seeing trip, that the guides will be armed, and that they don't need to lug theirs along, too."

"Eberhard won't go for it," Demetri said.

Jack looked at Kate. She shook her head. "Okay, so he

doesn't, that's still only one weapon in the bunch." He paused. "And you might want to keep watch. If he sets it down somewhere at the edge of a cliff, it'd be nifty if you could sort of accidentally knock it all the way over."

Old Sam winced. "I hope George insures these trips."

"Dieter will probably want to take his, too," Kate said. "I don't get a feeling from the rest of them that they'd much mind never picking up a gun again."

"Then that's two against two," Jack said, "and what I said about Eberhard goes for Dieter, too, especially if he's the one who pushed Klemens's button. If you can separate either or both men from their weapons, do it. In the meantime, like Kate says, don't turn your backs on any of these bastards, at least not unless you've got someone else with you."

"I heard that," Old Sam said. "There are three people I trust enough to turn my back on in this camp, and two of 'em won't be with me this afternoon." He grinned at Kate. "And sometimes I'm not so sure about you, girl."

The plan developed a snag right away, of course, as such plans always do.

Seven of the hunters acquiesced in the plan for their afternoon's entertainment, especially after Kate pointed out the band of gray cloud engulfing the eastern horizon and noted its progress toward them since morning. "Might be your only chance to look at the view this trip," she said. "Lots of critters to look at, too." Probably not the best argument to use, as some of them had already been as up close and personal with a variety of Alaskan critters as they cared to get.

No one said so, though. It would have been unanimous

except for Klemens, who declined the invitation to go sight-seeing politely but firmly. Kate frowned. This would mess everything up. "No, you should go, Klemens. The view is breathtaking, you can see all the way to Anchorage. It's a once-in-a-lifetime opportunity."

Klemens smiled but spoke with finality. "I have seen enough of the Alaskan Bush, thank you, Katerina. And the others won't want me. I will go to the creek and fish."

Before she could expostulate Jack pinched her on the ass. He had never before done anything like that, or at least not in company. He was saved from almost certain annihilation only when Old Sam and Demetri rolled out the four-wheelers and the trailers. When she turned back, Klemens had picked up rod and reel and was walking to the creek.

On first sight Kate had admired the way he carried himself, pride made manifest in the squareness of his shoulders, the straightness of his spine, the angle of his chin. Now there was a definite trace of a stoop, something awkward and uncertain about his movements. His face was devoid of feeling, the lines in it deeply carved, the eyes sunken and blank.

Jack's voice murmured in her ear. "Probably just as well. Better he should stay here where we can keep an eye on him."

She rounded on him. "If you ever pinch me like that again, I'll—"

His eyes laughed down into hers, and the words died on her lips. "I guess I can pinch my roommate once in a while if I want to."

She opened her mouth again to remove any such bizarre notion from his puny little mind, and heard some stranger say, a smile in her voice, "Only once in a while."

Good god, she thought afterward, watching him help load the trailers. Was this what cohabitation did to you, turn you into a simpering idiot, ready, willing and able to be pawed by the obnoxious male you permitted, under protest and only after long apprenticeship, to reside in your once supremely inviolate home? A home that had known no permanent testosterone since Kate's father died?

She grinned suddenly. Maybe it did.

Dieter and Eberhard, both armed, climbed into the first seat behind Demetri. Gunther got into the seat behind them, brown nose as usual never far from Dieter's ass. Senta chose to go with Old Sam, who saw her into her seat with devoted attention to how well her slacks fit. She smiled at him in thanks, giving it her all. Old Sam rolled an appreciative eye in Jack's direction. Hubert and Gregor got into the seat behind Senta, and Berg behind them.

Jack tucked a full pack, coolers of pop and beer and a couple of thermoses into each trailer. "Snacks and drinks," he said. "Enjoy the view. I promise you, it's a beaut."

There were a few strained but polite smiles. The engines on the four-wheelers turned over and the little caravan rolled out of camp and up to the top of the airstrip. Kate and Jack stood still until the sound of the engines had faded away. She jerked her head toward the creek. "Did you notice Klemens?"

"Not particularly," Jack said. "Why, what?"

She shook her head. "I don't know, he looked a little gray around the edges. All of a sudden older and kind of, I don't know, shakier."

Jack stared at the diminishing cloud of dust retreating up the strip. "It's one thing to kill in war, Kate. Usually whoever you're trying to kill is trying to kill you, too, and you can make it out to be a matter of simple self-defense. Besides, you're under orders, sworn to uphold and defend the constitution of whatever your country is from all enemies foreign and domestic. And usually your government has done a pretty good job of demonizing the enemy so that they're hardly human to you anymore."

He paused. "It's another thing entirely to kill, either accidentally or in cold blood, in peace time, someone you work with every day." He looked at her. "In my more fanciful moments, I like to think that when you commit a crime as heinous as murder, you lose some part of yourself. Some piece of you is forever broken, some ingredient essential to the composition of your humanity, that one thing that keeps you a step ahead of the apes is irrevocably lost to you, and you can't ever get it back." He paused. "Most perps never know it's gone. Some do, though. Klemens would be one of those guys. I'm not surprised he's looking old. He should."

"Maybe. Probably." Still, Kate was troubled.

"Let's get those rifles under wraps."

"I want to toss the cabins, too."

He grinned. "Great minds think alike. Although I doubt these bozos packed in a motive for murder with them."

"Probably not. I still want to look."

"Agreed. What do we do if Klemens catches us at it?"

Kate shrugged. "We don't let him." She eyed him measuringly. "What did you give them for snacks?"

He looked limp with innocence. "Peanut butter on pilot bread."

"Jack. Shame on you." Kate's voice was shocked. "Feeding someone peanut butter on pilot bread isn't just manslaughter, it's premeditated murder." She knotted a hand in his shirt and hauled him down to her level for a kiss.

The rifles were easy to find, most of them leaning up against the walls of the cabins with the ammunition stacked neatly on the floor or table beside them. Dieter's Purdeys were in their gray carrying case beneath his bunk. "Where do we put them?" Jack said.

There was a pile of old burlap gunnysacks in the garage, marked with the faded logo of the Mat-Su Valley Spud Co-op and the year 1968. Clouds of dust billowed forth when they were picked up and they smelled of mold, but they were still sound of fabric. Kate filled them with rifles and ammunition and tied off the mouths of the sacks with duct tape. There were six sacks when they were done, fastened together in bundles of two with another length of duct tape.

Jack regarded the result with satisfaction. "Some people say that the computer is the finest product of human civilization. Others argue that it's the VCR remote, or maybe Ziploc bags. I say it's hundred-mile-an-hour tape. I've seen it secure a splint around a bone, keep the roof on a house during a chinook and the strut of a plane together in the air."

"I feel like I should start singing the national anthem or something," Kate said, giving the duct tape around the mouth of the last gunnysack a final twist.

Jack held up a forefinger. "I'm not done. Duct tape, it is said by I forget who, is like the Force. It's light on one side, dark on the other and it binds the universe together."

Kate groaned. "Are you done now?"

"There is no finer example of the mind of man at work," Jack proclaimed. "Now I'm done."

A pair at a time, they carried the gunnysacks down to the empty fuel tank next to the runway. There was an access hatch on top of the tank, and after much sweat, swearing and the vigorous application of the largest monkey wrench to be found in the garage, they got it open.

Jack sniffed. "Smells like diesel."

"To fuel the generator," Kate said, nodding. "I thought I told you."

"No, I mean there is probably still some down there on the bottom. All sealed up like this, it hasn't had a chance to evaporate, and even if it had there would still be some residue."

They were kneeling side by side in front of the hole. He looked at her. "So how do you want to do this? You want to just toss them in?" He looked at the case holding the Purdeys.

Kate looked down into the black well of the tank. "If they are in this tank with the hatch on tight, they can't shoot at us with them."

"Works for me," Jack said, and didn't even flinch when the first bundle landed on the bottom of the tank, with not exactly a splash but certainly with a sodden sort of splat. The gray case was too wide to fit in and the Purdeys went in one at a time and the case was tossed into a thick stand of alder growing nearby.

"Okay," Jack said, standing at the foot of the ladder and wiping his hands on the seat of his jeans. "Where do we start?"

"With Dieter's cabin," Kate said. "And let's do a good

job, Jack. Eberhard isn't the kind of a guy not to have a second piece for backup."

"I've always loved the way your mind works," Jack said. "Thank God you never took up a life of crime."

She remembered thinking much the same thing when she was burgling his ex-wife's house the previous October and flashed him a brazen and totally unrepentant grin.

His heart skipped a beat. It didn't bother him. He was used to it.

The cabins were lined up on both sides of the trail paralleling the creek, bisecting the triangle of land between airstrip and creek bed. Six of them were in good repair. The seventh was falling into the Nakochna, restrained only by the same length of cable that was holding up a retaining wall built of all the junk George and his procession of lady friends and admirers had hauled from the camp and thrown over. There was an old boiler, a ton of toothed gear wheels and other engine parts, what looked like the rusted cylinders off an old steam engine, a dozen truck and tractor tires and other, less identifiable items mixed in with a lot of loose gravel. There were also half a dozen boulders two and four feet across. For now, the current had been balked of its prey.

"A good effort," Jack said, surveying the scene, "but one heavier than usual snowfall and a warm, fast spring and it's good-bye, cabin. Can you see Klemens?"

Kate grabbed a branch of an alder and leaned out over the bank, peering up the creek. The bank was ten feet high at this point and Jack winced and looked away as she swayed out over the edge. "Nope."

"Maybe I should check on him one more time."

"You've already snuck down there twice, Jack, and he hadn't moved from one time to the next. Let's just keep watch, all right? If we hear him we can duck into the brush."

"Fine," Jack said. "It's thick enough. Why doesn't George cut it back here the way he does the yard?"

"And ruin the berry picking?" Kate said, shocked.

"Forgive me, I don't know what I was thinking," Jack said, dodging a patch of devil's club at the last minute.

The cabins were lined up three and four on a side and staggered among the trees and brush. While no cabin was directly across from the next, neither was it more than twenty or thirty feet from its neighbor, thus satisfying the needs of both privacy and safety. Jack took a moment to admire the care taken in the arrangement.

"Yeah, yeah," Kate said, "come on."

Jack muttered something about ferrets and holes and dogs and bones. Kate ignored him and led the way into Eberhard and Dieter's cabin.

"Dieter likes toys," Jack observed, who in five minutes had unearthed a cellular phone, a personal pager and a Game Boy with a color screen loaded with Tetris in 3-D. He tried the phone. It wasn't working. The battery on the Game Boy was dead. There was a selection of tapes, all opera, mostly Wagner with a few Mozart thrown in for variety, or maybe just for Dieter to prove how cosmopolitan he was. Unfortunately, Jack thought with a hidden smile, there was no longer anything available on which to play them. Such a shame.

There was a Global Positioning System locator, a piece of equipment that worked out its position from triangulation with satellites twenty miles up. This toy did work, flashing their precise latitude and longitude on the digital display, and, when asked, giving the location of the nearest airport, Skwentna.

"This puppy looks high-end enough to pinpoint our position on the moon," Jack said, not without admiration. "Dieter likes his toys, all right, and he doesn't mind paying top dollar for them, either."

There was also a handheld computer that told the time in all twenty-four zones, changed deutschmarks into dollars, francs, pounds, lira, ringgits, won, yen and yuan, and had an address book with over three hundred names in it.

"What the hell's a ringgit when it's at home?" Jack said. He scrolled through the names without recognizing any. "I suppose we wouldn't, unless Dieter has been donating large sums of money to American political parties whose agents' names have been lately headlined in sound bites on the ten o'clock news."

"What?" Kate said.

Jack, seated on Dieter's bunk, looked at her for a pensive moment. "I think the sooner I move to the Park the better. The world is too much with me in Anchorage."

Boxes of ammunition with RWS markings were stacked haphazardly on the table. Jack tipped the only open one over, spilling out the nickel-plated shells. Kate fished out the round she'd found in the creek.

"A perfect match," Jack said.

"Perfect."

"In the immortal words of Linda Ellerbee, I'm whelmed by your enthusiasm. Hey. What's this?"

"What?" She peered around him.

There was a folded sheet of paper in the bottom of the ammunition box, as if someone had dumped the shells, put in the paper and loaded the shells back in on top of it. Jack opened it up and laid it flat on the table. They stood staring down at it.

It was a letter addressed to Herr Dieter Ulbricht with a logo at the top, and no matter how many times Kate read it, it still said the same thing: INTERPOL, in large black block letters.

"Interpol?" Kate said, stirring herself to speak. Awed silence was all very well but, really, it was just another law enforcement organization. "I feel like I've just wandered into the middle of a James Bond movie."

It was two sheets long with neatly spaced paragraphs, unfortunately all in German. "Shit," Jack said.

"Yeah, blueberry bear shit," Kate said, holding the letter down by the corners with the tips of her fingers. "Dieter must have had this on him yesterday. Look. Every paragraph begins with a name, and look at the names." Her forefinger traced down, flipped the page, traced down again.

Jack whistled. "What do you know, the gang's all here. Eberhard, Klemens, Hendrik, Fedor, Hubert, Gregor, Berg." He flipped back and forth. "But no Senta. Why not, I wonder?"

She looked up at him. "What does Interpol do, exactly?"

He shrugged. "I don't know, exactly. It's an international police organization, run out of Switzerland, I think."

"Can you hire them?"

"I don't know that, either." He hesitated. "But even if you couldn't—"

Kate picked it up. "Even if you couldn't, if you were involved in some kind of international conspiracy to commit embezzlement and fraud and evade taxes and dump products, stuff like that, maybe Interpol would come knocking on your door. And maybe you'd be scared enough you were going to lose those seaside frolics with Julia Roberts that you would voluntarily cooperate with the feds, or whatever you call them over there."

Jack stood still, an arrested look on his face. "You think Dieter's the stooge?"

"Jack, you said it. DRG is Dieter's meal ticket, hell, his party ticket. He's not going to let anyone sell it out from under him."

He nodded once, slowly. "Okay, that makes sense, I guess."

"Of course it does." She bent back over the letter. "Look here, something written in the margin next to most of the paragraphs. Like Dieter's been rereading it, making notes to himself. Notes on things to clear or incriminate his employees, perhaps? To corroborate evidence given, maybe? Look at all the notes next to Fedor's name." Her eyes narrowed. "And isn't this Senta's name next to Berg's, this scribble here?"

"In German, who knows," Jack said, adding succinctly, "Shit."

"You're repeating yourself." Kate flipped back to the first page. "Nothing next to the paragraph on Eberhard, I see."

"He trusts him?" Jack suggested.

"I don't," Kate said flatly.

"You don't like him," Jack observed. "It's not the same thing."

Kate ignored this and tapped the letter with a forefinger. "Why not Senta?"

Jack shook his head. "Beats me." The corners of his mouth quirked up. "No reason not to. In my experience the female is always deadlier than the male."

Kate ignored this, too, and tapped the letter again. "Should we keep it? Illegal search and seizure. Inadmissable in court. All that picky constitutional stuff."

Jack didn't hesitate. "There have been two violent deaths associated with this group. I say we take everything we find that has even the most remote chance of being rele- vant to those deaths and worry about the legalities later."

Kate's heart warmed to him. Her man. "Okay." She stuffed the folded paper into a back pocket. She patted it, and said, "I wonder why he didn't just carry it with him? Stick it in his hip pocket?"

"Those safari suits don't have hip pockets," Jack said. He held up a hand. "I know, I know, they've got pockets everywhere else. I don't know, Kate." He grinned. "Yester- day gave Dieter an object lesson in the wear and tear your av- erage Alaska big-game hunt will inflict on your clothes. Maybe he decided he'd better leave it behind from now on."

"Maybe."

"You're also underestimating the paranoid's need for secrecy."

"Who says Dieter's paranoid?"

"All CEOs are paranoid," Jack said. "Everybody's out to get them, the department heads all want their jobs, the IRS wants their records, their wives want alimony, their stock- holders want to hold them accountable." He gave a sharp nod. "Paranoid. Trust me."

"Just because you're paranoid doesn't mean they aren't out to get you, is that it?" Kate looked around the tiny cabin into which they had lately broken and entered. "Lucky we're so normal, right?" She reassembled the shells into their box.

Dieter's side of that dark little cabin was almost colorful in its disarray, clothes, sleeping bag, comb and brush and toiletries scattered all over the place, dirty clothes stuffed into a garbage bag tossed in a corner, suitcase spilling more clothes onto the floor, flashlight, extra rolls of film, film canisters and their lids, double-A batteries, everything was everywhere in a jumbled mess. Dieter didn't pick up after himself. He didn't have to; usually he had people to pick up after him.

Eberhard's side of the room looked like a monk's cell by comparison. There was a ditty bag with a safety razor, a toothbrush and dental floss in it. There was a towel and a facecloth neatly draped over the towel rod mounted on the wall at the foot of his bed. There was a small suitcase with spare underwear and shirts folded into precise creases inside it. There were two boxes of ammunition for the Weatherby aligned just so on Eberhard's side of the small table. The sleeping bag was lined up precisely on the center of the bunk with the pillow tucked carefully inside the head of the bag.

"Speaking of ex-soldiers," Kate said. "Klemens isn't the only one around."

She sat on Eberhard's bunk and looked at Jack. Jack sat on Dieter's bunk again and looked back.

"No family pictures," Kate said. "They're going to be gone two weeks, including travel time, and they don't put out pictures of their families?"

"Maybe Eberhard isn't married."

"He had a mother, didn't he?"

"Besides, I told you, they're European."

"Does Dieter have kids?"

"Yes. Two sons, I think."

"Even Europeans love their kids, Jack."

"Yeah. Maybe he's got pictures in his wallet." Jack gave the cabin a long, considering look. "No books, either."

"Nope."

"Not even the *Alaskan Almanac*, or the *Milepost*, or *Alaska Magazine*, or *The Spell of the Yukon*."

"Not big readers," Kate said.

"Doesn't look like it."

Another pause. "I tell you what it does look like," Kate said at last. "It looks like Dieter's on vacation."

"And like Eberhard's here to work," Jack agreed. "It doesn't fit, does it?"

"Or it's a good show."

"Or it's a good show," Jack said, nodding. "Who's in the next cabin?"

TWELVE

I'm just saying it could be an uncomfortable night.

The next cabin housed Gunther and Klemens. "Very tidy," Jack said.

"Very," Kate said, and proceeded to trash the room.

They surfaced five minutes later, disappointed. "Nothing," Jack said. "Gunther carries his security badge, but then he would."

"Explain."

"He's a kid, Kate, and he's the head of security for a major multinational firm. That badge defines him. He'd use it for everything, to show off to his parents, to impress security officers of other companies, to con special privileges out of cops." Jack grinned. "And to get girls. Definitely, to get girls."

Kate was indignant. "Girls don't fall for that kind of crap."

"Wanna bet?"

"Well," she mumbled, "not anybody you'd want to date."

He caught her up to give her a smacking kiss. "Got that right."

She wriggled free. "No personal pictures here, either. Klemens reads, though." She picked up a well-thumbed copy of a German translation of Henry David Thoreau. "I saw him reading this yesterday, or another book like it. Does a cold-blooded killer read Thoreau?"

"Oh Kate, come on. I've known cold-blooded killers who never missed the new Danielle Steel."

"Yeah. Yeah, I know." She put the book down where she had found it. "Next cabin?"

"Just let me check on Klemens first." Jack hotfooted it down the trail and disappeared. A few moments and he was back. "All clear. I think he's asleep, he doesn't look like he's moved an inch."

"He's got an awfully clear conscience if he can just doze off the day after he killed a friend and employee."

The next cabin was Hendrik and Fedor's. Only one bunk had been slept in. A handful of used Kleenexes were piled on the table, some falling to the floor, right in front of a picture in a gold frame. The picture was of Fedor and Hendrik dressed in identical cream-colored linen shirts, skin tanned an identical golden brown, hair bleached an identical blond, the sea a deep Mediterranean blue in the background. They looked very young, very handsome and very happy.

"Look," Jack said, on his knees next to the bed. He sat back on his heels and held out a notebook. "It was shoved in between the pad and the board."

Kate opened it, and gave an irritated sigh. "Great. It's in German."

"Of course."

"It's handwritten, and recently. The numbers are the same. Their dates are backward, though, the day before the month." She turned a page. "The last entry is September twenty-sixth. See? Twenty-six slash nine." She turned a page. "Wait a minute. Here's another entry in a different hand, dated September twenty-eighth."

"Fedor died on the twenty-eighth," Jack said. "Hendrik must have written something in it."

"Looks like. The Department of Education should never have dropped the foreign language requirement in high school." She held up the notebook. "We're hanging on to this, too. The troopers can find a translator back in town."

"Doesn't Demetri read German?"

"I don't think so," Kate said, tucking the notebook into her shirt. "He can speak it like a native, but I don't think he ever learned to write it."

"Terrific."

"Best thing we did was get that bunch the hell out of camp," Kate said, rising to her feet and dusting her knees. "Ten to one this notebook wouldn't have been here otherwise."

He looked out the door. "All clear. Who's next?"

Hubert and Gregor were next. Their cabin was a model of familial loyalty combined with just the right touch of Protestant work ethic. There were family pictures, one for each side of the room, and laptop computers with battery packs, one for each side of the room. Kate turned on one of the computers and was confronted by an unending screen of indecipherable text made up of unrecognizable symbols. "Hubert," she said. "Senta told me Hubert was in research and development."

Next to the computer was a jam jar filled with cut plants. There was a stalk of fireweed with one remaining blossom trembling at the top, horsetail, angelica, wormwood, sour-dock and one frond of field fern, among others. "Looks like Hubert's into herbs." She remembered him wading into the fireweed the night she had slain the boombox.

"Those are herbs?" Jack said with a quizzical look. "Look like weeds to me."

"You can make tea from fireweed and wormwood. Sour-dock paste relieves itching. Horsetail's a diuretic, some say an abortifacient."

"Come on."

She cocked an eyebrow. "You can use devil's club to treat burns. As handy as you are in the kitchen, I ought to plant a patch next to the cabin."

His heart skipped another beat. "I'd rather suffer the burn than have to pick the devil's club to cure it." Inwardly, he rejoiced. She was taking his presence at the cabin as a given. And she wasn't telling him he had to learn to cook. He wanted to ask her to marry him then and there. Nobly, he restrained himself. One step at a time.

Blissfully unaware of the euphoria her casual words had induced, she turned on the other computer, fumbled her way through the directory and was nearly blasted out of the cabin by the resulting color and sound. "Where's the volume control on this thing?" she yelled.

Jack found it and turned it down. "What is it?" he said.

"A commercial, I think," Kate said. "Or part of a promotional campaign. Senta said Gregor was the head of public relations."

"That would explain the boozer's nose," Jack said, nodding.

"Yeah, it does kinda look like it belongs on W. C. Fields's face, doesn't it? Bet we find a bottle stashed in here somewhere."

"Nah. He's carrying it." Jack saw her look and added, "It's a silver flask. I saw him take a nip out of it this morning."

They watched the screen for a few moments as a hearty male voice spouted a string of German while a series of pictures flashed the smiling faces of happy workers all sporting the snazzy DRG logo on a hat or a tie or a shirt pocket.

Jack turned it off. "Pretty picture, when the truth of the matter is that most of their work is probably done in Laos by people making seven cents an hour."

Kate surveyed the room and shrugged. "Looks like the temporary residence of a couple of hardworking family men. It might even be true, or it is when Gregor's at home. Let's move on."

The next cabin, and the last one in line that wasn't falling into the Nakochna, belonged to Senta and Berg. Berg proved to have, besides the usual clothes and toiletries, a secret stash of Hershey bars. "Plain," Jack said peevishly. "Why couldn't it be the ones with almonds?"

"That Berg, so inhospitable toward his friendly neighborhood burglars." Kate was looking for Senta's purse. In her experience, a woman's purse was second only to a man's mother in filling in the blanks of an individual's character. "Aha."

She found it under the bunk, a darling little mini-back-pack affair, probably the latest thing down the runway in Milan. It was made of real leather burnished a deep chestnut, soft and supple to the touch, and had two pockets fastened with a single and probably genuine gold buckle. The outer one was big enough to hold a passport. Kate opened it, and it was her turn to be peevish. "God, I can't believe it."

"What?" Jack said, unwrapping a Hershey bar and taking a bite with relish.

"She even looks good in her passport picture. That's against the rule."

"The rule?"

"The rule that says all passport pictures make people look like toads. They're usually worse than driver's licenses."

"Let me see." He swallowed and looked. "Yum."

"Watch it, big boy, she'd eat you alive."

He grinned. "I'd slide down kicking and screaming all the way."

"And this is the man," Kate told Mutt, who had reappeared to flop in the doorway and sleep off her midday snack, "who professed his eternal devotion to me on top of a fuel tank in the middle of the Alaskan Bush, beneath a full moon, and not even twenty-four hours ago. See?" she said to Jack. "Mutt thinks you're disgusting, too."

Jack regarded Mutt with a sapient eye. "Mutt is too stuffed to move out of her own way, let alone think anything of the kind. And it was a hunter's moon, as I recall."

Kate sniffed. "Hey, she's thirty-eight, four years older than me."

"So?"

Kate closed the passport and tucked it back into its

pocket. "So she's got that kind of a face, you know? The first time I saw her I thought she could be anywhere from thirty to fifty." She meditated. "I wonder why the guys took their passports with them."

Jack produced a wallet like a magician producing a rabbit from a hat.

"Even on a hunt?" Kate said.

"Even on a hunt," Jack said, deadpan. "It's a guy thing."

"Oh. Yeah. Right. Then why didn't Dieter put the letter in his wallet?"

"We may never know," Jack said, much struck.

She shook her head. Jack was not approaching the task at hand with what Kate considered an appropriate amount of solemnity. She returned to the backpack. At least women had enough smarts to leave their purses behind when they went out shooting.

The second pocket of Senta's purse was much larger, big enough to hold two wads of cash, one German, one American, a bottle of French perfume, a hair pick, a traveler's size bottle of mousse, another of hair spray and a third of shampoo, a makeup kit, a bottle of nail polish, a fistful of credit cards—all platinum—and a three-month supply of birth control pills. There was a business card case with Senta's name, job title, address and phone, fax and E-mail address printed in elaborately curliqued German lettering, all nouns capitalized, all umlauts dotted, all Fs and Gs serifed within an inch of their lives.

And, lo and behold, there was a picture folder. Most of them were of Senta, Senta in a crisp, tailored business suit either accepting or awarding some kind of plaque, Senta in a graduation gown, Senta in a bathing suit on a beach, blond hair shining gold in the sun and with just the right ratio of lean, hard flank to plump, soft breast.

"Woo woo," Jack said, breathing heavily over Kate's shoulder.

She elbowed him in the gut and flipped the folder. The last picture was of Senta as a girl of about eight, standing next to a boy on the verge of adolescence. Kate studied it. "Isn't that Dieter?"

"Who?"

"The boy next to her. Isn't that Dieter?"

Jack took the folder from her and frowned at it. "I don't know. Is it? They look like siblings, don't they?"

"Senta didn't say anything about it if they are." Kate remembered the look Dieter had given Senta when she had gone off with George. At the time, Kate had put it down to George poaching on Dieter's private preserve. If Dieter and Senta were brother and sister, that look had meant something else entirely. According to Jack, Dieter was a rounder. Rounders were notoriously straitlaced as regards the amorous activities of the female members of their families, much more so than they were about their own.

"Maybe she's family," Kate said. "Maybe that's why she's not referred to in Dieter's letter." And then she was struck by another thought. "What are European inheritance laws like, anyway, Jack? Do you know?"

"No idea. Weirder than ours, probably, they've had longer to work on them." He handed the picture folder back, and helped stuff Senta's belongings back into her purse.

They emerged from the cabin to find that the sun had been obscured by the encroaching band of clouds Kate had seen from the runway that morning. "You know what this means," Kate said.

"What?"

She jerked her chin at the gray sky. "It means George might really be weathered in in Anchorage and not be back with Demetri's cavalry today."

Jack looked toward the ridge. "It also means our guests will be back soon." He looked down at her. "They're going to notice that their rifles are missing. And probably that their cabins have been searched."

"I don't really give a damn what they notice." Kate stretched, joints popping.

"Me either. I'm just saying it could be an uncomfortable night."

"Well, if last night was any indication—" Kate began in a teasing tone.

Mutt's ears went up, and in the next second Jack and Kate heard it, too. They turned as one to look to the northwest and waited.

Nothing. Kate forced herself to relax, forced a lightness she did not feel into her voice. "What do you think for dinner tonight, moose heart or moose liver or moose tongue?" They had plenty of all three left over from the previous hunt.

"How about all three? Damn!"

She had heard it, too, another shot and then another. "Three altogether," she said uneasily. "But not three in a row."

"Nobody said they were good shots," Jack said.

Mutt was standing stock-still, nose sniffing the air, as if she could smell out the problem. Kate dropped a hand to her shoulder. "At ease, girl." She looked at Jack. "You think we should go see what's happening?"

"There are only two four-wheelers, right?" She nodded, and he shook his head and waved a hand at the sky. "The wind's coming up, Kate."

It was true, the wind was beginning to whip at the tops of the trees, to ruffle Mutt's fur, to pull at Kate's braid.

"I think we better stay here," Jack said, "close to shelter. They're probably already on their way back, anyway."

"Why?"

"Because the weather's socking in, because they've bagged something juicy and are ready to call it a day, because Demetri and Old Sam aren't idiots." He looked at her and said more gently, "They aren't, Kate. And there were only three shots."

Kate took a deep breath, held it and let it out slowly. "All right," she said, but she was still uneasy. "You know that gun rack on the west wall of the lodge?"

"Yeah?"

"Let's empty it out, hide the rifles. And we don't take these off" — she slapped the .357 pistols they had strapped to their waists — "for any reason whatever."

"Why don't we figure out a way to bar both doors while we're at it?" Jack said dryly, but he followed her to the lodge and helped to take the rifles down one at a time. There were half a dozen of them, ranging from a tiny .22 automatic rifle in pristine condition to a Winchester twenty-gauge shotgun with a tarnished barrel and a scarred walnut stock. "Where do you want to put them?" he said.

"Not where we put theirs," she said.

"Where then?"

In the end, they wrapped the weapons in more of the burlap potato sacks and climbed to the half-loft in the garage to secrete them in the center well of a spool of electric cable. They stacked half a dozen boxes of canning jars on top of the spool to hide the hole and what was poking out of the top of it. For good measure, they took the ladder down and hid it in the bushes on the side of the garage facing away from camp.

"Somebody could always shinny up the cable on that traveling block," Jack said. He caught her eye. "Sorry."

"It's not funny," she said severely.

"No, it's not," he said. "But for some reason I'm in a good mood anyway. So sue me."

He kissed her, a long, slow, savory kiss as the rising wind rippled through the campsite, setting spirals of golden aspen leaves to dance around them in a whirlwind of delight.

There was a shout from the creek, and as they looked Klemens came stumbling up the bank. "Come!" he said. "Come see!"

"Hell," Jack said. "You think he knows about the cabins?"

"Or noticed the rifles were gone," Kate murmured. She plastered a false smile on her face and stepped forward. "What is it, Klemens?"

"Come see!" he said. His face was red with excitement and for the moment at least he had forgotten his troubles. "Come now! I saw some moose fighting! Come see!"

Kate and Jack followed him to the creek and down the bank. The other side of the creek was thickly crusted with stands of spruce, cottonwood, alder, aspen and diamond willow, a thicket impenetrable even by light, but after five minutes walk it thinned to a small meadow fed by a tiny stream that was the last tributary to join the Nakochna before the Nakochna itself joined the Kichatna.

They heard it before they saw it, and they didn't need to follow his pointing finger to see it. Mutt heard it before any of them, and bounded ahead to watch avidly, quivering with interest.

"I heard noises," Klemens said, lowering his voice and half crouching behind a salmonberry bush. "Look what I found!"

They saw.

Two bull moose were squaring off, stamping and snorting and grunting, tearing the hell out of the trees and bushes lining the edge of the little glade. There were half a dozen cows grazing in the brush; the reason for the fight. They seemed unimpressed, sparing not even a glance for the ruckus being raised on their behalf.

And a ruckus it was, with the two bulls uttering cries that sounded somewhere between a drunken pig and a mad cow. "Old Sam was right," Kate said, "they are like drunks in a bar."

One bull was younger, with a fork on one side of his rack and a spike on the other. He was game, though, and he was almost as big as the other older bull, which was a good thing, because so far as rack size was concerned he was totally outclassed.

"What do you think, seventy inches?" Kate said

"Sixty, maybe," Jack said. "Okay, sixty-five. Not a record, but nice. I'm glad Dieter isn't here."

Klemens glanced at Jack, and then looked back across the creek.

The rack on the older bull was, in fact, magnificent, broad, evenly balanced brow palms and an equal number of brow tines, four to each side. The older bull was using his rack to advantage, ripping up what seemed to be quite half the trees in sight, yelling and bellyaching all the while, the noise rising in volume as feelings escalated. The object was to intimidate, to throw the opponent off guard, if possible to force a retreat before it came to blows.

The other bull, perhaps too young to know better, re-fused to back down. The older bull smacked its lips and charged. Seven feet high at the shoulder, nine feet in length and weighing close to a ton each, the clash of flesh and bone and antler when the moose collided was felt all the way across the creek.

"*Mein Gott!*" Klemens said. He'd forgotten to whisper.

It didn't matter, as the noise of combat was so loud that nothing could be heard over it. The younger bull, either too stupid or too horny to give, met a second charge head on. One of the brow tines of the older bull sliced open his forehead and blood flowed liberally down the young bull's head and neck. He didn't even notice, and tried to gouge his opponent with his single brow tine. The older bull treated this attempt with the disdain it deserved and stepped out of reach.

"Look!" Jack said, pointing.

Unbeknownst to either of the fighting bulls, a third bull, smaller in size as well as in rack, sidled quietly out of the trees and, while the other two bulls were preoccupied, proceeded to mount one of the cows. She stood where she was, accepting him placidly, her legs braced against the force of his thrusts. When he was done he dropped back to all four feet, gave her a friendly nuzzle, for all the world like a john taking leave of his Friday afternoon hooker, and ambled back into the trees.

Meantime, the battle between the two other bulls was still going on, with no quarter asked or taken.

Jack laughed so hard he had tears in his eyes. Even Klemens was smiling.

They watched until the younger bull received a second cut, this one on his flank from a point on the brow palm that would have impaled him if he hadn't jumped out of the way. He lost interest after that and headed for the hills. The older bull, tired but triumphant, gathered up his harem and began moving them upstream.

"You were right," Klemens said, staring after them. "It is good that Dieter is not here." He met Jack's eyes squarely.

"Klemens," Kate said impulsively, "did you mean to kill Fedor?"

Klemens looked at her, startled, but said immediately, "No, Katerina. I did not. I'm sorry," he said to Jack. "You told me to stay, and I didn't. I'm not like Berg, I don't wander, but I did this time. And then I was alone, and frightened, and I saw movement in the brush." He shrugged, a slight movement that betrayed his weariness. "I was frightened," he repeated. "I shot. I would give anything if I hadn't, but I did."

Kate hesitated, looking at Jack. He raised an eyebrow. "Was Fedor talking to anyone about the legal troubles DRG is having with the United States government?"

"What?" Either Klemens was the best actor who ever lived or this was news to him. "How did you know about that?"

"Come on, Klemens, it's been on CNN," Jack said. "We have cable in Alaska now, you know."

"You do?"

"Yes, and you haven't answered Kate's question. Was

Fedor talking to someone about DRG? Was he a secret witness for the plaintiff, any one of the plaintiffs?"

Klemens sat down heavily on a nearby stump. "Was he a spy, do you mean? No, I will not believe such a thing. He worked for me, he was a good worker, an honest worker, a hard worker. There was the relationship with Hendrik, of course, but Dieter said it was my department and that it was up to me. Fedor was a good worker in spite of his, ah, in spite of the way he was, and I kept him on because of it. I liked him," Klemens said defiantly. "He would not spy."

"You're the head of finance, right?" Kate said. He nodded. "I don't have to tell you, Klemens, it's all in the numbers. If a plaintiff wants information about a corporation he's suing, his best bet would be to hire him a spy in the finance department."

"Wait," Klemens said. Color crept into his face. "Wait one moment, please. You think Fedor was a spy, a—what? An informant, isn't that the word?"

"Perhaps."

On a note of rising wrath, Klemens said, "And you think Dieter found this out and had me kill him?"

"Perhaps," Kate repeated.

Klemens surged to his feet. The German fell from his lips in a steady stream, punctuated by savagely gesturing hands and reaching a decibel level to rival the outcries of the fighting moose.

He finished with a final, brief statement and stood glaring at them for a moment.

Mutt gave a low "Whuff." He jerked around and stared at her as if he might give her a swift kick in the ribs for her presumption. Don't do that, Kate thought, don't do it, Klemens, not if you like your foot the way it is now.

He didn't, swerving back to face them. "I did not kill Fedor for Dieter!"

"I think we got the message," Jack murmured as Klemens pushed past him. He looked down at Kate. "Do you believe him?"

"I think I do," Kate said thoughtfully. "Jack, I'd really like to know what Hendrik wrote in Fedor's diary. Do you think—"

"No," Jack said firmly. "We're not taking chances with any of these people. We'll wait for the troopers, Kate."

"Yeah, I know. You're right." She shivered. "The wind's picking up. Let's go make some coffee. They'll probably want something hot to drink when they get back."

A couple of hours later she began to get restless. "They should be back by now, shouldn't they?" She went to the door.

So far the storm was all wind and no precipitation, the gray clouds high above. She walked out into the yard and looked east. There the clouds looked lower and wetter and infinitely more threatening.

Jack followed her, sliding his arms around her from behind.

She turned and looked up at him, his face as well known to her as her own. He'd shaved two years ago after discovering that most mass murderers wore beards. Kate wasn't supposed to know that, but one of Jack's co-workers had told her on the sly, and she was saving the sliver of information for when it would do her the most good. He was tall, well over six feet, and burly, with untidy dark hair that continually fell into deep blue eyes, eyes that could on occasion see right through you and out the other side.

He was also loyal and trustworthy and brave and true. And he loved Jimmy Buffett only less than herself. Maybe this roommate stuff was going to be all right after all.

He smiled down at her. "What?"

"I thought you could read my mind."

He grinned appreciatively, and then his gaze shifted from her face to behind her and the smile faded. He opened his mouth and the back of her head exploded.

An immense shadowy pit opened up invitingly at her feet and she fell forward into its muffling arms.

Jack seemed to be falling with her, and the last thing she saw before they were enveloped in darkness was a gray streak arrowing toward her, ears flattened and teeth bared.

There was a boom that reverberated through her bones, a single, agonized yelp and then nothing.

THIRTEEN

May I have her as a pet?

Kate woke on her side in the dirt. The steady throbbing at the back of her head was the first thing she recognized, and it took several moments to understand that she was still at George Perry's hunting camp, that the sky was dark with clouds, and that she seemed to be alone. This bothered her, but she didn't know quite why.

She couldn't sit up. This puzzled her. Why couldn't she get her hands beneath her and push?

Investigation revealed that they had been secured behind her back. Her feet seemed to have been immobilized, too. She couldn't move, couldn't reach up to feel the back of her head, which felt as if a piece of it were missing and all the exposed nerve endings were screaming for help.

Since she couldn't move, she thought. At first there was nothing, a blank, black space devoid of faces, names, places. There was nothing there.

Panic gathered in her gut and threatened to rise up and choke her. She closed her eyes in fierce concentration. Her head throbbed with it but she wouldn't stop, not until she knew it all.

Who am I? she thought. Think, Kate.

Kate. Kate, that was it, Kate Shugak, star of the Anchorage district attorney's investigative staff, lover of Jack Morgan, granddaughter of Ekaterina Shugak, owner of a 160-acre homestead in the Park.

Or no. Emaa was gone, she remembered now. And she didn't work for the DA anymore. But she still slept with Jack Morgan every chance she got, and she still owned her father's homestead.

Tendrils of memory felt their way through the pain, one at a time. George Perry hiring her to guide the last week of August. The hunt before this one, which had gone off like clockwork, everyone had tagged their moose and shot enough ptarmigan and geese to fill up the rest of their freezers and gone home rejoicing.

The second hunt. The Germans. Fedor's death. Hendrik's. George taking the first body to town. Hiding the weapons and tossing the cabins. Klemens and the feuding moose. Jack. That gray streak, all furious yellow eyes and white teeth. The booming sound just before she blacked out. The subsequent yelp of pain and rage.

Her eyes snapped open.

She was facing the log in front of the lodge. The smooth white wood of the trunk was an inch from her nose. Spruce needles were digging into her cheek.

She waited, listening. There was no sound but the rustle of the wind in the trees overhead. A shift of her hips and she was rolling to her right, so that she could see the yard, a roll that should have been hindered by the presence of a .357 on her hip, but wasn't because the .357 was no longer there.

The yard looked much the same, with one exception. Jack lay sprawled on his face twelve feet away, a dark stain blotting the back of his shirt.

Something, some sound she did not recognize, ripped out of her throat. She launched herself toward him, wriggling, twisting, writhing, worming her way over rock, exposed roots, slivers of wood, ejected shell casings, cigarette butts, moving with agonizing slowness. Her universe narrowed to that one thing, all her ambition focused on achieving that one goal, to get to Jack.

Which was why she didn't hear the footsteps, and was totally unprepared for the hand that reached down and grabbed her braid.

The hand used it to haul her to her feet. Pain sliced through her scalp and an involuntary cry escaped her, a sound of which she was instantly ashamed.

A grinning face appeared in front of her own, a face she had seen calm, expressionless and unchanging but never grinning, hugely, as it was now. "Have I told you how much I like your hair?" Eberhard said.

In one of those quirky, quantum shifts of memory, she recognized the parody of Jack's nearly identical words the day before. Coupled with the sight of his lifeless body, the memory brought a welcome upsurge of rage, and with it a return of all her senses.

She masked it immediately. "No," she said. She couldn't quite manage a smile, but she was able to say, "How much do you like it?"

He took a fat loop of braid around his hand and jerked, and she stumbled forward until their faces were almost touching. In an odd way she was grateful for the support, as a wave of nausea seemed to begin with the dull pain in her head and roll over her entire body.

"A lot," Eberhard said. "I look forward to seeing it spread out on my pillow."

The rage beat back the nausea and this time she did manage a smile. "You'll like it even better then."

"And your brown skin, I like that, too. Very smooth. I will like to touch it. Too bad about the scar. It mars perfection." Eberhard looked over her head. "I like this one. May I have her as a pet?"

"Of course you may, darling," Senta's voice purred. Involuntarily Kate turned her head to see Senta smiling down at her. "So long as you kill her afterward."

Eberhard grinned again and stretched out his free arm to cup the back of Senta's head. He pulled her into a grinding, carnal kiss. She responded with little grunting sounds that reminded Kate of the rutting moose in the meadow. It was animalistic and entirely without affection or tenderness.

Eberhard used Kate's braid to muscle her closer, shoving his knee between her legs to rub her crotch with his thigh. Another, duller wave of pain radiated from her head and she fought back a second surge of nausea and willed herself not to shrink away.

Senta laughed at Eberhard when he let her go. They both looked at Kate, identical predatory smiles on their faces. "Perhaps we could share her," Senta suggested.

Eberhard liked this idea. "Perhaps we could. We have all night, *liebchen*, before the plane returns. And I think this one will do anything we ask of her, just to stay alive. Look at her, she hasn't even looked at her man, for fear it will make us think she cares for him, that she might want revenge for him. How much farther will she go? It could be—" he bent his head and ran his teeth along Kate's jaw "—amusing to find out."

He bit Kate, hard, where jaw and throat met.

She stood motionless in his grasp, enduring it because she had to, because for the moment there was nothing else to do. Now was not the time to fight.

Soon, but not now, not yet.

His hand cupped her breast and squeezed, not gently. Ruthlessly Kate restrained her instinctive shrinking, her cry of protest. Not now, not yet. She chanted the words over and over again in her mind, like a mantra, reaching for strength. She should have been encouraging his advances if she wanted to gain any herself, but she couldn't quite bring herself to do more. She looked past his shoulder instead of up into his face.

Her heart gave a great leap.

Jack's body was lying two feet closer to the trestle table than it had been the last time she had looked.

There were knives on the table.

The sight galvanized her, spurred her to action, the only kind of action available to her. She let her knees loosen and swayed on her feet, leaning against Eberhard for support. It was only partly an act. "Could I sit down?"

"Certainly, pet," Eberhard crooned.

He walked her to one of the deck chairs sitting near the fire pit, herding her like a wolf would a sheep. Someone had kindled a Sterno log, on top of which half a dozen chunks of wood had been inexpertly piled. The wind helped, whipping the flames up the sides of the logs.

She sat down. She forced herself to look up with a smile and say, "Thank you."

He chucked her beneath the chin. "You can thank me later, pet. In many, many ways. I'll make sure of it."

She looked past him at Senta, standing straight and proud, triumph glittering in her eyes. Most criminals shared the universal urge to brag about how clever they were. Kate said humbly, "May I ask where the others are?"

Kate had used the right approach, just the right touch of cringing servility, slave to mistress, peasant to patrician. Senta preened at this tacit acknowledgment of her authority. "Certainly you may ask, Kate."

"Later." Eberhard's voice was guttural. He was staring at Senta with narrowed eyes.

She met his eyes. Kate saw the instant of realization, actually saw her nipples erect beneath his gaze. Senta looked at Eberhard and ran a deliberately provocative tongue around parted red lips. One hand began to unbutton her shirt, the other slid over a hip and between her legs, part offer, part incitement.

It worked. Eberhard crossed the distance between them in three steps.

Kate tried not to watch what happened next, tried not to listen, but it was impossible. Senta and Eberhard wanted an audience. They took every care not to roll out of view. Kate focused on the trees at the edge of the clearing and tried not to show her disgust.

She didn't run because she couldn't, because her hands

and feet were immobilized, with duct tape she saw now, that force that bound the universe and her hands and feet together. She could have hopped, she might even have made the trees before they caught her, but Jack was taking advantage of their captors' distraction by inching forward again, and his hands and feet were free. If he could just get to one of the knives in time.

Unfortunately, it didn't take long to scratch Senta and Eberhard's itch. When they were done Jack was a foot closer to the trestle table, well within arm's reach if he were ordinarily mobile. How hurt was he? Was he able to wield a knife? Kate thought of the Swiss army knife in her pocket, pulled her bound hands first from one side and then to the other. Useless; she could not reach.

Senta, naked, hair loose around her shoulders, got to her feet and stalked to the fire. The logs were enveloped now in leaping flames two and three feet high. She nudged one closer to the flame with a bare toe.

In the fading light the flames gilded her hair, above and below, threw the lines and curves of her body into bold relief, flickered over her skin like sunlight on water. The wind rippled through the clearing and raised her hair from her face.

Kate had nicknamed her "Ice Queen" in her mind; the ice had melted now, to reveal the harpy within. All Senta lacked was the hooked beak, the claws and the stench, but as Kate very well knew, many if not most monsters looked as everyday as the girl next door. The Ice Queen had only been an image, carefully cultivated, to hide the putrefaction beneath.

Seeing her in those terms steadied Kate, concentrated her

attention on her options. Her focus had narrowed. It didn't matter what had happened on the ridge that day, or on the creek the day before, or on the hunt the day before that. It didn't matter why DRG was being investigated, or by whom, or if that investigation had led to murder, and what looked like mass murder at that.

Today, here, now, Senta had ceased to be human, ceased to be worthy of human regard, ceased, in Kate's eyes, to have any human rights whatever. With Jack, wounded, perhaps dying not six feet away from her, with Mutt missing, with Old Sam and Demetri and the rest of the hunting party unaccounted for, and Klemens, she remembered suddenly, where was Klemens?

She forced the thought from her mind.

No, she had no problem assuming the role of judge, jury and executioner.

It was time to make a move, to bring attention back to herself.

She stretched her legs, groaning, she hoped not too theatrically.

Eberhard turned his head. He, too, looked magnificent in the firelight and deepening dusk, powerful shoulders, well-muscled arms and legs, a strong neck. Kate had always liked a strong neck. "What's the matter, pet? Cramping up a little? We can't have that." He rolled over and looked up at Senta. "Shall we play with our new toy?"

Senta looked down at Kate. The feral smile and the purr were back. "Why not?"

Eberhard took that as a yes and rose effortlessly to his feet, padding toward Kate on bare feet. His penis, flaccid now, bobbed between his legs, a misleading statement of manhood.

It looked silly, as flaccid penises do, and she had to repress the bubble of laughter that rose to the back of her throat. He'd kill her if she laughed. He was going to kill her anyway, but if she laughed at the family jewels he'd kill her sooner rather than later. She couldn't laugh.

Eberhard knelt at her feet and began ripping at the duct tape around her ankles. "First let's get this off you," he said, his voice sounding too much like Senta's purr for Kate to find any comfort in it. He grinned at her. "Might be a little inconvenient later on, hmmm?"

Senta came to stand behind him, avid, amoral, ruthless. "Don't hurt our plaything," she said to Eberhard, looking into Kate's eyes and smiling.

Kate didn't flinch, either from the rapacious expression on Senta's face or from the way Eberhard twisted the duct tape to dig into her ankles even as he removed it. She wanted them to think she was beaten, without hope, that she had given up every thought but survival, that she would do anything she was told for that end and that end alone.

It seemed to work. "How well she is tamed," Eberhard said, sitting back on his haunches. "I don't think I like it."

Senta laughed, a wild, excited, animal sound. "I trust you, *liebchen*. You'll wake her up."

Eberhard's penis stirred and began to grow again. "Of course you are right, as always." He leaned forward to shove Kate's legs apart. Her feet slid back, too, parallel to and outside the legs of the chair, directly beneath her body weight and center of gravity.

In that moment Jack heaved his torso up from the ground and snatched not a knife but a box of twenty-two shells from the tabletop and tossed them into the middle of the fire. It landed with a sound like a log popping. Jack collapsed back onto the ground and lay without moving.

Neither sound registered with Eberhard or Senta, intent on opening up their new toy and playing with it until it broke. Kate took a deep, steadying breath as Eberhard's hands went to her belt.

The flames licked up around the box and the cardboard divider melted like wax.

Eberhard worked the buckle free and his hands went to the snap.

Suddenly the clearing was filled with the clamor of primer igniting and cartridge cases rupturing. Even to Kate, who had witnessed Jack's action and who knew that in spite of the noise the bullets weren't going anywhere, it sounded like a full-scale assault by an entire infantry division.

Eberhard leapt to his feet and ran not for his clothes but for the weapon leaning against the log. There was something wrong with that rifle but for the moment Kate couldn't think what it was, and she didn't have time to figure it out because it was at that moment that Mutt exploded out of the brush and over the log in one graceful, deadly leap, teeth bared, going straight for Eberhard's throat.

Senta, startled and gaping, had no time to get out of the way before Kate's right shoulder caught her solidly in the belly and hurled her backward onto the fire.

She screamed, a piercing shriek louder than the exploding shells, louder than Eberhard's yell as he fought off a set of sharp, snapping teeth. She rolled frantically out of the fire and kept rolling until she hit the side of the lodge, to lie there curled into a fetal position, moaning and sobbing.

Kate didn't hesitate; she jumped straight for Jack, who

was on his feet. Together they headed for the trees, giant steps awkwardly taken because of his wound and her bound hands.

The rifle boomed and there was a protesting howl from Mutt.

Kate screamed. She couldn't stop herself.

"Don't stop!" Jack roared. He gave her a shove. "Keep going, we can't help her now!"

The rifle boomed again, clipping the branch off the birch tree. It fell, missing Jack's head only to bounce painfully off Kate's shoulder.

Klemens rose up before them like a specter, blood streaking down one side of his face. He raised his rifle and for a split second Kate thought he was going to shoot her. "Klemens, no!"

The rifle cracked and the bullet sang past her shoulder. "Run, Katerina!" he said through clenched teeth, and fired again.

There was an oath from Eberhard, followed by another boom of the big rifle, and half of Klemens's face disappeared.

She plunged into the brush, crashing through the alder and the spruce, hearing Jack battling through behind her, knowing they had little time to gain a lead, that Eberhard at least would be after them as soon as he pulled on his pants.

In the meantime, she ran, lungs burning, heart pounding as hard as her feet, skin scratched and torn from the brush from which she had no hands to shield herself, her only thought to put as much distance between herself and the two killers as possible, to get Jack to safety, to see to his wound, to find a weapon and to return and exact vengeance for what had been done to her and hers.

She ran.

FOURTEEN

Light bright shining.

She burst out of the brush and brambles onto the banks of the Nakochna. She paused for a fraction of a second.

"Keep going," Jack growled.

His breathing was labored and she saw him clutching his belly. "Jack—"

"Keep going!"

By some sense of direction either accidental or deliberate they had emerged at the scene of Hendrik's death. Without pause she ran straight out across the log, jumping the stump of the branch that had been the instrument of his death and landing by some miracle safely on the other side. The trunk shuddered beneath her weight but she didn't stop until she had leapt to the opposite bank, where a patch of devil's club, broad leaves whose undersides were dense with tiny thorns, clawed at her exposed skin, leaving tiny red scratch marks behind that stung like fire.

"Oh fuck," Jack groaned.

"Never mind how high it is," Kate hissed, "get your ass over here!"

"Bitch," he said.

"Son of a bitch!" she said. "Get your ass over here now!"

With an uncharacteristic clumsiness that had her heart in her throat, he edged across. When he stepped off on the other side the pain brought him to his knees.

"Jack!" She dropped down in front of him. "Jack, we have to keep going! We aren't even a mile from camp! They'll be following! We have to keep going! Please, get up!" She nuzzled her face against his, nearly weeping. "Please get up, Jack!"

"Go," he said, his voice a thread of sound. "Just go, Kate. Get to Old Sam. Get to Demetri. Get their rifles. Go."

She was overcome by a sudden wave of overwhelming rage. "*No!* I will *not* leave you!" She butted him with her head. "On your feet, Morgan!" She stood and kicked him, hard. "Get up, goddamn you, get up!"

It terrified her that he obeyed. She nudged him up the creek. "That way," she said, crowding him forward.

"Wait," he said, his voice stronger. "Let me get your hands loose."

She was ready to yell at him again, but he was right. She turned her back on him.

He fumbled with the tape with feeble hands, cursing them and it in an exhausted monotone. Finally he went down on his knees again and bit at it with his teeth. Kate strained her wrists apart, and with a sudden jerk she was free, free, free, free to move, free to touch, free to feel.

Free to fight.

They were still without shelter, sustenance or weapon, but all joy is relative, and for a moment she wallowed in the sensation. She felt liberated, emancipated, as if she had just been granted the vote, unchained, like a dog trusted enough by its master to be let loose to roam.

She wasn't up to roaming at the moment, however, and neither was Jack. The best she could hope for was to find shelter for the both of them until morning. Shelter, she repeated to herself, willing her brain to function. There was a storm coming and Jack needed shelter, shelter and rest.

But before shelter, before they could allow themselves to rest, they needed more distance between themselves and those murdering bastards back at camp. How could they kill us all? she thought. How? And how could they think they'd get away with it?

She was unaware she'd said the words out loud.

"I don't know," Jack said. He leaned his forehead against the small of her back, worn out from the task of freeing her hands. She could feel the warmth of his breath through the fabric of her jeans. "Christ. Kate, I—"

"No," she said, turning and catching his shoulders. "On your feet, Jack. We've got to head toward the ridge, to the spike camp. George keeps a first aid kit in all his spike camps. And we can find out what happened to the others and bring back help."

If Senta and Eberhard had felt free to kill the both of them, chances were there was no one left alive on Blueberry Ridge to tell the tale, and Kate and Jack both knew it. Still, he managed to raise a crooked grin, his teeth gleaming white in the darkness. "Slave driver."

Her breath caught on a sob. She helped him to his feet and shouldered most of his weight, trying to ignore the wet, warm spreading stain dampening his shirt.

In another of those queer shifts of memory she heard her EMT instructor give the emergency medical technician students three rules of conduct upon their arrival at the scene of an injury. "First and foremost? Take care of yourself. Second, look out for your partner and third, your patient, but first take care of yourself. Remember, whoever shot your patient could still be hanging around, waiting to take a potshot at you, and I'm going to have to teach this course all over again to someone who'll respond and do it right."

He'd been a short, intense man with dark eyes that bored right through the bullshit when he looked at you, who had failed more students than he'd passed, but she was grateful for the memory. He'd been right then, and he was right now. Kate wouldn't be any good to Jack if she didn't take care of herself first.

All right. Her breathing was slowing, becoming more economical, more contained, quieter. The beat of her blood had subsided from her ears to the base of her throat. Her skin was clammy, and she realized she was shivering uncontrollably.

She could have applied those symptoms to someone else but not to herself. She didn't know it but she was in shock.

Kate had run up against evil before, the contractor the previous spring in the Park, the pastor the summer before in Chistona, the deckhand on the *Avilda*, the suspects without number before them whose parental and undeniably lawful rights Kate had had to force herself to respect, as they had not respected the basic human right of a child, any child to be warm and fed and above all, safe.

No, evil was not new to Kate. In her experience evil was not just a scarcity of good, it was a real, tangible quality that had to be fed, nurtured, coddled, encouraged, aided and abetted. In the course of her life she had met far too many foolish people who were blind to its presence in everyday life. "My husband?" a wife would say in surprise. "Oh no, my husband would never do such a thing." "My wife is the most loving mother in the world," the husband would say firmly. "I'm sorry, but what you are saying cannot possibly be true."

Ostriches, every one of them. Yes, Kate knew evil, but she had never in her life been bound before this night. What astounded her most was how ashamed she felt. Her sensibilities had been brutalized, her dignity affronted, her person assaulted, she had nearly been raped. It all combined in a general numbing of feelings of any kind, save a puzzled disbelief in how she, independent, autonomous, strong, smart Ekaterina Ivana Shugak, had arrived at such a state. There was also a pervasive and undermining sense of humiliation. She had been helpless, vulnerable, unable to raise a hand in her own defense.

It didn't matter that she had been knocked on the back of the head and woken trussed up like a Christmas turkey; she should not have allowed herself to be struck, she should not have permitted herself to be bound. She knew the value of her own strength, her own intelligence, her own quickness in action; how, then, had she been overpowered? How had Jack been wounded? Mutt? It was unthinkable, but it had happened, and Kate felt as if she had been translated into another dimension, where ability and experience had availed her nothing.

Jack's head went up. "What was that?" he whispered.

There was a snap of twig from across the creek and Kate froze. She was dressed in a Pendleton flannel shirt in a green-brown-gold check and blue jeans, colors dull enough to fade literally into the woodwork of an autumn forest, deliberately chosen to do so. Jack was similarly dressed. It was after dark besides, and she and Jack were standing at the base of the dead-fall, the remaining root structure splayed around them like an ungainly hundred-legged starfish. Her ears strained for movement, words, anything.

A woman's voice came from farther down the creek, angry, demanding, in German.

From directly across the creek, at the other end of the trunk, came a male reply, also in German, short and to the point. Kate didn't move, didn't breathe. Jack's arm gripped her shoulders.

Eberhard couldn't know they were there, not with any certainty.

Senta's voice came again, furious this time, imperious, filled with a passionate wish to be revenged that would have been translatable from any language.

Eberhard replied again, shortly. Kate caught the word "*nacht*." From the Christmas carol she was pretty sure that meant "night."

Yes, she thought, it is night, it's too dark for you to be out here stumbling around, go back to the lodge, don't find me, don't find Jack, go back to the lodge and let me find Jack some shelter, let me treat his wounds, let me regroup, find my strength, and then I'll be happy to face you down when and where you choose, you sadistic, raping, murdering sons of bitches, go back to the lodge, go back, go back.

Eberhard didn't move, and for a single terrifying moment she thought that the intensity of her feelings had reached him somehow, had halted him as he was about to turn and go back.

The voice came to her out of the night. "Good night, *Fraulein* Kate. Sleep well. In the morning light when we come you will have need of sleep. Senta is not happy with you, oh no."

A ploy, that's all it was. If he'd really thought they were there he would have crossed the log. Wouldn't he?

There was a deep, rich chuckle, and Kate found herself wondering if he could smell Jack's blood. She thrust the image from her mind and tightened her arm around Jack's waist.

The chuckle was followed by a step, another, the distinctive sound of careless, inexperienced feet traveling through the undergrowth, crushing twigs, snapping branches, mowing down bushes, letting everybody know for miles around who and what they were and where they were going.

Kate let out a soundless breath she hadn't even known she was holding and sagged against the roots of the deadfall only so long as Eberhard's heavy footsteps were still within earshot, Jack leaning against her.

The second they weren't, she pulled free. "Can you make it down the bank?"

"I'll try."

She didn't like the sound of his voice, rough-edged with pain, or the sound of his breath, which had begun to rasp, as if he were breathing through more than his nose. She dropped down the bank to the bed of the creek and turned to guide him down. He stubbed his toe on a rock and went down to one knee, unable to stifle a moan of pain.

"Come on, Jack," she said, pulling him to his feet. "Keep moving. They know this area, hell, we walked them all over it when we were looking for Hendrik. We have to get somewhere they haven't seen, that they aren't familiar with."

She urged him upstream, goading, beseeching, praising, scolding, her urgent need for haste hindered by his slow, halting progress. Moonrise wasn't far off, she thought as she guided him around a boulder. She didn't care if it was brewing up a storm; strong winds had a habit of pushing clouds out of the way as fast as they had brought them up in the first place. Eberhard had said they were headed for the lodge, had certainly sounded like it, but there was nothing to say he hadn't doubled his tracks and was after her right now.

If their positions had been reversed, Kate would have been.

Quartz made up a good part of the creek bed—it had been the site of a gold mine, after all—and she was grateful for it. White stones gleamed up at them through the darkness and guided their feet. As their eyes became accustomed to the dark they tripped less and moved faster.

Kate tried not to think that the creek bed would be a natural trail to take in following the two of them. At least the wind was loud enough now to cover the sound of their footsteps. If Senta and Eberhard were behind them, they wouldn't hear anything. Of course, Kate and Jack wouldn't hear them, either. They could be right behind them, just around the last bend in the creek, one of them could have somehow gained ground on the far side of the creek, they could be waiting—

She caught herself. It did her no good to think that way. She had watched a wolf pack pull down a caribou calf once,

cut it out of the herd and run it right off its feet, too tired to
be terrified any longer of its fate. It could happen to her, to
Jack, right here, right now, if she let it. Jack was moving in
dogged silence, placing one foot in front of the other with the
exaggerated care of a drunk, but his hand was clutching his
belly as if he were afraid his guts were going to spill out. Kate
was afraid they were, too. Maybe they should just find a convenient boulder and sit down, maybe—

No. Kate Shugak didn't give up, she didn't give in and
she wouldn't give out.

The wind whipped the tops of the trees back and forth.
The boughs rustled. The clouds scudded overhead, and as she
had thought it might, now and then a gleam of moon showed
through. It was as quickly extinguished.

The moon was a ghostly galleon tossed upon cloudy
seas. The line popped into her head from out of nowhere, and,
a little giddy, she went with it.

It was from a ballad, a form of poetry that in her opinion was greatly overlooked, from galloping the good news
from Ghent to Aix with Browning to riding to spread the
alarm to every Middlesex village and farm with Longfellow
to taking the oath of the Brother-in-Blood with Kipling. What
was this poem? For some reason she found it hard to concentrate. She hitched her arm around Jack's waist, took a firmer
grip on his hand and plowed on.

The Highwayman, that was it. Who had written it?
Hoyle? Royce? Noyes, that was it, Alfred Noyes. She began
to recite it in a breathless whisper, the way she had memorized it that semester of discovery at the University of Alaska,
Fairbanks, so long ago and so far away.

" 'The wind was a torrent of darkness among the gusty

trees,'" she whispered to the wind, bringing her feet into the rhythm of the words. One made the other easier; she wasn't sure which.

"'The moon was a ghostly galleon, tossed upon cloudy seas.'" The creek turned right abruptly, marked by a tumble of rock down a bank and three dangerously tilted spruce trees.

"'The road was a ribbon of moonlight, over the purple moor.'" There wasn't anything moorish about this landscape.

She recited it all, all the bits she could remember, Jack's body an ominously increasing weight. By the time the highwayman was shot down like a dog on the highway she was more than giddy, she was light-headed and unsteady on her feet, but they had covered a lot of territory, perhaps a mile, perhaps more. Was the highwayman riding, riding, riding, not up to her door but up her backside? Were they going to be cut down like a dog, too? Like Mutt?

She guided Jack around a pile of rock without either one of them falling on their faces and turned right with the creek. She could feel the ground rising, and was aware that the creek bed was leading her slowly but surely in the direction of the ridge. The ridge where Demetri and Old Sam might lie dead.

Or might be waiting for help.

Or ready to offer it.

She wouldn't know until she got there.

And she wasn't going to get there tonight. Her head hurt and she was exhausted. Ahead, a dense stand of what might be diamond willow loomed blackly against the bank.

"Come on, Jack," she said. "We'll crawl in there."

He let her tug him toward it, let her manhandle him up

the bank, let her haul him into the heart of the thicket. Leaves lay loose all around. She pushed together a pile between two low-lying limbs and bullied Jack onto it, lay down next to him and scooped up more for cover. He was out at once, his breathing stertorous. The wet spot on the front of his shirt was crusting over. She stripped her shirt off, cut the sleeves from it with her Swiss army knife and cut them into clumsy strips, operating mostly by touch. She wadded the body of the shirt against his wound and tied it down with knotted-together strips of sleeve.

It was too dark to do anything more. Careful not to touch his wound, she wrapped herself around his unconscious body, one leg across his thighs, one arm across his chest, her head snuggled into his shoulder. Her nostrils were filled with the smell of his blood. She was still shivering.

She closed her eyes and concentrated on the down comforter on her bed on the homestead back in the Park, a thick fluff of feathers between some smooth linen blend that kept her warm on the coldest nights of winter. If she tried, she could remember just how toasty it felt to lie beneath that comforter, how safe, how secure, how very, very warm, and how much warmer it was when Jack shared it with her.

She slept.

Something cold pressed against her cheek. Rain. There was a soft, keening sound. Wind. The storm was on them. She murmured an inarticulate protest and burrowed her face against his shoulder.

"Kate." His voice held only the weakest echo of its usual deep assurance. "Wake up. We've got company."

The meaning of his words penetrated her consciousness and she shot upright in a shower of leaves, ready to fight.

Mutt was lying next to them.

"Mutt!" Uncaring of the loudness of her shriek, forgetting for the moment the danger they were in, Kate threw her arms around Mutt's neck and buried her face in the thick gray fur. "Mutt," she said, her voice muffled. Unbidden, hot tears slid down her face and soaked Mutt's neck.

She pulled back and ran her hands over Mutt's body. One came away sticky with congealed blood. Mutt's left side just forward of the haunch was laid open, fur and flesh parted in a four-inch gash to show the white gleam of bone beneath. "Christ," Kate breathed.

Mutt's right eye was almost swollen shut, and cautious investigation revealed a hard knot halfway between eye and ear. A blow from a rifle butt, perhaps. Painful, but not fatal.

Not fatal to the receiver, she thought. She welcomed the red wave of anger that swept over her this time, warming, animating, inspiring.

She became aware of the quality of silence on the other side of her and turned to see that Jack's eyes were closed. "Jack?"

No response.

Fingers made clumsy by dread searched for a pulse in his throat. It was barely there, faint, erratic, but there.

His legs and hands were cold. Everywhere she looked was blood, matting his shirt, her makeshift bandage, the grass, the leaves, her hands, the left leg of her jeans where it had rested against his thighs.

"Jack, come on, wake up." She pulled him toward her, trying to discover in the pale light of dawn how badly he'd been hurt. "Jack? Jack?"

His eyelids fluttered open. "Kate?"

"Jack!" Kate was ashamed of the tears that sprang to her eyes and blinked them back. "God, Jack, you scared me, I thought you were dead."

A faint smile crossed his face. "Damn near."

"Can you roll toward me? I can't see—" His face twisted and he groaned as he turned. She raised the shirt padding his wound to peer beneath, and her words stuck in her throat. Most of his left side had been shot away. Part of an intestine was falling out of his stomach, and something else she couldn't identify.

She looked around frantically for anything to hold him together until she could figure out how to get him into the lodge and get some fluids into him. George had to be on his way back by now, he had to be. "Jack, I've got to get you back to the lodge," she said. "Put your right hand here and press, can you do that? Jack?"

His eyes opened again, and this time they were very clear, the clearest, the surest, the most loving she'd ever seen them. One hand raised as if to touch her cheek, didn't quite make it. He said something in a voice too low for her to hear. She leaned forward, tears sliding down her cheek to fall on his. "What?"

The words were little above a whisper. "Light."

"What?"

He struggled for breath. "What you are. Light bright shining." He tried to smile. His hand dropped.

"Don't," she said fiercely. "Don't you dare die on me, you miserable bastard, don't you dare!"

One corner of his mouth turned up in the parody of a grin. "You'll give orders to Peter at the gate, girl."

"Bet your ass." He winced and she said immediately, "Does it hurt? Where?"

A ghost of a laugh drifted out. "Everywhere. Don't worry about it. We can't go back to the lodge. What about Eberhard, and Senta?"

"I'll fry their livers and serve them to you for breakfast," she said fiercely.

His grin was a real one this time. "That's my girl. One more reason why I love you, Kate."

"Why this time?" she managed to say.

"Your fine-tuned sense of justice. Look out for Johnny for me, okay?"

"Look out for him yourself!" she shouted, breath catching on a sob.

"Promise?"

"I promise." Her voice broke over the last word.

He shivered suddenly, grin fading. "I'm cold."

All she had to put over him was leaves and those she heaped high over both of them, cuddling close, giving him all the heat from her body she had. Mutt struggled to her feet and dragged herself to his other side.

"Mutt?" he murmured.

"Right next to you," Kate said. Mutt was watching quietly, yellow eyes knowing.

Jack turned his head and saw her. "Good girl. Good girl, Mutt. You got a piece of one of the bastards, anyway. Good girl."

Mutt gave a "Whuff!" of acknowledgment and touched her nose briefly to Jack's cheek before turning to lick again at her injured side.

Jack smiled up at Kate. "See? Life goes on."

"Not without you," Kate said.

It was a plea, a prayer, an appeal, please don't go, please don't go and leave me here all alone.

"Someday without you," he said. "But not today."

The tears came in a flood then, she couldn't stop them. "Jack—"

"I love you, Shugak," he said.

"I love you, too. Goddamn you, Jack, I love you, too."

"Jesus, now I know I'm dying," he said.

This time he actually managed to laugh out loud, a shadow of its former self but a real laugh nonetheless.

A laugh cut off abruptly by a guttural, phlegmy choking sound. His body stiffened.

The last breath rattled out as his body relaxed on the long exhalation, and it was as simple as that.

He went slack in her arms, everything that was him going somewhere else, somewhere from her.

She pulled him to her with frantic hands, head cradled to her breast, kissing him, hungry, frenzied kisses on his lips, his eyes, his cheeks, again and again as if she could forcibly breathe the life back into him, as if her love must be enough to make him live.

"No," she said, at first in disbelief.

"*No*," she shouted angrily, defiance in the face of death.

Her head fell back and she screamed it out loud to the sky, the earth, Calm Water's Daughter and the Woman Who Keeps the Tides, Agudar, Raven, Buddha, Jehovah, all the gods old and new who had ever made useless promises to believers and failed yet again to keep them.

"*No!*"

FIFTEEN

I was afraid you were dead.

Time passed.

It began to rain, at first only a gentle pattering against the leaves above, increasing to a hard, cold, steady downpour that penetrated even that dense canopy before it ceased, to leave everything wet and dripping.

Kate sat with her arms around Jack, rocking back and forth, rocking, rocking, rocking.

Mutt whined, a questioning sound. Kate didn't hear her. Rocking.

Mutt heaved herself painfully to her feet, staggered a few steps and fell heavily.

Kate didn't notice.

Rocking.

Mutt hauled herself across Jack's body, crowding Kate.

Kate didn't notice.

Rocking.

Mutt whined again, licked Kate's cheek, rough tongue scraping damp skin.

Nothing.

Rocking.

Mutt barked once, sharp, right in Kate's face.

She'd never done anything like that before in her life, and Kate blinked at her.

Mutt did it again.

The rocking stopped.

Kate looked down at Jack, eyes closed, slight smile on his lips, gaping wound in his side, warmth leaving his body even as she tried to hold it in with her arms, with her spirit, with her love.

In that moment she almost gave up.

"Jack," she said. "Jack."

The words were torn from her lips by the increasing wind, which ruffled the tops of the trees, the boughs creaking and groaning with the strain. A stray draft blew through, although she could barely feel it, which seemed odd. All she had on on top was the t-shirt she had worn beneath her flannel shirt and jeans and tennis shoes, and everything was soaked from the dew and the rain. She should be freezing. Instead, she felt warm. Warm and sleepy.

Lassitude crept over her and her eyelids drooped. Never mind, she thought. Her eyelids drooped, her shoulders sagged, her head nodded. Never mind. Let it go, just let it go.

A momentary silence fell, a lull between gusts.

In the single, still moment of serenity that followed, Kate heard, or thought she heard, the call of a bird, three notes only, descending, one after the other, a pure descant of sweet, trilling sound.

Kate stiffened, coming back as if from a long, long distance.

The three notes repeated, three long trills, separate, piercing, true.

"Emaa?" Kate whispered. "Emaa?"

The notes were not repeated a third time, or were obscured by the resumption of the wind, escalating in speed from a boisterous laugh to a bad-tempered growl.

It couldn't have been, anyway; the golden-crowned sparrow was a spring bird, and this was fall.

There was more rain coming; she could smell it. If the temperature dropped enough it could even be snow. If it caught her like this, she would die of exposure. She had to find dry clothes, and food, and she had to do it now.

She had to try.

She stripped the shirt from Jack's body and put it on, noting in some detached portion of her mind that the bits of gut and the blood had dried hard. She covered Jack's body with leaves piled high. "Stay," she said to Mutt when Mutt would have followed her out of the clearing.

Mutt whined.

"Stay," Kate repeated.

Mutt growled, something else she had never done.

"Stay," Kate repeated, her face a frozen mask. "Stay. Guard."

In some detached portion of her brain she noticed that she was thirsty. She weaseled her way toward the sound of the creek, that detached portion of her mind that had seemed to take over rational thought ensuring that she made no unnecessary noise. She reached the edge of the bank and peered out from beneath the concealing branches of the willows. There was no one to be seen, and the bend in the creek was far enough down that she should have warning of someone coming.

She slid down the bank and went to kneel next to the stream. The water was clear and cold. It felt good on her torn wrists, better on her aching scalp and best of all in great sweet gulps, numbing the inside of her throat. She felt as if she could inhale the entire creek. She found a rusty tin can and filled it and carried it to Mutt, leaking all the way. She didn't look at the still mound beneath the dead leaves.

Afterward, she found a seat on a boulder just inside a fold of earthen bank, providing shelter from the rain, easy access to both bank and stream bed and a vantage point from which to keep watch upstream and down.

When she emptied them out, the contents of her pockets seemed meager indeed. The Swiss army knife, a quarter, two nickels and a penny, an aged stick of gum, a box of matches with two matches in it, a couple of rubber bands, and the otter, still in its little velveteen bag. She took it out and put it on a rock, where it perched, looking at her expectantly.

She should go back and rifle Jack's pockets but she simply couldn't bring herself to do it.

She unwrapped the gum and chewed it slowly, stolidly, entirely without enthusiasm, extracting the last bit of sugar for the minuscule amount of energy it would provide. It flooded her tongue and taste buds with warmth and sweetness and an odd flavor of normality, and in some strange way provided a kickstart to her brain.

Jack was dead.

Mutt was wounded, perhaps fatally.

She acknowledged both facts. The resulting feelings of pain and rage and grief almost brought her to her knees.

Almost.

She recovered, slowly, manhandling them into one corner of her mind and locking them there for the time being. If she let them escape, they would sap every last bit of her endurance and her will to survive. Contained, they would goad her into action and once she was moving, keep her moving.

She wrenched her mind to what she might find on Blueberry Ridge, excluding everything else.

Nobody got the drop on Old Sam, nobody, not in eighty-odd years, and Demetri had an extra edge in that he spoke fluent German. He could have caught any signals in time to run for cover. They might even be on their way back right now, and they might even be coming down the creek, especially if Senta and Eberhard had run off with the four-wheelers. The cliff from ridge to creek bed was formidable but with care, negotiable, up and down, and the creek bed at low water was practically an interstate from the foot of the cliff to the lodge.

And if they were dead, she had to know. She owed it to them, and to Edna, Demetri's wife, and to his children.

And if they were dead, and there was no help for her there, there was always the spike camp at the top of the ridge. It would have at the very least food, a tent and a sleeping bag.

And if they were dead, they had both been armed, and she might find a weapon.

Of course, Eberhard and Senta had probably already figured this out and could be waiting for her at the ridge.

On the other hand, it was just as possible that Senta and

Eberhard would let Kate run herself into the ground and trust
to the Bush to take care of her.

There was a hubris that accompanied the perfect crime,
or what was thought to be one, the almost uncontrollable urge
to brag, to share and celebrate the triumph in however perverse
and unconscionable a manner. The night before, Eberhard and
Senta had been swollen with pride, boastful, vain even.

They had been fearless, Kate thought, secure enough to
strut naked around the campsite. Why?

She sat up. Was there a third member of the party, back-
trailing them, backing them up, lending them that security?

If so, who? Gunther, the eager beaver with the brown
nose, so young, so inexperienced, so easily led? Hubert the
herbalist? Gregor the lounge lizard? Berg, obviously in love
with Senta, equally obviously too stupid to make a useful tool?

Whoever it was, it wasn't Dieter. One thing she was
sure of; everything that had happened on this trip was tied
into the discoveries made in the cabins. From the bullet in the
stream, it looked like someone wanted to frame Dieter for
Hendrik's death. If it was a frame, Eberhard and Senta were
pulling it. Maybe Dieter was supposed to have run amok and
shot up all his hired hands, corporate and sporting, and Senta
and Eberhard were the only two to have escaped.

And if they were the only two survivors, who could dis-
prove their story? The Alaskan Bush was often loath to give
up its secrets. Look at Baker Bob, the serial killer from Anchorage who had kidnapped strippers and hookers and turned
them loose on the Mat-Su River delta so he could hunt them
down again. It was years before he'd been caught, and the
bodies hadn't been found until he led the authorities to them
himself.

For that matter, look at Crazy Emmett, with all those alleged trespassers six feet under his property. Would anyone ever really know? Most likely not until he was dead and gone and someone went into his property with a backhoe, and Crazy Emmett was a long way from dead.

She looked up. A low ceiling of impenetrable gray rested on the tops of the trees. George, not knowing of any reason to rush, might fly as far as Skwentna to check out the weather. He'd fly partway into this soup to see how thick it was and how far it extended, after which he'd go back to Anchorage to sit out the storm, so no help there. After all, George wouldn't be worried, it was only the—what?

She looked at her watch, a Seiko automatic with a black rubber wristband and a scarred crystal face. Was it really only the thirtieth, only the fifth day of the hunt? Kate felt as if she had been on the run for a week, and instead, time seemed to be passing with glacial slowness.

The thirtieth of September. Tomorrow would be the first of October, when they should have ended the hunt for moose and begun the hunt for bear.

Jack. The memory slipped beneath the mental roadblock she'd thrown up against it. Jack lying over her, moving in her, coming with her, the hollow roof of the empty diesel tank sounding out his need. Jack, the roughly planed angles of his face dissolving into laughter in the moonlight.

Jack, lying facedown in his own blood, moving slowly, painfully toward the trestle table, intent on making an opportunity for her to escape.

Jack, his life's force seeping out even as she held him in her arms and begged him not to go.

And Mutt. Her right side, Mutt's side, felt naked.

No. She forced the thoughts back into their place, shut them in again, this time twisted the key off in the lock. Her head throbbed with the effort. She touched her scalp gingerly. Her braid was fraying from its weave and very sore at the base. She felt again Eberhard's hand using her braid like a leash, to haul her to her feet, to drag her across the yard, to sling her into a chair. The rope of hair felt like the rein on a horse, the chain on a slave, ready for the next master, or the same one, when he caught up with her again.

She gave her head an angry shake and looked again at the contents of her pockets. So. A box of matches, a watch, a knife, some change, a couple of rubber bands and a talisman. She had the water from the creek. She didn't have food, but she knew where she could find some, and until then she'd make do with what she could find in the woods.

She flexed her hands. They seemed to be working properly, all senses restored, although her wrists looked as if she'd gone for them with a dull knife. Eberhard had wound the duct tape tight, tight enough perhaps to leave scars. She felt for the scar on her throat, the roped line of tissue rough to her fingertips. What were a few more to add to the collection?

She stood up and pocketed the matches, the change, the rubber bands and the otter.

To the ridge then, as quickly as possible, to look for other survivors and weapons and food.

And then back to the lodge.

Definitely back to the lodge. Alone or with help, hungry or fed, empty-handed or armed.

Back to the lodge, and retaliation.

They would pay for what they had done, Senta and Eberhard.

They would pay.

It was an oath taken by a warrior.

It was a curse laid by a witch.

Senta and Eberhard would not survive a day longer than Jack Morgan.

"This I swear," Kate said, raising her face to the rain, which had begun again, a slow drizzle that oozed out of the air and coalesced into fat, oily drops in leaves, bark, stone and skin.

"This I swear!"

Her words echoed off the mist.

Only one more thing to do and she could be on her way to fulfill her vow.

Stony-faced, she grasped her braid in one hand, and with the big blade on the Swiss army knife sawed off the thick rope of hair at the nape of her neck. The blade was sharp. The braid thumped to the rocks behind her.

Never again would Eberhard be able to haul her around by the hair.

No one would.

Ever.

She folded the knife and pocketed it and walked out of the shelter of the creek bank and into the rain.

She didn't look back.

The creek bed narrowed after two miles and the banks steepened, forcing the water into a confined channel much deeper than the downstream flow. To keep her drying feet from getting wet all over again she had to climb the bank and re-enter the trees.

She did so cautiously, knowing the makeshift road that led first to the old gold mine and then followed the creek up to the ridge was very near at this point. She listened, but there was nothing to hear other than the rain on the leaves overhead, no footsteps, no four-wheelers, no cocking of triggers. Good. Between the fog and the dense undergrowth she couldn't keep Blueberry Ridge in sight as a landmark and a goal, but so long as she kept the sound of the creek on her left she would know she was going in the right direction.

She fought her way through the brush, pausing when she came to a stand of highbush cranberries. They were tart but she gobbled handfuls of them, ravenous. The tangy taste burst inside her mouth, making her stomach growl for more. Farther on there was a patch of wild rose hips. She ate those, too, seeds and all.

She was looking for blueberries when she stumbled into a clearing and nearly fell in a pile of brush and leaves and deadfall. A powerful stink emanated from the middle of the pile.

The hairs on Kate's neck rose. She raised one branch and peered beneath. It was a dead moose, with its stomach and genitals missing. Bear always went for the soft parts first.

By all the mercies she had managed to stumble into a bear kill while the bear was away, drinking out of the creek maybe, or sleeping off the first course. There were at least two and probably three courses left, so he wouldn't be very far away, or away for very long.

She moved smartly out of the area. She would have run if she'd had the room, but the game trail she'd been following vanished almost immediately, and the trees and the brush began to close in on every side. She ran her shoulder into the branch of a low-hanging birch, wriggled through a stand of close-knit alders, and was scratched until she bled by a patch of devil's club.

It took ten minutes to travel twenty-five feet. She stopped, gasping for breath. The light was dimmer, the air seemed closer, the oxygen rarer in here. She was going to have to take to the four-wheeler track after all. It more or less parallelled the creek, both traveling north from the camp toward Blueberry Ridge, the first real foothill of any size in the Alaska Range closest to the lodge.

Putting the bear cache at her back and walking directly east, or what she hoped was east, she bulled her way through the brush. The trail eluded her long enough for her to wonder if she was lost. She pressed forward dully, pushing brush out of her way, tripping and falling over a tangle of soapberry, stinging her hand on a patch of nettles.

And suddenly there she was, on the west bank of the trail, nearly over it before she caught her balance. She slumped down and gulped in great, grateful breaths, face turned up to the low-lying fog that, gray as it was, was still lighter than the twilight darkness of the all-enclosed brush.

Her wrists ached, the slashes from the devil's club stung her cheeks, her shoulder hurt where she'd run into a branch, and she had long since stopped feeling the cold and the wet, but all that was better than being shot for carelessness, and she waited.

This section had been cut, and banks four and five feet high rose on either side. The track itself ranged from eight to twelve feet wide, a great, gravelly scar inflicted on the landscape by the sharp, pitiless blade of a tractor thirty years before. Alders, those prolific, subarctic weeds, were growing up along the middle of the track, threatening to take it back, in company with wild roses and berry bushes and devil's club. Its roots exposed by erosion and its white bark peeling away in crumbling rolls, a white birch leaned over the road-way at a forty-five-degree angle, ready to fall at the slightest provocation.

After twenty minutes of hearing and seeing nothing more alarming than a raven soar overhead, Kate slipped be-neath the birch's trunk and down the bank to kneel and ex-amine the tracks on the road: two four-wheelers with trailers, day old, indentations puddled with rainfall. She tried to re-member the tread on the four-wheelers. Would this be going or coming? Going, she decided. There was a third set, newer and coming back. Eberhard and Senta on their triumphant trip home. She repressed the surge of rage the sight caused, and forced herself to concentrate. No new tracks since, wheel or shoe, other than an occasional cloven hoof or bear claw, nor-mal enough for the area and a far more reassuring sight.

She set off up the track at a stiff jog, willing her limbs, which had become stiff and sore with the wait, to warm again. Her clothes had dried on her body but she didn't seem to be able to get warm. Cold she was, cold from the inside out, so cold she couldn't even shiver.

She was numb in more than mind.

After half a mile the road became a series of switchbacks up the face of the three-thousand-foot ridge. Kate paused and tried to think. It had taken forty-five minutes the last time she'd hiked from the base to the ridgetop.

The last time she'd hiked it had been the week before, with Jack, when—

No.

Kate hit the slope with grim-faced determination, emptying her mind of anything else but the need to get to the spike camp. The grade was steep and punishing and her legs were aching before she reached the first hairpin turn. The good news was that she was definitely warmer.

She concentrated on putting one foot in front of the other, in mastering the dizziness brought on from fatigue and hunger, on ignoring the loud thump of blood in her ears. The switchbacks helped, giving her a short, attainable goal, and hindered, by giving her what seemed to be an endless series of more goals each time she gained a turn. If she'd had the energy, she would have been glad of the overcast. She couldn't see through it to tell how much farther she had to go.

Two-thirds of the way up she came out of the tree line to emerge on the tundra. The banks of the track fell away and the trail became a four-foot-wide, hard-packed dirt path between lichen-covered rocks and thick, low-lying vegetation. The fog was right down on the ground now, but it wasn't so thick that she couldn't see the blueberries for which the ridge had been named, clustering close to the edge of the trail's banks and ripe and ready to fall into her hand. She swept up handfuls as she passed and they burst on her tongue, so tangy, so sweet. She thought she'd never tasted anything so wonderful. They made her thirsty, though, and she was sorry she'd left the creek behind.

When she got near the top of the ridge she ducked down and scuttled up the few remaining feet. There were bushes thickly clustered along the edge, berry bushes mostly. She didn't see any bear, but she knew they were there. They always were this time of year, the salmon mostly spawned out and the berries ripe. Time for dessert before the long winter snooze.

She caught herself. She must be a little light-headed. She had to get some real food in her, and soon.

Again, she peered over the top of the ridge. She listened. She sniffed the air. She wanted to climb over the edge and head for the spike camp, where she knew there was food and a stove and fuel and a sleeping bag. She could taste the tea, sweetened with a cube of sugar, she could smell the freeze-dried stew boiling on the little Sterno stove, she could feel the warmth of the tiny flame on her hands and face.

She waited, motionless.

Nothing. Nothing except the continuing, monotonous pattering of rain falling all around her in a steady, unceasing flow, not just a shower but not quite a downpour, either. It didn't matter; by now Kate was soaked through to her skin. She'd been keeping warm by keeping moving. It hadn't taken long after she stopped for the chill to set in again. She needed food, hot food, and dry clothes, or at least a sleeping bag in which to regain some of her body heat.

Still she waited, listening, the memory of the assault at the lodge fresh in her mind, making her wary of coming out over the edge of the ridge and into the open.

Again, she heard nothing, saw nothing, smelled nothing.

Except—she thought for a moment she heard a muted groan off to her right.

Nonsense. But—

No, she had definitely heard a groan, because she had just heard another.

Flattened to the ground, she slithered over the brush, soaking up quantities of water with the front of her shirt, Jack's shirt, trying to peer through the mist that had closed in around the top of the ridge.

The moan came again. "Hello?" she said in a low voice, conscious of the way sound carried in a fog. "It's Kate. Who is that?"

In the next moment she bumped into a body.

It was Dieter. He was lying with his head twisted at an odd angle, eyes open and staring at nothing, all the arrogance and bombast drained away, leaving only the empty shell behind, a shell someone hadn't had even the decency to bury.

Again she felt the welcome flicker of rage, but the flame seemed much dimmer and less powerful. She put out a shaking hand and closed his eyes. She looked for his rifle and couldn't find it.

The moan came again, galvanizing her into action, crawling through the brush, getting wetter and wetter until at last she ran into another body.

It was Old Sam this time. He lay still, unmoving as Dieter. "Uncle?" she said, her voice quavering. Her hand went to his shoulder.

Quick as a snake his gnarled old hand flashed up to grab her. Pain radiated down her arm from the broken skin of her wrist, and she only just managed to bite back a whimper. Still, she was so glad to see him that she almost burst into tears. "It's me, it's Kate, uncle."

He blinked at her. "Ekaterina."

"Yes. Let go, you're hurting me."

His grip relaxed. With a fair imitation of his normal acerbic style, he said, "Where the hell you been, girl? It ain't like I'm having a whole hell of a lot of fun lying out here getting pissed on by Mother Nature."

"What's wrong with you?"

He shifted. A spasm crossed his face. "Leg's broke, I think."

His right leg was broken, just below the knee. Kate could feel the lump beneath his jeans. "It's a closed fracture," she said, relieved.

"Gee, that makes me feel a whole hell of a lot better."

"Less chance of infection." But his leathery brown skin looked flushed. She put the back of her hand to his cheek. It was hot. "What else is wrong with you?"

He gestured toward his left arm. "Got shot."

The bullet had passed through the flesh of his inner arm, punching holes through shirt and T-shirt on both sides. "You were lucky, uncle. Missed your humeral artery and didn't hit your chest."

He grunted. "Yeah, well, I was moving fast enough. Was probably only luck she got me at all."

"Senta?"

He nodded.

I will kill her for this, Kate thought. Among other things. It was a vow, and it steadied her. "What happened, uncle?"

"Beats the hell out of me," he said.

"Sssshhh," she said. "Keep it low. I don't know who else is around, or what side they're on."

He looked at her, awareness sharpening his eyes. He noticed the blood on her shirt. "What happened to you, girl?" He struggled to rise. "Are you hurt?"

She pushed him back firmly. "No. You first. Tell me what happened. I want to get to the spike camp as soon as possible and get you a sleeping bag and some food. Did you go to the ridge?"

He let her push him down, which frightened her, and answered her question without prevarication, which frightened her even more. "Yes. Rode the four-wheelers all the way up. Took damn near three hours, because we had to stop every five minutes for Hubert to pick his friggin' plants."

Kate remembered the jar on the table next to Hubert's computer. "He's into herbs."

Old Sam met her eyes. "He was."

She took a deep breath. "I see. I found Dieter, uncle."

"He dead?"

She nodded.

"Figured. Anyway, it didn't hurry us along any when Senta started following old Hubert into the brush. Helping him, she said." Old Sam snorted. His voice grew stronger in the telling, and Kate had to shush him again.

"We all knew what kinda help she was offering. He wasn't buying though, old Hubert wasn't. The first time she followed him he came a-roaring outta the bushes like a nun with a crusader on her tail, his shirt unbuttoned and his glasses crooked and his face all flushed."

"She made a move on him."

"She tried." Even Old Sam, who boasted all the moral fiber of an alley cat on his eighth life, appeared slightly scandalized by Senta's blatant behavior. "And then they argued the second time, and he came out of the brush even faster. That was the last time he made us stop."

"What were they arguing about?"

"They were arguing in German, so I don't know. I thought I heard Hendrik's name, though."

Kate thought. "Fedor and Hendrik were a couple. Fedor

worked for Klemens in finance, Hendrik with Hubert in re-search and development."

Old Sam shifted. "Whatever. I thought I heard his name. I don't know for sure."

"So you get to the ridge. What happened then?"

"Everybody got out their cameras. Somebody opened the knapsack and passed out the snacks and drinks. It was windy, but the clouds were holding off in the east, and you could see Denali, big as life and twice as natural. There was a lot of oohing and ahing, as you might expect. Myself, I went up the hill a ways to take a leak."

And to get a better look at the view, Kate thought, but Old Sam would never admit to taking a purely aesthetic plea-sure in anything, fearing that it would downgrade his status as one hundred percent manly man.

"I wasn't gone that long, maybe ten minutes or so, when I hear shots from the ridge below, three of them. One's that Weatherby of Eberhard's, the other two sound like they might be from that elephant gun of Dieter's. I hadn't seen any game on the way up, but you don't figure to when you're roaring through the woods on a four-wheeler, so I come on the run, thinking something four-legged snuck up on Demetri and he might need some help."

He stopped. "Are you cold, uncle?" Kate said. Her hands went to the buttons of her shirt. Jack's shirt.

One gnarled fist closed over both of hers. "I'm fine. Let me finish, and then I want to hear what happened to you."

"All right," she said, letting her hands fall.

"Like I said, I come on the run, but I must of went higher up than I thought because before I get all the way back I hear one of the four-wheelers start up and somebody else start to scream in German. Sounded like a man. Then I hear this god-awful crash, bang, thump, crunch and some more screaming, and what sounds like somebody beating on somebody else. Well, hell, Kate, it was beginning to seem like I might maybe oughtta slow down a little, but by then I was going so fast I couldn't stop.

"So I bust out of the bushes and Senta's standing there with Dieter's gun and one of the four-wheelers and its trailer is just going over the side of the ridge and Eberhard's throwing Hubert after it."

He paused. "Goddamndest thing I ever saw," he said, not without admiration. "Just stiff-armed him up and over, pitched him the way you or me would pitch a fish. That is one big tough son of a bitch."

"I know."

The sharp old eyes examined her face, but he didn't comment, not yet. "So I managed to put some turn in my forward motion and kept on going, right over the edge of the ridge about twenty feet from where the four-wheeler went over." His lips tightened. "I woulda made it, too, except for that goddamn blonde. She shot me just before I got over, and I fell and broke my goddamn leg." He fumed.

"You're alive," Kate said. "Right now, I'll settle for that."

The lack of animation in her tone alerted him. "What happened your end?"

She told him, voice flat, face expressionless. When she got to where she'd been knocked unconscious, Old Sam noticed her missing braid for the first time. "What the hell happened to your hair, girl?"

"I cut it off," Kate said.

Old Sam was very old and very wise. "Jesus," he said with a disgusted look. "Women. I get shot up right, left and center and you take time out for a new hairdo."

"When I woke up, I had my hands and feet tied with duct tape. Someone had dumped me next to the log. Jack was lying in the middle of the yard. He had been shot. I thought he was dead, but he wasn't. Senta and Eberhard showed up then, in a celebratory mood. They invited me to join in. Jack tossed a box of cartridges into the fire and when they went off, Jack and I lit out."

Old Sam frowned. "I underestimated that old gal," he said finally. "I figured she was just another pretty face."

So did I, Kate thought.

Never again.

"How the hell did they think they could get away with it?" Old Sam demanded.

"If they're the only ones left alive, uncle, who's going to say any different? If Senta had Dieter's gun, they must be thinking of framing him for the whole business. It makes a weird kind of sense, if you don't have any evidence to the contrary—his company is being sued by everybody and his brother for what sounds like everything under the sun. Jack —" Her breath caught. "Jack," she went on evenly, "Jack said Dieter wasn't the most stable person at the best of times, partying with the jet set, stuff like that. My guess is they're going to say he lost his mind and started shooting everything that moved." She added, still in that odd, flat voice, "They'll probably sue George for not providing adequate safety mea-sures on the hunt."

"Where is Jack?" Old Sam said bluntly.

"Let's see to that break, uncle." She found an alder limb of the right length and size and used his boot laces and Dieter's shirt to splint his broken leg. "There." She sat back. "You hear anything I should look out for?"

He shook his head, disgusted with his own weakness. "I been in and out. All I been hearing is my ears ringing."

She looked up. The rain was tapering off but the mist was becoming thicker and hanging lower. "Stay here, uncle. I'll get you that sleeping bag."

"Kate? Where's Jack?"

She left him without answering.

It took ten minutes to gain the ridge, and by the time she did the mist had closed in, a solid, disorienting pall. A couple of times she had to stop and think which way was up, and when she at last emerged on level ground it took another five minutes to feel her way to the group of fifty-five-gallon Chevron barrels that constituted the spike camp. They were only twenty-five feet away and stood next to the largest tree on the bluff, to make it easy to find. It was only easy if you could see the tree, and she couldn't.

She was shivering uncontrollably, wet, cold, a hunger too long ignored gnawing at her stomach like acid. Somehow she was at the barrel, somehow her numbed hands were unclipping the lid. She raised the flat circular metal disc and grabbed the first thing she found, which was a sleeping bag.

A voice said chidingly, "My, how cold you look, *meine kleine* Katerina."

She looked up and saw Eberhard emerge out of the mist like a ghost traveling between dimensions. He had in his hands what Kate now recognized as not his own Weatherby

but Dieter's Merkel. It was the same gun he had had the previous night at the lodge, the gun whose appearance had bothered her so fleetingly.

"At least you're alive," Eberhard said. He smiled. "I
was afraid you were dead. That would have spoiled all my
fun."

SIXTEEN

Who knows what goes on in the mind of a man like that?

She let the sleeping bag fall back into the barrel and stood very still, hands grasping the lid so tightly that the edges cut into her skin.

"How did you get here so fast?" she said stupidly, the first words to come to her mind.

He shrugged, that terrifying grin unimpaired. "When I got back to camp last night, I doctored Senta's back. She is not happy with you, Katerina. She doesn't want you for a toy anymore, she wants you dead, and dead right away. So I took the four-wheeler and drove here and camped. I know you will come here to look for your friends, food, a weapon."

"Where's Senta?"

His smile was rueful, his shrug self-deprecating. "Senta does not camp. She says such things are not good for the complexion. So she gives me her blessing, in a manner of speaking, and sees me off." He eyed her slyly. "She has taken a dis-like to that man of yours. I pity him."

Kate couldn't stop flinching at the words, but she was shivering so hard it was undetectable.

"What have you done to your hair?" He looked at her critically. "I liked that braid. I shall have to punish you for cutting it off without my permission." He gestured with the rifle. "Now come here. We have some unfinished business."

"What happened here?" Kate said, trying not to let her teeth chatter. "Yesterday? What happened?"

"An accident," he said piously. "One of the four-wheel-ers drove too close to the edge of the cliff. And poof!" He demonstrated, one hand arcing a graceful, swooping swan dive that ended with a flat smack of palm on palm. "That Dieter, he was always a little—what is the word for the tem-perature? Mercurial, yes. The legal problems were increasing, and the stress was beginning to show. He has been very de-pressed. And then poor Fedor, and Hendrik. They were so young, such valued employees, so close to him. For them to die in such horrible accidents. I blame myself. I should have been watching him more closely."

He shook his head sadly, a gesture belied by his unre-pentant grin. "But now Senta, as the nearest blood relative, will inherit control of the company, until his sons come of age." The grin widened. "Somehow I feel neither one of them will make it that far."

Kate felt sick, and knew she looked it. Good. The last thing she wanted was for Eberhard to think she had heard this before, and to go looking for who had told her. "All of the party went over? Everyone?"

Eberhard nodded cheerfully. "Everyone." He grinned again. "Eventually."

"What about us? What about the guides? Why kill us, too?"

Eberhard shrugged. "Like I said, Dieter was depressed. I am sure we can find a doctor to say that he was verging on the insane. Who knows what goes on in the mind of a man like that?" He motioned with the rifle again. "Enough talk. Come here."

Instead she threw the barrel lid, slicing through the air like a discus to catch him squarely in the chest with a solid thunk.

It was hard to tell who was more surprised, him or her, but he dropped his rifle and it gave her time to run and she did, and that wonderful fog closed in behind her as if someone had drawn a curtain, thick and enfolding, like a lover's arms.

The edge of the bluff was reached in a dozen giant steps and she launched herself into the air blindly, going into a tuck and praying for a nice thick stand of brush wherever she came down. As she dropped the rifle boomed and a bullet passed close enough for her to feel a hot rush of air against her cheek. A lucky shot; he couldn't see her, he could only hear her, and he was running, too.

The ground came up and hit her in the knees. She ducked head and shoulder and continued to roll until she came up hard against a sharp-edged, lichen-covered boulder. The breath was knocked out of her, and she lay where she was just long enough to get it back and no more. She heard footsteps above, along with some swearing in German. They halted abruptly, and in the resulting silence Kate couldn't understand why Eberhard didn't hear her heartbeat and zero in.

In the few brief seconds that followed, Kate realized two things: one, that Eberhard must not be allowed to learn that Old Sam had survived, and, two, that he must therefore be led away from the ridge. There was also three, she'd better do it quick before Old Sam decided to take a hand.

She stood up and kicked the rock deliberately. "Ouch!" she said, raising her voice, and began to run straight down the hill. The fog parted before her and swirled together again behind her.

Behind her, she heard the footsteps again, hurried, crashing through brush, stumbling over rock, but always, always in pursuit.

She eschewed the switchbacks and ran straight down the steep side of the ridge, taking great leaps and horrible risks in the enclosing mist, barking her shins on boulder and branch, catching her shoulders and arms against the limbs of trees. She let the angle of the slope guide her. He was bigger and stronger and probably faster than she was, and he had undoubtedly eaten and drunk well both the evening before and that morning.

Kate was smaller, dizzy with pain from her throbbing head and faint from hunger, but she was lighter on her feet, she knew where she was and she had a plan. It depended on him following her, so she made as much noise as she could and when she couldn't, deliberately made more by breaking branches and kicking rocks loose as she ran. He started a dozen mini-avalanches of his own, dirt and rock tumbling down with him.

As the ground began to level out, the fog began to thin, so that she could see maybe twenty feet in front of her. A regular line of brush indicated that she had stumbled on the last of the switchbacks and without pause she jumped a rock, yanked her sleeve free when it was snagged on a branch of white spruce and pounded down the road.

There was a crash and a curse behind her and she paused at the turn, gasping for some much needed air while he disentangled himself and got back on his feet. It wouldn't do to get too far ahead of him. By now he knew he had no choice but to follow, that he would never find his way back up the ridge until the mist cleared. And Kate was headed toward the lodge, and Senta was at the lodge. He had to come after her.

The second after his first footfall sounded she was off again, running flat out, as fast as she could go, straight down the middle of the trail, taking her chances that Senta wasn't coming up it from the other direction. She didn't think so; Senta didn't seem the type to head out after a lover/co-conspirator, but it was still a risk. Kate took it.

The switchbacks ended suddenly. It was astonishing how much faster it had been going down than going up. It wasn't far now, half a mile or so to where the peeling bole of the birch leaned precariously over the trail. Kate took the track at a steady trot, head down, arms pumping, lungs burning, ignoring everything but the need to cover distance and cover it fast. She was no longer cold and the mist was her ally now, refreshing her, encouraging her, urging her on.

She felt rather than heard his footsteps pounding behind her and she put on speed, the last she had in her. If she'd still had it, he was near enough to have caught her braid and brought her down.

He still might. Had she run too slowly? Had she allowed him to catch up too soon?

Would she make it?

There! There was the leaning birch. She scrambled up the bank and plunged in, leaving him cursing and clawing the foliage behind her.

The trail she had left behind that morning was faint, he wouldn't have been able to see it but she could, oh, she could. A broken branch here, a footprint left in a pile of leaves there, a crushed clump of horsetail. She ran, knocking her shoulders against tree trunks that seemed to jump into her path, tripping over roots, tangling her feet in devil's club.

Behind her there was a loud thump and more cursing. Pursuit ceased. Eberhard must have run into a tree.

Kate skidded to a halt, waiting, listening. Moments passed, while her heartbeat slowed and she caught her breath. Had he knocked himself out? A groan answered that question.

Perhaps he needed encouragement. She fished out a quarter and a penny and tapped them together, clink, clink, clink. Nothing. Clink, clink, clink-clink, arrhythmic but continuous. A muffled curse came wetly to her through the mist and she pulled out a rubber band. One end around her left thumb, the other stretched around the quarter. She waited until he was almost on her, a dark figure looming up out of the mist, and let fly at where she hoped his face might be. The quarter hit some part of him with a satisfying fleshy chunk. He cursed and broke into a stumbling run, arms reaching blindly. It looked like he'd lost the rifle.

She turned and ran flat out through the trees, taking the most dangerous risk of all, and burst into the clearing with the brush pile.

She paused long enough to register the outraged expression on the face of the grizzly as he reared up on his hind feet, muzzle bloody from his latest feeding, front claws extended to defend the kill he had returned to, as grizzlies always have and always will, until the last bit of meat was gone, until the last bone was cracked and sucked dry of marrow, until all those delicious brains had been licked from the inside of the skull.

Kate took the brush pile and his putrefying kill in one colossal leap, clearing his outstretched claws by inches—she couldn't have done it again if she tried for a hundred years—and crashed into the trees on the opposite side of the clearing.

Eberhard stumbled out of the trees. Kate had startled the grizzly, had alerted him to trespassers, but she had been too quick for him, and now here was another trespasser blundering onto his private cache of meat. It was bear season, all right, but this time the bear was doing the hunting. He was ready and waiting when Eberhard ran straight into his arms.

Eberhard's screams were louder than the bear's.

Smoke curled up from the chimney of the lodge, but it could have been a trap, set to lure her in.

Eberhard had been gone a long time, however, and Senta must be getting worried about him.

It had taken Kate three hours to make her way back to the lodge, inching her way to avoid a possible ambush, and another thirty minutes to crawl in close enough to survey the situation. Senta probably thought he couldn't live without her that long, and if his story was to be believed, he'd been gone since the previous night. Senta must be getting a little antsy.

There was only one of her.

But she had a rifle.

Rifle. Rifles. There were a bunch of rifles in the garage. But to get to the garage Kate would have to circle around behind the lodge, and there were windows on every side of that building except the one facing the garage. And they'd left the ammunition in the lodge.

Kate lay in the thick brush at the edge of the clearing and considered.

With the splint, Old Sam was marginally mobile. He could make it up to the spike camp, and maybe even look for other survivors. But he'd need some help, soon.

She considered for an hour, waiting, watching. She listened for the sound of voices, anything to indicate that Senta wasn't alone, but there was nothing.

One of the four-wheelers had gone over the edge, again according to Eberhard. That left one more, and that had been left at the top of the ridge that morning. So Senta was on foot.

Kate eyed the smoke again. Senta was also warm and dry and fed.

Bitch.

Kate was still cold and still hungry and still exhausted. The sky was gray overhead, the ground sodden beneath. A flash of red caught her eye, and she turned her head to see a troop of ptarmigan parade past. She had been lying so still for so long they had mistaken her for part of the landscape.

They looked to her hungry eyes like a bunch of drum-sticks marching in step. Her mouth watered.

This was ridiculous. Senta couldn't be in six places at once. Seven of the eight shelters had to be empty, and empty long enough for her to sneak in and grab some dry clothes and maybe one of Berg's Hershey bars before her stomach crawled right up her throat and out of her mouth.

She made up her mind and backed soundlessly into the brush again, wriggling backward on her stomach. It didn't take any particular skill to move soundlessly in the forest, no matter what Zane Grey said. All you had to do was take your time. Take it slowly and carefully and be aware of where every part of your body was and what it was doing. Kate was very slow and very, very careful. One leg stretched straight out in back of her, toe down, both hands raised her torso and pushed up and back, her toe took the weight and she was six inches backward from where she had been. She had to feel carefully for purchase and for anything that might make a noise before she put her weight on it, but so long as she didn't get in a hurry, it was possible.

It took her twenty minutes to thread her way back to the creek. She crept down the bank path, worn smooth so close to the lodge.

Exposure and exhaustion must have taken their toll, because she never did figure out how what happened next happened.

What happened next was that a bucket came crashing down on her head, a water bucket wielded by the man filling it at the water pump. He brought it down hard, too, and only the fact that it was half full of water and unwieldy saved her. She ducked out of the way of the bucket but not of the water, and it was very cold water.

"You son of a bitch," Kate said. She came to her feet with a surge of anger and kicked him as hard as she could right square in the balls.

He folded up like a collapsed balloon, his rosebud of a mouth an "O" of surprised agony, his hands going protectively to his crotch, his ass hitting the ground with a solid squelch. Glasses, thick and unwieldy, slid down his nose.

It was Berg. Kate blinked the rain out of her eyes and

looked again. Yes, it was Berg. But Berg was just a fool, a buffoon, a nonentity, a nonstarter so inept he took naps under bear bait. What the hell was he doing here? "What the hell are you doing here?" Kate said out loud. "I thought you went over the cliff with the rest of them."

"No," a new voice said. Senta emerged from the trees, Eberhard's Weatherby in her hands. "No, Berg works for me."

"Son of a bitch," Kate said again. She was more angry than afraid. She glared at Senta and said furiously, "Is there anyone at DRG you weren't fucking?"

Senta smiled, the familiar predatory smile, full lips carefully outlined in carmine. "No," she said simply. "Except for Dieter. He wouldn't. We were cousins. He said we shouldn't."

"Why, Senta?" Kate said. "Why come here? Why involve us? You wanted DRG, fine. You couldn't find an easier way to get it than stage a mass murder in the Alaskan Bush?"

"But it was the perfect solution," Senta said proudly. "Far, far away from home, isolated in the wilderness, no one left to say what really happened. I could do anything I wanted."

Keep talking, Kate said, just keep talking. She let her eyelids droop in a half-bored way that said, Impress me, I dare you. It had impelled the truth out of more perps than Senta had shades of lipstick. She shifted her weight unobtrusively from one foot to the other, keeping her balance, staying ready. Tell me all about it, Senta, about how clever you are, how brilliant your plan was, how everything would have worked if only you'd had smarter people working for you.

Senta obliged. "You see, Dieter has family. Two sons." She smiled again, this time at a fond memory. "They are both in love with me, and they are both underage."

Johnny, Kate thought with a pang. How was she going to tell Johnny?

"They can be managed," Senta said. "His wife—" She shrugged. "She is nothing, she could be managed, too. They would all lean on me if Dieter was gone, and then I would have all that lovely money to play with. So Dieter had to go."

"At first all you were going to do was discredit him, right?" Kate said. "You were the source for the investigation, weren't you?" With a sudden inspiration, she added, "And I'll bet you were framing Fedor to take the fall."

Berg groaned at their feet, his hands cupped against his crotch. Both women ignored him.

"That little fag." Senta's lip curled again. "Always poking his nose in where it didn't belong, wanting to know where every penny went."

"Ah," Kate said with a thin smile. "You've been embezzling, too, have you, Senta?"

Senta shot her an angry glance. "He was a deviant, who could believe anything he said?"

"What's the matter, Senta?" Kate said. "Did Fedor turn you down?"

She thought for a moment she'd gone too far; Senta half-raised the rifle.

"What made you change your mind?" Kate said quickly. Why take us with you down this road to hell, you homicidal bitch? "Why did you decide to kill Dieter? Why kill the rest of them, too? And if you'd decided to kill him, why plant that cartridge in the creek next to Hendrik's body?"

"What is this about planting a bullet?" Senta said with some surprise.

The rifle lowered again, as she was reminded that Kate

was of an inferior species, less quick than herself, less intelli-
gent, less swift of perception, less of everything all the way
around. Senta forgave Kate's obtuseness with a generous
smile. "Dieter was always mad for the hunting. Shoot, shoot,
shoot, elephants in Africa, tigers in India, jaguars in South
America." She gave an elaborate shudder. "You should see his
office, full of the heads of dead animals. He was going to come
to Alaska anyway, he had always wanted to."

It didn't matter now how many guides Dieter had pissed
off on how many continents. "Who suggested that he make it
a corporate retreat?"

"You know men." Senta tossed her head. "A word here,
a word there, and he thought of it all by himself."

"And then Fedor died."

"Opportunity knocking," Senta said lightly, smiling.

So it was an accident after all, Kate thought. Poor
Klemens. "What happened to Hendrik?"

Senta sneered. "Another deviant. He heard us talking."

"You and Eberhard?"

"Yes. We met down by the creek the evening Fedor
died." She smirked. "I think Fedor must have been suspicious
and told Hendrik something. We saw him hiding. Eberhard
went back to follow him, and saw him talk to you." She
shrugged. "Hendrik was always a little clumsy. He slipped,
he fell. Who is there to say it was different?"

"And that's when you decided it would be so much easier on everyone if Dieter died too, and the rest of them as
well."

Senta beamed, delighted to prove Kate wrong yet again.
"No, Eberhard had the idea first when he took the safety off
Dieter's rifle."

"What——" It took Kate a moment to catch up. "You mean Eberhard clicked the safety off Dieter's rifle after he shot the moose?" Kate tried to remember. Dieter had constantly been handing things to Eberhard that day, and yes, the rifle had been one of them. "I guess it was bad luck he only shot himself in the arm."

Senta's face clouded. "Yes. And then Hendrik hears us talking about it, down by the creek, and about other things. And then Eberhard saw him talking to you, so Hendrik had to go. That was when we thought of turning Fedor's death to our advantage, you see."

"Yes, I see."

Kate did see, all too well. The conceit that comes with killing once successfully had intoxicated the killers to the point that any solution up to and including mass murder looked reasonable, even necessary to them. And, of course, foolproof. No annoying witnesses left to cloud the issue. The perfect crime.

Senta proved it with her next words. "What could be more believable than two deaths, accidents, of course, followed by a ride up to a high place in the wilderness, a depressed corporate officer loses his grip and they are all dead except for a few—a very few—fortunate survivors?"

Senta smiled. "It happens in United States post offices all the time. But this, given the international nature of DRG, would make headlines all over the world. And," she added, "think of the publicity, the sympathy it would generate. The investigation into DRG would vanish. The stock would rise, too," she added. "You watch."

Kate didn't think Senta had any intention of letting her. Berg groaned again, louder this time, and began muttering in

German beneath his breath, the same phrase over and over again, probably the words "Ouch ouch ouch" repeated.

"Get up, Berg," Senta said sharply. She motioned with the rifle. "Let's get in out of the rain while we wait for Eberhard." She smiled at Kate, and this time her teeth seemed sharper somehow. "I promised him a pet. You remember."

She looked disappointed when Kate didn't break into a sweat at the very thought. She looked past Kate, in the direction of Blueberry Ridge. A suspicion leapt into the blue eyes and she opened her mouth.

At that moment Berg began a lurching movement to his feet. When he was just coming up off all fours Kate kicked him again, this time right under the chin.

The force of the blow carried him backward into Senta.

The Weatherby went off.

Berg screamed.

Kate ran.

She felt like she'd been running for most of her life.

She ran straight past the squirming jumble of bodies, one of which had a spreading stain on the front of his shirt and was screaming in a hoarse voice. The other, swearing furiously in German, was punching and kicking and hitting to get him off her.

Kate ran, but not too fast, not so fast that Senta would lose sight of her.

It had worked once, why not a second time?

Besides, she'd had another idea, an even better one this time.

SEVENTEEN

He's not dumb enough to starve his plaything.

The trestle table seemed to float by as she ran through the yard, the table from which Jack had tossed the bullets into the fire. She scooped up a roll of duct tape as she passed and dropped it down the front of her shirt, Jack's shirt. It seemed the thing to do, somehow. Duct tape always came in handy; hadn't Jack said it bound the universe together? Kate curled a hand around it through the flannel fabric of her shirt and ran.

She had run south this morning, south along the mine road, south to lure Eberhard to his death.

She ran east now, toward the first day's kill. She ran, and again she heard the sound of pursuit, and again she ran just fast enough to elude capture. She wasn't worried about Senta shooting her on the run; Senta could accidentally blow the guts out of someone at close range, always assuming she could manage to get the safety off first, but she wasn't a marksman. It was one thing to shoot at a bull's-eye, it was another to have an entire side of moose to aim at, it was a third and completely different thing to sight in on a much smaller target that kept moving out of your sights, especially when you had to move to keep them in those sights.

As if to prove her point, the rifle boomed. There was a thud as the bullet impacted the trunk of a white spruce twenty yards to Kate's right.

No, she wasn't in any danger, not at this distance and not at this speed.

Kate had led Eberhard away from Old Sam and now she led Senta away from the lodge.

She ran, an easy loping stride, arms pumping, chin up. It was almost habit by now.

After all the foot traffic of the first day's hunt the path was clear. It was after noon by now and there was a brightening on the southern horizon; better weather coming. Better weather and the cavalry. She had to hurry.

Senta helped by staying on her trail like a hungry hound dog. Kate didn't ask for more.

She ran through stands of aspens, golden leaves drooping and falling beneath the weight of accumulated moisture. She ran through clumps of hemlock and spruce, of alder and birch, of berry bushes and diamond willow and devil's club and the eternal and endless fireweed and a hundred other trees and plants she lived with every day and which she didn't know by name.

She ran until she was too far ahead and had to stop and wait until Senta could see her again. Senta, like Eberhard, was angry. The anger spurred her past exhaustion. The humiliation of defeat at the hands of a lesser being could not be allowed. She had a clear trail to follow and a prey that didn't seem to be able to get that far ahead of her.

And of course, she had the gun. That made all the difference.

Another shot came, this one lopping off the limb of a quaking aspen fifteen feet to Kate's left. Her aim was improving.

Kate's stride didn't falter. She ran straight up the little ridge where Berg had met his bear and Dieter had been shit on by it and over the top. The instant she was down the other side she ducked into the brush and waited.

Senta came thudding along behind. Kate was pleased to hear that she was wheezingly out of breath.

She waited until the other woman was abreast of her and then she stuck out a foot and tripped her, as simple as that. Senta went sprawling on the path. Kate, knife at the ready, was on her in a single pounce, one knee in Senta's back, one hand knotted in Senta's hair, pulling her head back, the other holding the knife to her throat.

"Don't move or I will kill you," Kate said.

Senta believed her implicitly.

After all, it was what she would have done.

Kate pulled the duct tape from the front of her shirt and bound Senta's hands behind her back. Another strip went around Senta's mouth. She objected. Kate kicked her in the side, not too hard, just hard enough to get her attention. It worked.

The rifle had skidded partway down the path. She picked it up and checked the magazine. Two rounds left.

She held in her hands the weapon that had killed Jack

Morgan. It was a heavy weapon with a smooth stock and flip-up sights.

She wanted to flip them up. She wanted to use one of the rounds in the magazine. She wanted to blow a hole through Senta's side and leave her guts to spill out onto the trail, to leave her lying there to the tender mercies of the jays and the seagulls and the ravens and the eagles. She wanted it so desperately her hands shook so she couldn't have drawn a bead.

Instead she motioned with the muzzle. "On your feet."

Senta's blue eyes burned over their silver gag, but she got up, maneuvering awkwardly because of her hands. Kate smiled without humor. "Not very comfortable, is it? March."

Senta turned toward the lodge.

"No," Kate said. "Other way."

The blue eyes looked momentarily confused. "Other way," Kate said and prodded her for emphasis. Senta flinched and groaned behind her gag. Kate remembered her burned back, burns it had been Kate's pleasure to give her, and prodded her again.

An hour and twenty minutes of forced march later they walked into the tiny clearing where Dieter had shot the moose. Senta stumbled over a long leg bone picked clean and fell heavily to the forest floor.

"Get up," Kate said.

Senta, moving more slowly now, got up.

Kate nudged her again with the rifle. Senta screamed behind her gag. What a shame. Kate prodded her again. "March."

Senta marched.

Crazy Emmett had hid his trail well but not well enough, not today. Half an hour later they halted just inside the ring of trees clustered at the edge of the clearing surrounding Crazy Emmett's cabin. It was built of logs, chinked with moss and roofed with what looked like a spruce thatch. A wisp of smoke rose up from a chimney made of weathered black stovepipe.

"Lay down," Kate said in a low voice.

Senta refused. Kate hooked a foot behind one of her ankles and shoved her hard with one hand planted in her back. Senta fell face forward. Before she could move Kate had her ankles strapped with duct tape. Senta was immobilized.

Kate leaned down and spoke, her voice flat and expressionless. "First off, Eberhard is dead. I killed him." Senta rolled over and stared. "No one is coming to your rescue, Senta. In fact, no one even knows where you are, or that you're still alive. And I'm not going to tell them, so they never will."

It took a moment or two for the import of that statement to sink in. When it did, Senta's face turned a congested red. Kate remembered Dieter's face turning that exact same shade. Must run in the family. She said, "There's a man we call Crazy Emmett who lives in this cabin. You can see for yourself, it's got a roof, but I don't imagine there's any hot water, or any running water at all for that matter, and certainly no electricity. He doesn't go hungry, but he doesn't have much time for any of the finer things in life, like, oh, I don't know, say baths, for instance."

Senta closed her eyes, and Kate nudged her again, this time even less gently. "This is important, Senta, so you'd better listen. We call Emmett crazy because he's hiding out from the feds and their black helicopters, thinks the United States is about to be taken over by the United Nations and a one-world government. He doesn't take to the idea. So he hides out in the Bush, lives off the land. He doesn't see anybody if he can help it."

Kate paused. "There are a lot of stories about the bodies buried on this place, stories of people who poked their noses in where their noses had no business being. Nobody's ever had the guts to ask him straight out if any of those rumors are true."

Kate slung the Weatherby over her shoulder. The unfamiliar weight settled against her back like it had found a home.

"One thing I can tell you that isn't a rumor. Crazy Emmett's been a long, long time without a woman. He made that real clear when I saw him last. I was lucky I had a rifle with me. Real lucky."

She patted the strap of the rifle. "You won't be."

She saw a dawning awareness in Senta's eyes, followed by a kindling rage and a faint but gathering fear. "You can fight him or not, it's up to you. He'll fuck you regardless, but he'll feed you, too, he's not dumb enough to starve his plaything. He might even let you go eventually, if you work hard and be real, real nice to him."

She shook her head. "I doubt it, though. He's had a long dry spell, and once he gets his hands on something as fine as you I expect he'll do his best to keep you.

"But you can always try."

Kate stood up. "I'll just let him know you're here."

She stepped into the clearing. Behind her she could hear thumps and grunts as Senta fought to free herself. "Hello the house!"

A thin husky lying next to the cabin woke up and be-gan barking hysterically, lunging the full length of his chain. "Emmett, it's Kate Shugak. I've got a present for you."

It took a good five minutes before curiosity got the bet-ter of him and the door cracked open. "What do you want? What do you mean, a present? I skinned out that bull; you said I could."

"Doesn't have anything to do with the bull. I got a woman here for you. No one knows she's here, and no one will know. You don't tell anybody, she's yours as long as you want."

The door swung wide and he stepped out, rifle held in two hands across his chest. He looked at her suspiciously. "I don't see any woman except you."

Kate jerked her head backward. "She's right here. Be-hind this stand of spruce."

He hesitated, took a cautious step forward, wanting enough to believe, not credulous enough to believe too quickly, too suspicious to move too fast in any case.

Kate moved down the trail about ten feet and turned to wait.

Before too long Emmett sidled into the trees. He saw Senta and halted, an amazed expression on his face.

Senta took one look and began loud grunting noises of protest, writhing to throw off her bonds and escape.

Kate wondered briefly if she should warn him. No, she decided. No need. Poisonous as Senta was, Crazy Emmett hadn't spent all these years in the Bush without learning to watch his back.

She watched Crazy Emmett kneel and begin to unwrap

the duct tape from around Senta's ankles. Over his head, Kate met Senta's eyes.

She smiled.

As she walked away, she could hear muffled grunts and thrashing sounds as Senta fought in vain to free herself before Emmett could lay hands on her.

Like Jack had said, there was no finer example of the mind of man at work than duct tape.

Ten paces up the trail she stopped as if she had run into a wall.

No, she thought. No.

She stood stock still, deliberately conjuring up the dead face of Jack Morgan, the memory of the life leaving it, the inanimate sprawl of his limbs, limp hands that had caressed her, cold lips that had kissed her. Klemens, his head gone. Mutt, gut-shot. Old Sam, wounded, perhaps mortally. Dieter, staring lifelessly at the sky.

No, she thought. Kate, don't do this. Leave her. She deserves it. Leave her!

Against her will, she felt herself turn around and head back down the trail.

Senta's charms were so overwhelming that Crazy Emmett's vigilance was not at its normal peak of efficiency. With a faint feeling of regret Kate hit him once at the base of the skull with the butt of the rifle, and he slumped down without a sound, his head lying on Senta's breast in a parody of repletion. Over the duct tape gag, Senta's eyes glared at Kate with a mixture of fury, fear and relief.

With one foot Kate nudged Emmett off her, and he rolled

to his back, his mouth slack. At the cabin the dog set up a
frenzy of barking.

"Get up," Kate said. Her voice was flat and expressionless.

Shakily, Senta rose to her feet. With rough movements,
Kate pulled up Senta's pants and fastened them. She rose. "If
you fight me, I'll kill you. If you run, I'll kill you. If you do
anything but exactly and precisely what I tell you to do, I will
kill you."

She took a step forward and went up on her toes, trembling with rage, and glared at Senta. "I want to kill you, you
crazy fucking bitch, I want to kill you so bad my teeth ache,
so I'm praying you're stupid enough to do any one of those
things. Do you understand?"

Senta, cowed by Kate's wrath and her near escape from
rape and lifelong slavery, gave a jerky nod. After all, Emmett
wasn't dead, and this short, skinny little brown woman with
the awkwardly cut hair and the crazy eyes could change her
mind again.

And of course, she now had the gun.

Kate motioned at the trail. "Walk."

Senta walked.

EIGHTEEN

Leave her be.

By morning the rain had stopped, the fog had vanished and the clouds had dissipated into the west and south, and hard on their heels came the sound of two engines. First a Super Cub landed, and then a helicopter. George had come back, finally, and he had brought Alaska state trooper Jim Chopin with him, brave and immaculate in his blue and gold.

The first thing they saw was Old Sam, bloody but unbowed.

"Took you long enough to get back," Old Sam said. "I suppose you both had a girl in McCarthy who just couldn't wait?"

The old man sat propped against the tire of a four-wheeler, rifle held loosely in the crook of one arm. Two other people lay bundled into sleeping bags nearby. One was Demetri, the other Hubert. Both were unconscious but breathing.

Senta and Berg had been duct taped to chairs from the lodge and were sitting next to each other. Berg had lost his glasses and messed in his pants, and the bandage wrapped around his middle was red and sodden.

At the edge of the trees there was a fire, and at its side sat Kate, hair cropped, face and hands cut and bruised, shirt stained with blood gone brown with age. Her eyes were dark and staring, lacking soul or spirit. An endless, keening sound came from her throat as she rocked, back and forth, back and forth, cradling the lifeless body of her lover in her arms.

Next to her on the bare patch of ground lay the great gray halfbreed, coat encrusted with blood, panting in short, labored breaths, raising her voice now and then in a frail accompaniment. One voice was strong, one weak, the two united in sorrow and rage and protest and lamentation.

"Christ," Jim breathed.

"Kate," George said, starting forward. "Kate, what happened? Let me—"

"No," Jim said, holding up an arm to block his way.

"Jim, come on, that's Jack. We've got to help, we can't—"

"No," Jim said, voice as stony as his face.

"Leave her be," Old Sam growled.

Jim passed a shaking hand over his eyes and turned away as if he could no longer bear to look, which indeed he could not.

The tuneless lament drifted up like smoke and hung there like a grieving wraith in the clear autumn air.

It was a sound none of the men would ever forget, no matter how hard they tried.